Paper Ghosts

PAPER GHOSTS

A NOVEL OF SUSPENSE

Julia Heaberlin

MICHAEL JOSEPH
an imprint of
PENGUIN BOOKS

MICHAEL JOSEPH

UK | USA | Canada | Ireland | Australia
India | New Zealand | South Africa

Michael Joseph is part of the Penguin Random House group of companies
whose addresses can be found at global.penguinrandomhouse.com.

First published in the United States of America 2018
First published in Great Britain by Michael Joseph 2018
001

Text copyright © Julia Heaberlin, 2018
Photographs copyright © Jill Johnson, 2018

The moral right of the author has been asserted

Paper Ghosts is a work of fiction. Names, characters, places
and incidents either are the product of the author's imagination
or are used fictitiously. Any resemblance to actual persons,
living or dead, events, or locales is entirely coincidental.

Text designed by Dana Leigh Blanchette
Printed in Great Britain by Clays Ltd, St Ives plc

A CIP catalogue record for this book is available from the British Library

HARDBACK ISBN: 978–0–718–18134–5
TRADE PAPERBACK ISBN: 978–1–405–92131–2

www.greenpenguin.co.uk

Penguin Random House is committed to a
sustainable future for our business, our readers
and our planet. This book is made from Forest
Stewardship Council® certified paper.

FOR STEVE,

WHO NEVER GAVE UP ON ME OR THE CUBS

"A picture is a secret about a secret. The more it tells you the less you know."

—*DIANE ARBUS (1923–1971)*
American photographer

Before

When she was twelve, my sister fell into a grave.

We were two children by ourselves in an empty cemetery, old stones jutting out of the ground in all directions. The grass was dead, the same straw color as my sister's hair. I remember the terrific flutter in my chest. How her fingertips barely brushed mine when I reached my little hand down to try to pull her out. It was freshly dug earth, waiting.

She was laughing down in that hole.

I was five.

My sister loved to roam that cemetery in Weatherford, Texas. Peter Pan was buried there, although the stone said Mary Martin Halliday. So was someone named Jimmie Elizabeth and someone else named Sophronia, which is also the name of a moth in England and a purple lily and a character in Charles Dickens. My sister told me that. She was going to name her first daughter Sophronia and call her either Sophri or Phronia for short.

There were hundreds of graves. A million bones under our bodies as we cartwheeled across plots.

Death came to her like a summer's dream. That was etched in script on one of the ancient white markers. I don't remember the rest of the epitaph, although my sister read it to me every time.

I ran a half-mile back to our grandmother's house for help.

My sister climbed out of that grave by herself without a scratch on her.

I look back and think that's the day, the moment, she was cursed. When she was nineteen, she disappeared, like a lasso dropped from the clouds and snatched her up.

I know it was the day I became afraid of things.

NOW

1

"Who the hell are you?"

I slide my queen one space closer to his king. "You know who I am."

He swipes his right arm, the one that still fully cooperates, across the board. A single, swift movement. Pieces fly, bounce off the carpet, rattle into corners fuzzed with dust from a past decade. I don't flinch, something I'm practiced at. Neither does the only other occupant of the room, a deaf woman knitting an infinite patch of blue. Or green or gold or pink. It could be any color.

She doesn't have needles. Her hands work the air methodically while her invisible work piles up like an accordion. A wedding veil sits crookedly on the silvery threads struggling out of her scalp. The second hand on a plastic clock above her head jerks.

I've wanted to rip that clock off the wall on every visit. Time for the people in this house is meaningless. No need to travel beyond the triple-locked front door or wonder who or what made the three long white scratches that run down its wood veneer. No good reason to think about the people who never visit you or the horrible things you've done. So what if you can't remember that you never liked dark bananas or the canned laughter of *I Love Lucy* but now you eat one while watching the other?

I wonder what Carl is thinking. Maybe about how he'd like to kill me. I'm twenty-four, in the age range. White. Slender. People say I look like my sister. The difference is, she was lit from the inside. Dramatic. Gutsy. A performer. People drifted to her. Loved her. *Carl* drifted to her, and snatched her life.

Maybe he thinks I am my sister come back to haunt him.

I am the understudy, Carl. A shell of her, loaded with dynamite, set on revenge. The nervous one in the wings about to jump onstage. You and I, we will be co-stars.

I am also a perfect stranger every time I come here, or he's lying. Each time, he claims to forget my name. He won't answer when I ask why, in June, he is wearing a Christmas tie leering with Grinch faces, or tell me where he bought his leaden, ancient boots, or the prettiest place he remembers they last took him. Boots always remind me of vistas. Of standing firm and steady on a dangerous precipice while beauty unfolds for miles before your eyes.

He's unimpressed by any of my random musings on boots, or the Walt Whitman and John Grisham I read him by the only sunny window in this house, or the series of jokes about talking cows that I tell while we take walks around the neighborhood. Things any loved one would do. This afternoon at IHOP, I watched him drown his pancakes in strawberry syrup and knife them into a precise patchwork of bites. I wanted to ask, *Does the syrup remind you of blood?*

He's trying to make me think his eyes are glimpses into a dark solar system where he retreats, alone, but I won't be fooled. I wonder what he sees in mine. Anything familiar?

He's a hell of an actor, according to old court testimony.

Right now, with a harmless bit of violence, he's reminding me that he's still strong. Relevant. I already know. I've studied him carefully. Weighed the risks. Searched his room while he was in the shower and found his secret stash hidden in a battered suitcase under the bed—the red rubber exercise band that keeps up that knotty little bulge on his right forearm, and the ten-pound free weights. The sharpened pocketknife and the silver lighter with the engraved *N,* tucked into the zipper pocket along the back with a single cigarette.

The 8X10 photograph, pressed carefully flat, under the lining. It could be 1920, or two years ago. Carl the photographer, whose *Time Travel* book of surreal images once hit the bestseller list, specializes in timeless. The corners of the paper are soft, and there's a white crease in the middle that cuts the girl in two. She's standing on a barren rusty landscape that's probably never sucked up a drop of rain.

A tiny silver key charm nestles in her throat. The same key that I know hangs out of sight, somewhere in the graying curl of his chest hair. I saw it once, when it slipped out of his shirt and dangled over the chessboard. Is she one of his victims, too?

Old serial killers who roam free have to land somewhere, of course. I've thought about this a lot. They must get tired. Decide to pamper roses or grandchildren. Break hips and suffer heart attacks. Go impotent. Run out of money. Don't see the car coming. Put guns to their heads.

The killers who publicly beat the system, and the unseen monsters who are never caught and slip around like silent, pulsing background music. Screeching oboes and pounding drums. Only a few ever hear their soundtrack, right at the very end, and then it's too late.

It took a long, long time to find the man I believe killed my sister. Years. Dozens of interviews. Hundreds of suspects. Thousands of documents. Reading, stalking, stealing. It's been a singular, no-holds-barred obsession since I was twelve and my sister's bike didn't make it the three miles in broad daylight from our house to her summer babysitting job. It was *morning.*

Two sweet little boys, Oscar and Teddy Parker, were waiting for her on the other end. Hard to believe, but they are in high school now. Several months ago, their mother found my address and mailed

Oscar's college application essay with a note saying she hoped she was right to send it.

I wasn't sure. I didn't unfold the piece of paper right away. I had no idea what it would say—I just knew that my sister was the subject. I tucked it in the frame of my bathroom mirror. I didn't like thinking of her life as something to be critiqued and rated by college admissions personnel.

It took me a month to work up the courage. *Nothing*, Oscar wrote, *was ever the same. I was only five, but her disappearance changed everything. I wore the friendship bracelet we made together until the threads wore through and it fell off. No babysitter ever lived up to her. If I'm honest, no girl ever has. No assurance will make me feel safe again, yet I think of her every time I need to be brave. She's the reason I want to major in criminal justice.*

I'd always thought of how deeply my sister's death affected my family. *Me.* Even my physical body never felt the same, as if every cell was chemically changed, forever tweaked to high alert.

I'd never once thought of the pain of the two little boys who begged her to read Harry Potter because she was so good at the voices. When Mrs. Parker called at 9:22 A.M. to ask why Rachel hadn't shown up, I was getting out the flour to make chocolate chip cookies.

My parents, both accountants, had left for work fifteen minutes before. I was twelve, charged with cleaning the house and making dinner in the summer. It was a normal day in a normal house.

Is Rachel sick? Mrs. Parker had asked on the phone. She wasn't mad, I remember, just concerned. *Does she have a fever?*

An accident, I thought immediately. *A car ran into her bike. She's unconscious somewhere.* The canister fell out of my hands onto the floor, scattering its powder across the black tile.

No one cleaned it up for a long time. In the chaos that followed, people tracked flour all over our house, footprints that stayed for weeks. Months later, there was still the light whisper of them. It was like Rachel was there with us, walking around as a ghost.

Now that I'm finally here with Carl, making my move, I wonder for the last time if I should call it all off. I've told no one of my plan to steal him out of this place and find the truth.

It wouldn't be the first promise I've broken to myself. The girl in his suitcase, with the tiny key to nothing, seemed to be begging me with her eyes to leave and not look back.

I don't want to think about what Carl could still do with two good hands.

The air conditioner clunks on. A lukewarm breeze is blowing out of the vent in the ceiling. The wedding veil drifts, a cobweb caressing a wrinkled cheek.

I kneel down to pick up the chess pieces and disappear under the card table.

"Who the hell are you?" He's shouting now, pounding the card table so it jars the top of my head. His boot shoots out, and he presses down purposefully on my hand until it hurts. I jerk my fingers back, refuse to cry out, open my fist to the lowliest piece on the board. A pawn, of course.

"I'm your daughter," I lie.

It's the only logical way to get him in my custody.

Who the hell are *you*?

2

Ten visits in, I set my plan in motion. Carl is still adamant I'm not his daughter, but he's remembering my name now, at least the pseudonym I gave him. I casually suggest that we take a little vacation. *A couple of weeks,* I promise him. *A breather. We can get to know each other better. You can have a break from this claustrophobic prison.*

"If I go, will you let me use a pen?" he asks. "Mrs. T has banned me from pens. She figures I might stick one in somebody's throat."

"And that would be a damn mess for me to clean up," Mrs. T confirms from the doorway to the kitchen. Her "jiggling Polish behind," as Carl calls it, always shows up silently and perfectly timed.

But it was Mrs. T who took him in thirteen months ago. Hers was the only halfway house of old felons that would say yes to a possible serial killer with dementia after a Waco cop found him rambling the highway.

The famous documentary and fine-art photographer Carl Louis Feldman, suspected of stalking young women and stealing them for years, said he couldn't remember his own name. It took fingerprints and a sample of DNA to do that. A local hospital guessed a diagnosis of early onset dementia and sent him back out into the world.

Because even if he was "damn-sure-fire a sick Ted Bundy with a camera and a Ford pickup truck," as a prosecutor once pounded out to a Texas jury, the state just didn't care anymore.

He was declared not guilty in that missing girl case—the only one he was tried for, the only one with a bit of incriminating DNA evidence. Two days of deliberating, and the jury said he was good to go. And go he did, hiding out for years like a brown recluse in some dark corner while I patted my foot impatiently until he crawled out.

Who knew I'd end up here—crammed so tightly on a sagging couch with my sister's killer and a woman who knits imaginary things that we can feel each other's heat. The wedding veil is missing today, but her fingers are flying in frantic rhythm like there's a whip at her back.

The other occupants of the house are scattered in the kitchen, the bedrooms, the bathrooms—away from the soundtrack of the TV, which starts the day at 6 A.M. The relentless, high-pitched buzz from deep inside its guts lives in my head for hours after I leave.

Carl rips his eyes from the screen in front of us, a Discovery Channel special. We have just learned about a tarantula that can exist for two years without eating.

Carl twists toward me, the bone of his knee purposely jutting into my thigh. I imagine that same knee holding Rachel down. I'm suddenly glad, for her sake, that the woman beside me is deaf and, for my sake, that her dangerously sharp needles are imaginary.

Carl's hand drifts up. Mrs. T is gone. He's going to touch me. I'm going to let him. Whatever he wants. Whatever it takes.

He slides the rough pads of his middle and index fingers lightly down my cheek while I stare ahead at the hairy spider on TV, now warring with a lizard.

Carl traces my chin, my ear. He drifts to my neck. When he reaches the hollow place beside my windpipe, he presses his two fingers into my flesh harder than he needs to.

"Bump, bump," he says. "Bump, bump. That's your carotid."

I nod, swallowing hard. I know intimately about the carotid artery from reading hundreds of medical examiner reports. Its three layers—the intima, media, and adventitia. How the two carotids in the neck carry ninety percent of the blood to the brain. The TV shows aren't lying. A ruthless jab to one of them can cause death in bare minutes.

Carl keeps his fingers glued to my throat even when there's a rapid knock on the front door. Two shrill rings of the bell.

I bend down for my purse so Carl is forced to pull his hand back. So I can catch my breath and smooth out the loathing and humiliation on my face that I hope he hasn't seen. My fingers scramble in my purse. I hear the creak of floorboards, the swish of Mrs. T's skirt, the noisy clanks as she opens the myriad latches on the front door.

When I sit back up, the visitor is stepping over the threshold, a dark-haired teenager named Lolita with a rose tattoo etched on the delicate underside of her wrist. Lolita visits every Wednesday—the granddaughter of one of Mrs. T's boarders. She has done a good job of trying to forget that her grandfather once set a house fire with six people inside. He's docile now. Only out of prison because no one died.

I've noticed that Lolita keeps her head down around Carl. Today is no exception. As usual, she's wearing a scarf stamped with pink and white snails. One time, the scarf was tied around her ponytail, another, scrunched through her belt loops. Today it dangles loosely around her neck. I overheard her tell Mrs. T that the scarf was a Christmas gift from her grandfather. She wears it to help him remember who she is.

Mrs. T and Lolita drift out of the room, chattering, without speaking to us. I hand Carl the pen from my purse, a favorite one with the ink that glides like blue oil.

"As requested," I say. "So you will come?" I sound a little more pleading and hopeful than I'd like. Maybe more like a daughter. Maybe that's good.

He jams the pen in the waist of his jeans, baring the intimate flash of black hair below his belly button. My heartbeat punches against my throat, harder even than when he pressed his fingers there.

"Cute girl, cute scarf," Carl says matter-of-factly. "Did you know the cone snail has enough venom to kill a human being? People call it the Cigarette because once it stings, you have just about enough time to smoke a cigarette before you die." He pokes me in the ribs. "Oh, come on. Smile. I've heard that's an exaggeration." Carl pulls his fingers to his lips and pantomimes a drag. "I wonder if Lolita likes to smoke."

3

The first time I saw a photograph of Carl, I felt a sharp sting of the familiar. It was a partial view, an artsy portrait shot in half-shadow. I had a feeling I knew him from somewhere. Still do. When I concentrate, it's like searching for the name of a bit character in a book I read years ago or trying to latch on to a genetic memory. And yet it is a defiant reason I'm so sure Carl is the one.

It's been two more visits, and Carl hasn't said yes to going with me. He is crawling around in my head all the time now. Waking me up. At night, alone in my bedroom, I feel his fingers roaming my body, searching for pulse points.

Now fury pounds my chest, the same insistent rush I'd felt on the way over today. Our bodies are slanted in battered Adirondack chairs in Mrs. T's dirt backyard. In the corner, there's a ragged patch of garden where Carl eagerly told me three cats and a squirrel are buried. Honeysuckle and vines creep wildly out of control up the sturdy ten-foot fence, fusing a thick cage.

"I don't see a thing in this so-called vacation for me," Carl is complaining. "You could be a lunatic. The female lioness does ninety percent of the hunting. Learned that yesterday on Nat Geo. I have to give it to Mrs. T, she doesn't skimp on cable." He's sucking at the straw of the Big Gulp I concocted at his request: one-third Sprite, one-third cherry Coke, one-third Dr Pepper.

In that instant, I decide on a new script. I manage to keep my voice low so it stops before it reaches the shuttered windows of the house. *"I need to know."*

Carl calmly tugs a square of yellow paper out of his pocket and begins to unfold it. "I want to hear you say it."

"I need to know if you're a killer. As your daughter, I need to know what kind of blood runs in my veins. You owe it to me." The first and last line, at least, are true.

"That wasn't so hard, was it? So we're clear this trip isn't about bonding or breathing fresh air. If you were really my daughter, you would have told me that from the start. You would have talked about how you don't want your babies to be killers. You would have cried big tears. And you would have gotten out of here just as fast as you could. That's what normal girls do."

I open my mouth to disagree and close it. Carl is right. I am not a normal girl. He is being extremely lucid for a change. I don't want to interrupt.

"Just so you know, this is an exercise in madness," he continues. *"I can't remember.* Every now and then, a cop drops by here to be sure. He thinks I'm giving him shit. If he can't break into my head, how do you think you can?"

What cop? Someone I know? For a second, I feel another man's fingers.

"I have a plan to help you remember," I wheedle. "Places. Photographs. Don't you want to know?"

"Why *would* I want to know? You're much prettier than that cop, though. A lioness on the hunt."

On the wide arm of his chair, he's smoothing out the wrinkled yellow paper he pulled from his pocket. I can't make out the words from here, just that he's been putting my blue pen to work. Then he holds the paper in front of his face like an earnest child. It shakes ever so slightly even though the air is hot and still.

When Carl begins to read, I realize he's been planning to go with me all along.

He's naming conditions—all the things he wants in return for getting in the car.

Sweet tea every day like his dead grandmother made.

Books.

A shovel.

It's a fairly long list. I stop listening about halfway through and start thinking about the next step—cajoling Mrs. T into springing Carl, which I've hinted at. I've told her my birth certificate says "unknown" for the father—that I found him through a DNA match. I'm hoping she won't ask for paperwork again.

When he finishes reading, Carl says magnanimously: "Don't feel like you have to get this stuff before we hit the road."

He folds up the paper neatly and tucks it back in his jeans. "You're an odd little duck. Emphasis on *little*. And *odd*. I wonder why you don't seem worried that I'm going to kill you, too."

Conditions

Camera

Ghost pepper salsa

Sweet tea (daily)

Dairy Queen

Whataburger

Ruby Red

New nail clippers

1015s

Pulled pork

Baby Head

Muleshoe

Mystery Lights

100 percent feather pillow

CFS

Tito's

Case of Shiner

Hiking boots

Rope

Shovel

11/22/63 (Stephen King)*

Lonesome Dove*

Ulysses*

Mexican Dr Pepper w/real sugar

Waterproof watch (resistant @ 300 meters)

Flashlight

WD-40

New York Times

Glad Press'n Seal

Bible

*Hardcovers only!!!!

DAY ONE

How to be as brave as my sister

1. Make a notebook.

2. Research fears.

3. Test fears.

4. Sneak out the window at night like she does.

5. Don't be afraid.

4

I'm dizzy with hope. He's finally packing to go with me. Perfect T-shirt squares. Socks balled into a plastic bag. *Borderline obsessive-compulsive,* claimed two psychiatric reports. Carl adds one pair of sweats, two pairs of pajama bottoms.

The drawers in this narrow blue room are hanging empty; the closet, a skeleton of bare hangers. He's packing every item of clothing he brought when he was dismissed to this hell of last resort, and they won't even fill up a suitcase.

Where is his stuff? Right after the trial, after he was acquitted, when he sold his house and disappeared for years, there were rumors he kept a secret place, the proverbial cabin in the woods. It was hinted at between the lines of a glossy magazine spread on Carl titled "Darkroom," which I thought was a spot-on headline for a documentary photographer who was a suspected serial killer.

Mrs. T is watching with me from the door, arms crossed, a disapproving sergeant in a fading apron. It took a week, but I convinced her. She'd bargained me down to ten days instead of fourteen.

"You're still sure about this, right?" Mrs. T says, interrupting my thoughts. That's what she likes to be called, tired of people mangling her consonant-riddled Polish surname.

More than once, she has reminded me how brave she is to give refuge to outcasts and criminals "as Christ commanded." I despised her until the day two weeks ago I passed by a bedroom and saw her hugging the lady with the veil. Mrs. T was reassuring her. *Your man will make it back from the war in time for your wedding.*

"It will be fine," I say to Mrs. T.

"Ten days is longer than you think. I can't say it enough. You *have* to keep up with his meds. He gets these tremors sometimes but other times he's just fine." She gestures to the pharmacy in the Ziploc bag in my hand. "He'll lie, you know. Forget. It's not good when he forgets. You saw it yourself last week. How old are you again? You don't look the right age to be his daughter. A little too young. Are you nineteen? Twenty? If I do that math, it ain't going to add up."

So, I say silently. *Stop me. Someone probably should.*

". . . but I'm putting my trust in you because you seem like your heart's in the right place. Just don't forget our deal. I cut you slack on the red tape. I don't want to be cut short for the days you've got him if he's not here when that tight-ass from the state does her little monthly bed check. I don't get enough money as it is. The state must think *halfway house* means I deserve half as much." She likes this line of hers. Wears the same smirk every time she says it.

". . . what they don't realize is, tending to six half-crazies is like having twelve. Half their head is still sharp as the devil, making plans to sneak out for donuts and tequila. The other half is time-travelin' to God knows where. It can get real busy around here. Right, Mr. Feldman?"

I keep silent throughout her speech, because I've heard it a few times. Carl is curling up his Christmas tie and tucking it in a corner near the underwear. I'm relieved it's not around his neck. Better if nothing attracts attention.

20

An hour ago, when he thought I was busy with his landlady, I had watched him carefully through the kitchen window as he buried his ten-pound weights in that untended garden out back. I don't know what has happened to his other treasures. I will deal with them later.

The knife that could cut skin like paper and spill the strawberry syrup. The long red rubber band that could choke. The lighter with the N that still fires. I had stared into its flame before I put it back.

The photograph of the girl in the desert that makes my mouth dry.

"Don't know what y'all expect to do on this little family bonding trip," Mrs. T says, "but don't expect some hallelujah father-daughter moment. Neither of you."

"Has he had a violent episode here?" He's only six feet away. I want him to hear me. *Violent* wasn't on any of Mrs. T's daily reports, at least the ones she let me see.

She tugs me into the hallway. "You said you already know all about his history." Her face works for a few seconds. "Here's the deal. My nephew's paying me to rent his room through the rest of this month."

That answers my little worry about the cop showing up to see Carl while we're gone. If this cop exists, Mrs. T has her own reasons to keep him away.

She's working the angles. Concerned that I'll back out. I've nosed around. *Where does the money go, Mrs. T?* Certainly not into the sticks of Goodwill furniture, the pantry of pork and beans and generic-brand peanut butter, the two bathrooms with corroding handicapped bars and *Reader's Digest* stories taped on the wall.

Only the locks on the doors and the medicine cabinets are gleaming and solid. The TV is the newest equipment in the place, but it's an off brand, on duty fourteen hours a day, already signaling its death with that relentless buzz. I want to report her but that could backfire. I plan to slip into her life, and out.

And where would the woman with the veil go? Who would hug her?

"He's coming with me," I assure her. "I just would like to know if he's attacked anyone since he's been here."

"Depends what you mean. I lower my standards for this crowd. Not everything gets reported, you know? And Carl here, he don't get antagonized much. My residents got a sense not to mess with him. They don't like his weird friends." She chuckles.

I'm thrown again. Mrs. T and Carl haven't mentioned any friends visiting before. *Will someone else miss him?* I can't think about that now.

Carl is pulling something metal and shiny from under his pillow. It's disappearing into the suitcase.

He snaps the case shut. "I'm ready." He's wearing Levi's, a tucked-in blue work shirt, a worn leather belt, and those finger-crushing boots. The nicest things he owns, which I know because I tried to search every inch of his space. The effort he's made today on a public appearance both scares and tugs at me.

He's not hiding it. He's looking forward to this.

I've prepared myself as much as I can.

"Last day of the month at the outset," Mrs. T repeats. "That's when he needs to be all tucked in." She turns to speak directly to him. "Mr. Feldman, don't get any fancy ideas about freedom. This will be your first and last vacation from Mrs. T's bed-and-breakfast."

She escorts us to the door. A conga line of ex-criminals is waiting, two men and three women. One wedding veil, one Cubs baseball cap, two pink fuzzy slippers, one bare chest, one aloha shirt with palm trees. Two murderers, one arsonist, one child molester, one rapist. All diagnosed with dementia and a pre-existing tendency to snap. I researched their trials on the Internet, called up social workers, gossiped with a late-night, tipsy Mrs. T.

Pink Slippers is the nicest. She shot her son-in-law five days after he violently raped her daughter. By the time she got out of prison at seventy-four, her daughter was dead. No one was around to step in and knock off the next brute she married.

Mrs. T leans in, her breath licking my ear. "He's going to want a camera. You don't need me to tell you that's a bad damn idea. For emergencies, don't forget the bottle with the red mark on the lid. Say hi to Florida." She shuts the door on us firmly. Done.

Endless aqua sea. Salt in my mouth, on my skin. No clocks.

Except that's not where we're going, and Carl knows it.

He's already fifty feet ahead of me, whistling in appreciation at the black Buick parked by the curb. I don't tell him it's a rental, or that we'll be dumping it. There will be no part of me he will ever be able to hunt down. When this is over, I will be one of the million feathers in his brain he can't catch.

I pop up the trunk and move to take the suitcase out of his hand. He ignores me, lifts it easily, and tosses it inside. Slams the trunk. I'm not surprised. He is strong. Already, he seems taller, more substantial. Mrs. T marked him at 5'11" on her admittance form. The old police reports said 6'3". Both listed a birthdate that makes him sixty-two years old next Thursday.

He pulls open the door to the backseat and glances back at Mrs. T's prison, a two-story Victorian with gray paint peeling like fish scales. The houses on either side stand like abandoned carcasses, fish bones licked clean.

In an upstairs window, one of the shutters moves.

Carl delivers a jaunty two-finger salute in return.

Significant paralysis in the left arm. I was counting on those words, typed with such officialdom and clarity on one of the reports. Except Carl just saluted, no problem, with his left hand. Until now, he's never lifted anything but his right hand in my presence, the one he's using now to hold open the door to the backseat.

I walk over, shove the door closed, and yank the handle on the front passenger side. "Not the backseat. You're riding shotgun. Up here." I almost add *Dad. Up here, Dad.*

"Just bein' polite," he says.

He slides into the seat. Rolls down the window. Grins at its fluid silence. Rolls it up. Rolls it down. Tasting freedom.

He lays the familiar yellow piece of paper on the console. "My list of conditions. In case you forget."

"I won't forget."

I thrust the car in gear. I've spent half my life getting ready for Carl. I'm suddenly terrified ten days isn't going to be enough.

5

Rachel was lying to my mother.

"I already said *we won't leave the house*." Each word, taut with fury.

My sister was imprisoned because of me, missing a birthday sleepover, ordered to babysit so my parents could attend the wedding of a twice-divorced friend.

A storm was predicted.

When my parents left, the sky was still clear and light.

As soon as she tied on her most battered Nikes, I knew where Rachel wanted to go—a culvert in a nearby creek bed that she liked to explore. You had to traverse a row of fourteen stones jutting out of the water to get to the mouth of the dark tunnel where random treasures floated in and got stuck. An old bottle, a silver ring, once even a soggy coin purse with fifty-two dollar bills.

We were halfway down the incline, rain slashing the creek, when the anger drained out of Rachel. "This is a mistake. We're turning around."

That's when we heard the yell. And another. A hundred yards below, I could make out a small boy standing in the mouth of the culvert, waving his arms. The rain was falling in sheets now, the creek at a frothy boil. The water in the man-made cave, normally just an inch or two of muck, was already halfway up to his knees. The boy seemed too scared to cross the creek to solid ground.

Rachel gripped me possessively by the shoulder. No one could sense my fear like she could. "Wait here. Do not *move*. Do you hear me? I will never, ever let anything happen to you."

She was at the water's edge before I could beg her to stop. I didn't move. I couldn't take my eyes off Rachel as she performed a dangerous ballet, leaping from stone to stone. Except the stones had disappeared, swallowed by rising water. Rachel was jumping from memory.

I'm sure it was only a few minutes before she led the boy across the creek. It felt like forever. He fell off a stone at one point, and they waded the rest of the way, the water up to the boy's neck.

The three of us climbed back up the embankment, soaked and silent, Rachel in the middle holding our hands. We dropped the boy off at his house about two blocks from there, not knowing what story he'd tell. He hugged Rachel goodbye. I don't remember ever seeing him again.

Rachel and I kept that night a secret. We'd gotten home well before my parents. She had immediately thrown me in the shower, made me cocoa, helped me slip on one of her soft T-shirts and into smooth sheets.

"Are you awake?" I whispered later into the gap between our beds. "Yes," Rachel replied sleepily. "What is it?"

"I thought you were going to die. Please don't die." A sticky sob emerged from my throat. Rachel slipped into my bed and wrapped her arms around me. I still feel the imprint of her body at my back when I curl up.

Maybe every child has a story like this, where something really terrible almost happened. Maybe the water wasn't rushing as fast, the space between the stones wasn't as great, the danger to Rachel not as imminent.

I just know I saw Rachel walk on water that night.

6

I've neatly placed a collection of snapshots in rows of five on the motel room's desk. Wide eyes and closed ones. Baby toes and yellowed teeth. Cut-off heads and the blur of legs, running. Some are filler, to sift out Carl's lies. Some are mute witnesses who can speak only to him.

This is Carl's first test. After a couple of hours of my driving, he fidgets in the chair, eager to get this over with and watch TV without having to barter with Mrs. T's other houseguests.

There are twenty photographs in all. Nothing arty, just normal point-and-shoot. There are at least fifty others in the lime green Tupperware container in the trunk of the rental car.

Family picnics and birthday parties, Christmases and Easter egg hunts, graduations and weddings. When the camera sees happy smiles, I imagine the worms wriggling underneath. The mean daddies, the cheating brides, the rotten eggs, the thoughtless presents.

"That's me." This is true. I point to an adolescent girl reveling in the corn chip smell of two puppies my dad let Rachel and me pick out at the animal shelter. I named one Biscuit because he was the color of a biscuit. My sister instantly named the other Gravy.

No response from Carl. I push aside a scratchpad on the desk that unabashedly reads *Waco's Dollar Inn: By the minute, by the month* and spread some of the pictures a little farther apart. "That's you in college." I stab at an image of five boys in Kappa Alpha T-shirts, raising Bud Lights in the air. "You're the one on the far right." He stares at the face blankly. I'm lying. I have no idea who these boys are.

I pick up the picture next to it. "This is Uncle Jim and Aunt Louisa in front of their house." True. Someone has written *Uncle Jim & Aunt Louisa* in pencil on the back.

"Pretty crappy house," he says. "Are they dead? Bet they wish they were dead."

It's after nine, a very bad time to be starting my project if he "sundowns" as the books say. The word sets me on edge. Dementia isn't a pretty evening sky. It's an ocean fog, an endless midnight beach run and a stalker you hear padding in the sand behind you. Keep running, or wade into the black waves. The correct verbification of dementia would be "Stephen Kinging."

I can't help myself from pushing Carl tonight. We didn't get out of Mrs. T's until six, wiping out almost a whole day. He napped or pretended to on the hour-and-a-half drive from the halfway house in Fort Worth to the outskirts of Waco. He wolfed down a Dairy Queen dinner in near-silence, complaining briefly about how the sweet tea tasted like creek water laced with pancake syrup.

This, even though I know for a fact he loves Dairy Queen. It is No. 4 on his list of conditions. I had caught him staring at me from the booth while I placed our order with the teenage waif at the counter. Not a benign stare. A cold, memorizing one. He was sizing me up, making his own plans.

He begins to stack the pictures squarely on top of each other. "This motel is a dump."

"Well," I snap, "you're not paying." The books say, *Don't snap.*

When I pulled $4,000 out of my savings account two days ago, it seemed like a fortune. $2,000 of it is now rolled into wads in the spare tire in the trunk, another $500 tucked behind my underwear in one of the mesh pockets of my new suitcase with the combination lock. I stuffed the rest into the wallet next to the credit cards in my real name that I won't be using on this trip except for an emergency exit.

But already I am worried. Counting. $12.62 for the Dairy Queen Dudes, fries, and iced tea. $100.29 for two bare-bones rooms with beige plastic bathtub liners and scratchy maroon-striped polyester bedspreads. $38.66 to fill up the car because I set rules for myself on this trip and one of them is to never let the tank fall below half.

Another $3,000 from my savings was shot when I made a little run to Houston a few days ago. I'd handed off the cash to the preppy college student who met me behind an Indian restaurant in Houston's Rice Village. In person, he struck me as the guy at the top of his class in business school, or maybe the kid giving the mafia of Asian pre-med girls a run for their money.

I'd hooked up with him on the Dark Web, where the cockroaches of the earth do their untraceable Internet business. It took only three minutes to download a search engine that allowed me to skip in the shadows like a schoolgirl alongside terrorists and arms dealers, libertarians and twenty-something entrepreneurs.

About a year ago, a hairdresser named Tiffany, who had a "bit of a boyfriend-and-Discover-Card problem," told me about an illegal website she was going to use to reinvent herself as a Lola or a Francesca. She was trying out a blue-black rinse on me at the time, and I listened out of one ear. I wondered if the "bit" referred to her boyfriend's penis.

I never returned to her salon again, but I typed the password she mentioned—*Pamperzzz*—into mommyzhelper.com. For a careful planner like me, it was a risk. A tip from a Tiffany.

I could have been contacting a baby-napping adoption ring, a guy with a diaper porn fetish, a cop on the other end ready to sting. How could I really be sure that *all* the signals in the Dark Web bounce around like grasshoppers on cocaine?

A chat box had popped up almost instantly: *"I'm Tom, your Texas Helper. Can I change you?"* I didn't get the diaper reference until days later, after I'd sent three headshots into the ether. I was told I could pick up my package in Houston.

At our rendezvous time, I'd brought a Subway bag stuffed with $20 bills and a toasted ham and cheese with lettuce, mayo, black olives, green pepper, jalapeños, and Swiss. Tom's special order. I traded for a manila envelope that contained three fake driver's licenses, three MasterCards with names that matched, and three sets of shiny new Texas plates. Three's always been a good number for me.

"I threw a little Larry G in there for the road." Tom had gestured toward the envelope. "Customer appreciation. Spread the word." I didn't know if Larry G was like a Flat Stanley for adults or something moody for the CD player.

I didn't ask because my head was filled with other questions for him. *Don't you know you could go to prison for a very long time? Don't you know you could ruin everything and never, ever recover?* They are questions I constantly ask myself.

Before I could deliver a little food for thought, Tom touched my shoulder and advised, "If you think someone isn't buying what you're selling, don't panic." He gestured to the manila envelope. "The pic of you as a blonde? It has the least cred."

My cheeks had gone hot—a grateful rush of emotion at the idea that this stranger cared about my outcome. Instant intimacy, like with the doctor who sees you in a blue paper gown and kindly lays a hand on your shoulder but would never recognize your face in an airport. The warm feeling hung on until he snaked his way back across two lanes of Houston rush hour traffic and disappeared.

One of the credit cards and a driver's license worked like magic a few hours later on the ditzy Avis agent who rented me a car at the Dallas/Fort Worth airport. I don't know if they will fool the police if I get stopped. Absolutely no speeding, that's another rule.

I'd switched the license plates in the back of a Walmart parking lot on the way from DFW to Mrs. T's. I'd cut the first fake credit card, whose job was done, into sharp, jagged bits and let pieces fly out the car window at thirty-second intervals. Maybe all of this is overkill, but how can I know? I want a life after this. Ten days, that's how long I have. Almost down to nine.

We will need gas and food and two motel rooms every night no matter the cost because I am sure as hell not sleeping in the same room with him. I'm already adding in other items I didn't account for ahead of time. Things that will make him blend in. Good athletic shoes, toiletries, and a haircut. There are the extra conditions he added at the last minute. And miscellaneous.

My father had always reminded me to be sure to add a separate line for miscellaneous when I was making budgets. What would that be in this case? Bribes? Extra bullets? Bandages? Shovels? Red licorice and BIGS Dill Pickle Sunflower Seeds from every Buc-ee's truck stop along the way?

The pictures are back in a tidy pile. Carl didn't really study the images, just organized them by size, the largest ones at the bottom. Landing on top, a wallet-size school picture of a boy with sleepy eyes and a crooked part in his hair. The boy is Alexander Lakinski, the son of Nicole Lakinski, the woman Carl was put on trial for kidnapping from a park in Waco. Alexander was left behind with a broken arm. He said he fell off a swing. His mother was never seen again.

Carl stands up. Stretches both arms in the air.

"May I go to my room, please, ma'am?" He's already halfway across the carpet to the door that will stand between us tonight.

"You promised, Carl."

"Promised what?"

"To try. You promised to try. You told me you didn't remember what you did, but you wanted to. That you were all in. Never mind. Just take your pills, OK? I'll get them. They're in my purse."

He's fiddling with the chain lock on my side, sliding it gently back and forth on its track. Considering.

"You have to take your pills, Carl. That's the deal. If not, you're back at Mrs. T's watching insects on the Discovery Channel."

"Did you know houseflies hum in the key of F?" he asks. "I'll be happy to take my pills."

He's going to give me this. Carl knows I'm lying—that I'm not about to throw in the towel on our very first day.

He told me once that my gray eyes remind him of someone he used to know. *Smoke and mirrors,* he said. *Makes it hard to know what either of you will do next.* Rachel had green eyes with a sprinkle of gold.

I've caught intelligence, *sanity* in Carl's. Over the chessboard, at Dairy Queen, while we drank canned iced tea in Mrs. T's backyard that he said tasted like Triaminic, whatever that is.

Carl used to be a talented artist. His eyes remind me of a mossy pool of muck in one of his photographs. The police dug around at that spot and several others, trying to link Carl and his camera to other disappearances in Texas. But they gave up too soon.

Carl knows I'm lying about why we're on this road trip. There's not an ounce of him that buys that I'm his crime-solving long-lost daughter compelled to know what kind of DNA is churning in her blood. That once I know the truth, I'll just walk away.

He's putting the pills in his mouth one at a time, swallowing them dry, even though I offered to unwrap the cellophane from the cup on the dresser and fill it with water out of the bathroom faucet.

I could lay it all out—that every time I look in his face, I feel a merciless itch in my brain. How it's just one reason I'm sure he's the one who took my big sister when the sun was shining. Rachel was going to French-braid my hair that night for a party. She was going to be a famous actress. I was going to have a niece named Sophronia.

Don't feel.

Keep his mind dancing.

Carl is a curious man.

Why is my puppet string.

He's on the other side of the door now. Starting to hum.

7

I'm inching open the door. A faint slice of light spills like bleach from my room to his, across the floor and up the stripes of his bed-spread.

It's after eleven. I'm worried the light is going to strike his face and wake him up if I nudge the door open much more.

Did he really swallow the pink pill that makes him sleep? Or did he spit it out? It seems ridiculous to treat him like a child, although Mrs. T said, *You have to treat him like a child.*

I slip through the crack as soon as I can fit, raking my belly on the doorknob. Push the door behind me as far as it will go without click-ing in place. I'm perfectly still, not breathing, letting my eyes adjust. I can't see much. The curtains are pulled shut. The air conditioner under the window is rumbling like a truck that wants to die. I'm as-saulted with the smell of mildew and feet, the *fuck you* of underpaid maids.

I don't sense any movement or sound from his bed, but would I? The window unit is laboring, working both for and against me.

In my own room, while Nigella yapped from the TV about gou-jons of sole, I practiced six times. Carl and I have duplicate spaces, as cookie cutter as prison cells. There are ten careful steps from this spot to the foot of the bed. I take them. My knees fall to the scratchy carpet. I lift up the bedspread, thrust my head underneath, flip on my tiny flashlight, and cast the beam around.

I'm not disappointed. There's a trail of popcorn, a child's Mickey Mouse pacifier coated in hair, and Carl's suitcase just where I thought it would be. Habits are hard to break for dementia patients and ob-sessive compulsives and serial killers. He is at least one of these things, maybe all of them.

I slide forward on my stomach so I can reach it. The suitcase lies flat under the right side of the mattress, which means less chance of disturbing him when I slide it out. Carl sleeps on the left. I saw the indent in his pillow at Mrs. T's more than once, and it was an odd detail in the testimony of his cleaning woman, Irma, who had worked for him on and off when he lived in Fort Worth, about six miles from my childhood home. *What serial killer has a maid?* Carl's defense lawyer had asked that excellent question of the jury.

Irma, in a forlorn little apartment with her well-dusted pig figu-rine collection, had nothing useful to say by the time I got to her. She clearly had residual affection for Carl, who'd paid her $25 an hour. Her apartment smelled like collard greens. I couldn't stop staring at the pig in the center of the mirrored shelf above her head with the chipped white ear and the near-fatal hairline fracture around its neck. Irma had made an extreme effort to save it. What did this pig say about Irma? That she loved the person who gave it to her too much to throw it away?

Irma made me leave after an hour of fruitless questioning so she could get back to a good part in her erotic romance. "Sex every fifty pages, like clockwork," she'd told me. "It's a rule."

I turn off my flashlight and pick up the case by the handle. *One-two-three-four-five-six-seven-eight* steps to the bathroom door. The tile under my feet is cold and sticky.

I shut the bathroom door until it clicks and lay the case gently on the bathroom rug. The suitcase zipper sounds like a buzz saw. I pause for a good two minutes to make sure Carl didn't hear before I travel the flashlight over his clothes, so tidy and creepy.

On top, one of Mrs. T's sauté pans, which must be the shiny thing I'd seen him slip into his suitcase. My hand wriggles into every crevice, every pocket, between every layer of clothing. I feel the soft edges of the picture of the girl with the key. But I can't find the lighter or the knife, the red exercise band that I have imagined around my throat.

I had planned to steal these one at a time, hoping he would forget, think he misplaced them.

I don't believe he abandoned any of these things along the way. He's hidden them in this motel room, somewhere in the dark.

Another round to Carl.

In less than a minute, I'm back at the adjoining door, ready to leave, the suitcase snugly back in place.

Movement. Not from the bed.

From the other side of the room.

He's awake.

My heart begins a steady punch to my chest.

I picture my room, so I can picture his.

Carl's in the darkest corner, sitting in a plastic chair that he said was the color of a Dreamsicle when we first walked into the motel room four hours ago. He had then added a Dreamsicle to his conditions. After he explained the cool collision of vanilla and orange in his mouth, I wanted one, too.

I reach for the knob and yank. The door opens two inches and revolts. He's thrown the chain.

I flip around. I can't make out anything but a shadow, so my imagination sketches in the details. Maybe he's found my gun. Except a gun would make a noise, and Carl wouldn't want that, would he?

There is only ominous stillness from the corner. I close the door because I have no choice. I'm counting how many steps it might take for him to reach me in the dark and slip the red exercise band around my neck or jut the pocketknife under my ribs. All the while, I'm fiddling with the fragile necklace on the door.

And then I'm falling into my room, slamming the hollow door between us, twisting the tiny lock in the knob, working at the flimsy chain on my side three times before my shaking fingers get it right.

I press my ear to the wood. The air conditioner's rumble swallows everything.

I stagger to the bathroom. In the mirror, my pupils, dilated and glassy, look nothing like Rachel's. I turn my hands over and over in running hot water, until they stop trembling. In the bedroom, I snap off the TV. I straighten the pen and the Bible on the desk. I grab my dirty clothes off the floor and begin to painstakingly fold them to put away. Anything to keep my hands busy, to make this night pass faster.

When I lift the lid of my suitcase, I choke down a scream.

Carl has left me a present.

Lying on top, the scarf that was wrapped around Lolita's pretty neck at Mrs. T's.

For seconds, I don't breathe. The pink and white snails march innocently across the fabric, their smiles like tiny eyelash curls.

I remember another piece of fabric, swirling in water in one of Carl's photographs. A missing girl named Violet. My head jerks toward the door that connects my room to Carl's. Chain in place. Knob, still. When I turn back to my suitcase, Lolita's sweet, youthful smell drifts up and with it a silent, panicked prayer that she's alive, that I have not stirred up a hibernating killer.

In the bathroom, I grip the scarf by its edges and hold it up to unforgiving light. I search every happy snail for a spot of blood. There's nothing. Just a faint mustard stain, the scratch of a pencil mark.

I picture the muscled knot in Carl's forearm. His chuckling face when he heard my muffled scream through the door. The taut shape of him in the darkness, waiting. This scarf, torn from my hands, drawn tight across my neck until I see the glimmering, sunny spots of the end. *Would you like a cigarette first, dear?*

I curl up on the bed. Coil my hands into fists.

I want my sister.

8

I was in third grade when I kept my first secret from my big sister.

Rachel was fifteen, always hanging out at theater practice, making faces, flirting with boys. I was lonely. I obsessed a lot. Anthrax and shark attacks were big news.

I was also odd, with rituals. Kids sniffed this out no matter how many times Rachel tried to fix my hair like hers or picked out my clothes in the morning for school. I insisted on carrying a hiking backpack with a hidden pocket for my survival notebook instead of a sparkly one with Lizzie McGuire's face. Once, when a teacher brought in a black kitten, I crossed my heart and spit over my shoulder onto the desk of the boy behind me.

My mother worried about me. She had hammered up a Matisse poster on my bedroom wall, insisting it was bright and cheerful enough to scare away all the ghosts I invented. She didn't know I closed my eyes every night worried that the yellow cat dabbing its paw in a vase of fishes was eventually going to succeed. That when I woke up, the cat would be gone and the water would be bloody. *Le chat aux poissons rouges*. Even its title sounded ominous.

I'd found the old photograph in our house a month later in an envelope taped to the bottom of the attic stairs. My mother had sent me up with a flashlight to retrieve the snowman wreath she always hung on our door.

A sliver of paper was peering through a crack on the step. When I reached around the side and underneath, I thought the envelope probably held directions to the attic fan or the furnace. The elderly woman who lived there before us was forever taping envelopes with instructions to the bottoms of drawers and cabinet doors. Rachel and I hadn't quite given up hope that one of them would hold hundred-dollar bills.

This one, though, was thinner, sweated with brown water stains. It held a black-and-white picture of two girls in a forest, about my age, little brides with white dresses and veils. They looked like twins. One girl was a blur of white motion, like she had just stepped out of the other. On the back of the print, there was another blur, of blue writing. Their names, the date—whatever had been written there—obliterated.

I never considered this photograph strange. It felt magical, special, just for me. I was drawn into that forest like Alice to Wonderland. I taped the picture carefully to the wall at the back of my closet where no one would find it. I could tell that these were the kind of girls I wanted to be—girls who wandered unafraid, climbed trees too high, trapped creatures in jars, back-flipped across every open space, spit on boys on purpose.

I used to part my hanging clothes like stage curtains, and they'd be waiting to play. I'd make up stories. Sketch their picture. Sometimes I pretended that one was me and one was Rachel, that we weren't seven long years apart, that we had exploded into life at the same second and curled up to each other in the womb, that I never spent a single moment being alone or needing to be afraid of anything.

Eventually, I made a real-life friend—a gawky, sweet girl who sat with me at lunch and only ate things that were orange. She kept secrets, too. She stole food out of her kitchen and concealed it all over her bedroom, never eating it. Once, I found a melted, unopened carton of chocolate ice cream under her bed. She made me feel normal.

The picture curled up and fell on the closet floor.

I forgot about the twins.

I had no idea they would someday lead me to Rachel's killer.

DAY TWO

How not to be afraid of spiders

1. Read *Charlotte's Web* every night.

2. Draw a picture of one wearing eight tennis shoes.

3. Hold a fake one.

4. Capture a real one.

5. Call it Barney or Marshmallow.

6. Admire a pretty web.

7. Walk through a web without screaming.

9

I've yanked the curtains open as far as they'll go so that the sun floods the motel room. Carl's sprawled in the orange plastic chair like a taunt, with jean-clad legs stretched out. Boots made out of a nasty snake crossed at the ankles. Lazy expression that has probably fooled a lot of people. Clear-eyed, in a good mood, like last night was just a freak event where we bumped into each other in the netherworld of dreams.

Carl had banged his fist six times on the adjoining door at about 9 A.M. I'd been dragging out my minimal packing, hoping the longer I took, the more chance I'd find his bed made smooth as a cardboard box and Carl Feldman gone.

Just one day in, and I'm thinking this way. *One* day in.

I don't bring up his little present. If Rachel's death taught me anything, it is the tormenting power of silence. When I'd opened the door to the motel room, Carl had waited politely, suitcase in hand, until I gestured him over the threshold. He said he was getting worried about me. *Do you always sleep this late?* I couldn't detect any

43

guile. In fact, I hadn't closed my eyes until after a call to Mrs. T, until the first dull light of morning whispered *safe*. Two uneasy hours of shut-eye, tops.

I'd debated the merits of waking Mrs. T from a dead sleep. My panic won out. "What the hell time is it?" she'd screeched at me. "Why in good God do you care? No, I haven't seen Lolita. Today is Tuesday. Girl's regular as a clock. Not due to show until tomorrow." And then, grumbling: "She did call at suppertime last night, looking for that hideous scarf."

I am already counting the extra money it will take for better hotels with real dead bolts. Texas posts speed limits of eighty-five miles an hour on some roads. I was shortening my timeline—*eight days? seven?*—and wanting to discount Mrs. T's warnings about close sleeping arrangements. *Make sure you can hear him holler. If he wakes up and doesn't remember what's on the other side of the door, that's trouble.*

"I'm going to check the bathroom," I say to Carl, "and then we can go."

He doesn't acknowledge, just leans over and picks up the map I've spread out on the bed.

I like to see Texas all at once, every vein and artery, because it is a body that will fool you. I won't be relying on a bossy GPS voice to find my way. I don't want to be tracked. Carl and I, we are both ghosts.

Carl seems mesmerized by the three scattered red dots on the map, each like a fresh drop of blood, each representing a spot on earth where he stood and snapped a picture near where a girl disappeared. I'm hoping it's going to be an eventful and fluid journey— that Carl will erase dots, add dots, whatever makes him talk, feel control, *remember*.

Besides Rachel, I've linked ten missing girls to Carl's photographs. For the purposes of my plan, I ruthlessly narrowed the list to three. I did this based on my gut and which girls' eyes begged and dared me when I stared at their photographs. On which families touched me the most with their grief.

These girls—these cold cases—are my insistent, beating hope, the only way I know to jog Carl's conscience. I have to follow their stories, because in Rachel's case, there is no story to tell, no dot. No one remembers a girl on a silver mountain bike that morning. No one knows if Rachel was on a new route to her job or took a short-cut. *No one saw anything.* She was simply gone.

I close the door in the bathroom. Flush the toilet, run the tap water. Give the map time to gestate in his brain. Glance to the scarf tossed on the hook on the back of the door. I hadn't wanted it to touch my clothes all night. For a second, I consider leaving it.

When I come out, there's no Carl. No map. The adjoining door is ajar. I give it a tentative push. At some point this morning, he has stripped his sheets, blankets, and bedspread and folded them into a stack of squares. A crisp twenty-dollar bill sits on top of the pile.

Mrs. T said he didn't have any cash.

Both suitcases are gone. So is my purse. He's taken everything but the change I'd strewn on the dresser for the housekeeper.

I'm outside in seconds. The car is still parked in front of the room, exactly where it was when we pulled in last night. Carl's in the passenger seat, his mouth moving animatedly. When he sees me, it snaps tight.

I walk toward him, slowly looping the scarf around my neck.

10

Carl hasn't said a word about the scarf. I adjust it so it doesn't drip into my coffee and slide the laminated menu back behind the sugar shaker. Our waitress is edging up the aisle with a tray, a couple of booths away.

All night, my head was flooded with faces. Lolita, Violet, Rachel, the anonymous girl in Carl's suitcase surrounded by a flood of red sand. I picture her pretty hair, hanging in a black snake down her back, the curly tip flipped up like it was about to strike.

She's one more enigmatic piece. One more possible victim.

I'm stuffed to the bursting point with Carl. Photographs, criminal evidence, psychiatric reports, rumors, supposition, anything and everything I could hunt and find on the killer sitting across from me in this crap diner.

The immense pressure of it rises into my throat.

I pick out one tiny thing.

"Why were you nicknamed the Rain Man?" I ask.

"Why do you want to know?"

"Just breakfast conversation."

"Sure it is. I guess a little *breakfast conversation* doesn't hurt anything. At one time, I was only shooting pictures in the rain. It turned out to be a dumb idea. Difficult and limiting." He shrugs. "It was the period after someone I loved died in a storm."

There isn't a sliver of emotion on Carl's face.

It's not the first time I've heard the story. The prosecutor told the jury it was *pure public relations fairy tale. Don't be fooled. This isn't a romantic man, folks.*

Before I can follow up, Carl leans forward, his elbow scattering the six pills I laid out in a line in front of him on the blue-and-black-speckled Formica tabletop. "Let *me* make a little conversation. I'd remember if I ran around killing people. That's what dementia patients do. They remember the past like it was *fucking yesterday.* I remember the first picture I ever shot, and I sure as hell remember what iced tea is supposed to taste like. So I'm pretty sure I'd remember what it was like to slit a throat."

I involuntarily jerk my head so that my hair falls over my left eye and cheek. Since childhood, this has been my tell, the one nervous tic I can't seem to control no matter how much I practice. Carl knows. He's eyed my hair tosses before, at Mrs. T's.

"Don't worry," Carl says. "Nobody's listening. More privacy in an egg joint like this than on a computer. Me, I listen. I see every frame of life in pictures. Freeze here. Snap there. Can't turn it off. The teenager in the booth behind me? She's knocked up and wants an abortion. She'll get it way before her belly pops up. The woman back of you? She got smacked again last night. Thinks she's really getting a divorce this time. She won't. By the way, I want a damn phone. Add it to my conditions."

This is the longest speech Carl has made in my presence. It's both intelligent and predatory. A week ago, Carl told me he couldn't remember ever being a documentary photographer, or even exactly what one was. The next day, he'd topped his conditions list with *Camera.*

The diner is noisy, its booths packed. It was Carl's idea to get

47

right back out of the parked car at the motel and eat at this restaurant only steps away. Sixty-eight steps, to be exact. It bothers me, this new counting obsession of mine—of steps, of days, of money, of the pills that Carl is now tucking out of sight under the edge of his coffee saucer. Of the 4,566 days since Rachel vanished, the 94 days since my mother assured me she'd stopped drinking again, the 38 days since I signed my real name.

I need to wrest back control. "You can't keep adding conditions, Carl. Where did you get the twenty-dollar bill you left on the bed at the motel?"

"Here you go, honey." The waitress, interrupting, clanking down Carl's breakfast.

"I remember you from somewhere," he tells her. "Your name is Annette. No, *Lynette*. Pretty name. Pretty lady." She flashes beige teeth. I want to shriek, *It's on your name tag, you idiot. He will eat you alive.*

I'm watching Carl unfurl into catnip for an aging waitress wearing a button that says *Don't go bacon' my heart*. I feel a violent urge to mark out the apostrophe. I can tell that Lynette is unsure how to proceed with Carl because of me. *Competition,* she's thinking, *but what kind?*

"This is my *daughter*." Carl, helping her out.

"You sure you don't want more than that little box of cereal?" she asks, refilling my coffee. "You're such a tiny thing."

"No, thanks. I'm good." *Being nice to me won't get you into Carl's jeans and out of that one-bedroom, Lynette.*

I'm unsympathetic to her lifetime plight of picking dangerous men, to the teen who may hustle Texas out of an abortion, to the middle-aged woman alone with her *black-no-cream-please* cup of coffee whose head is softly brushing the back of mine, to myself for already feeling vulnerable when I've trained so very hard for this.

"Stop playing around," I hiss at Carl as soon as Lynette moves down the row.

"What? You want me to lie about us, don't you? She's not my type anyway. Has one of those Shit Yous that barks like a girl. Drives a junker. Bad dancer."

"How do you . . . ? Never mind."

"Dog hair on her pants, key to an '87 Malibu hanging off that ring at her waist, which I also saw sitting in the parking lot. And she's got high arches. They always come with some curly toes."

Carl wets his $6.99 Texas Slamski liberally with blueberry syrup, forks a chunk of Polish sausage and pancake, and slathers it around. "Delicious," he proclaims too loudly. "Mrs. T is a burnt Eggos woman."

"Do not draw more attention to us," I say.

"Not trying to."

"Just keep your voice down."

"I've been thinking. You could be another cop, tricking me. A reporter writing a book."

"We've been over this. Do I look like a cop, Carl?"

At the word *cop,* the teenager flips a third of the way around, thinks better of it, and goes back to tapping on her phone.

"We made a deal," I tell Carl. "You said you would try. That you'd be honest if I fulfilled your conditions. That you'd keep an open mind about our relationship." He didn't say any of these things.

"I'll be as honest as you are, how about that. So far, you are two for thirty-one on the conditions. Maybe we *should* write a book. A man with dementia and his long-lost daughter toddle off on a road trip across Texas solving cold cases to figure out if he's really a serial killer. Clint could play me in the movie. Or the Bridges brother, the younger one, The Dude. Elizabeth Taylor could play you if she had a nose ring and vanilla wafers for boobs and she was alive. I'd like to walk into the desert at the end. I know just the spot."

He pours more syrup in the blank space where his pancakes were. With his spoon, he traces either a heart or Elizabeth Taylor's boobs, then smears it all away.

The cheap material of the scarf is starting to itch the back of my neck. Send shivers.

Still, I don't remove it. Still, Carl does not say a word.

"Is this just a big joke to you?" I hiss. "Women *died*."

"How do you know, if no one ever found them? I've read a few things about me, too."

Before this can register, Lynette is back, snagging up his plate, her chest murmuring against his shoulder. "Who gets the check?" she asks cheerfully.

"My daughter here will take that," he says. "I'll be leaving the tip." He lays a ten in Lynette's palm. Keeps his hand there for a few beats, marking her. When she's gone, he starts popping the pills like they were peppermints she dropped off.

"A jury declared me guilty of taking pictures," he says. "I've decided I have no reason to doubt them."

My eyes are on Lynette, pulling away plates from a table of men in trucker hats. Breasts at work again. Money changing hands. I'm feeling bad about my snap judgment. Lynette is probably way less of a fool than I am.

She's pausing at the register with her stack of dirty plates, now doing double duty as cashier. The woman who had been sitting behind me is paying her bill. Her pillowed waistline and Clarks shoes say *mom*. Her demeanor to Lynette says *kind*.

And if Carl's right, the size of the square-cut diamond on her left hand says there's a lot for her to lose. Carl and I, we're into the details.

She's slipping off sunglasses so she can sign her name, a bruise the color of blueberries under her right eye.

"Cute scarf," Carl says.

11

When I was eight, three years after my sister fell into that grave, I wrote down every fear I could think of in a notebook. I already had a bunch by then. I worked my way methodically through them. I started with the little ones—picking up a tarantula by the leg, eating a jalapeño whole, lighting firecrackers—and moved on to riding the most vicious roller coasters hands-free until I didn't scream anymore.

Every year, I crossed off two or three and added four or five more.

At twelve, after my sister vanished, I dug deeper. I held a gun in my hand until it wasn't shaking anymore. I flopped like a pushed cat into the deep end of aquamarine pools until I could knife my body into a lake, drive down through black muck, brush the bottom, and swim up with my lungs boiling.

At nineteen, I skydived from a prop plane, zip-lined across a thin crevice that dove to hell, slid in Nikes on a frozen pond where catfish slept. At twenty, I chased an ominous funnel until my old Toyota gave up and shuddered to a stop, defeated, willing to be swept away.

Every time, my heart was exploding out of my chest.

My last boyfriend told me I had a death wish right before he broke up with me. He didn't understand: I have a *brave* wish.

I glance sideways at Carl in the passenger seat. We left Lynette and her diner less than ten minutes ago. His lips are a tight line. If he only knew. For the last year, I've upped my game. I've paid someone to scare me to death. To be suspended in air, blindfolded, and dropped, not knowing if the next seconds would bring the lash of glacial water, the taut rejection of a trampoline, a desperate tumble down an endless hill.

I've been tied up in a closet until I lost track of time, slammed to the ground in a parking garage, tailed by a Mercedes at one hundred miles an hour. I've practiced for hours so I can shoot somebody deliberately in the head. None of this left me unscathed. But that wasn't the point. The point was to redefine how I viewed bravery. Bravery wasn't a character trait I was born without, thank God. Adrenaline and muscle memory and mind control, that's all it is.

We're rumbling over the first red dot on my map, the 17th Street bridge in Waco. A muscle in Carl's cheek twitches as he stares out at the corroded view of abandoned buildings and factory clutter like he's never seen it before in his life. If he remembers what's under this bridge, he's not saying.

"You're sweating like a pig." Carl punches the air-conditioning all the way to max. I have no idea what he's talking about—there isn't a bit of perspiration on me.

In fact, the Buick is an oasis of cool after the sausage-coffee perfume and bird chatter of the diner. Maybe Carl's brain craves the white noise. One at a time, he flips every vent at me. My hair tickles my face, blows in my eyes. I feel goosebumps rise on my arms, a tiny rumble of last night's panic. I see Carl, sitting in the dark refrigerator of his motel room, listening for my frantic rattling of the chain.

Fear like this has always nipped at me like a pack of rats. They say we arrive on earth innately afraid of only two things: loud noises and heights. Babies and kittens refuse to move around on a clear glass table for fear of falling, but a duck will waddle across because he knows he can fly. It's instinct. So they say. I think we fall to earth afraid of everything. We just pretend we're brave until the monster wakes.

Carl's fiddling with the radio, zipping across the stations, filling the car with discordant snippets of music, baseball announcers, weather reports.

Loves me . . . chance of rain . . . hallelujah . . . fly ball . . . oh my rose.

I want to slap at his fingers. Fingers long and delicate enough to strum classical guitar, or clip off an aneurysm, or tie a vicious knot. On the witness stand, Carl said he used his hands for printing pictures and drinking whiskey sours, *sure as hell not to kill anyone.* Back at the diner, Carl had mentioned *slitting throats.* Details. They're important.

"Jesus Christ, I'll listen to country crap if you insist," Carl mutters. "Just shut up about it already."

We've finished crossing the bridge. I haven't said a word to Carl in the last two minutes, certainly not about my taste in music. He was so cogent in the diner. Is he just messing with me? Or something else? *Don't ever get lulled,* Mrs. T had warned. *Dementia is a clever cat. It will walk out the door like it's totally lost interest. But it will always creep back. It will never give up until the mouse is eaten.*

Carl doesn't comment when I pull to a stop in the weeds on the side of the road.

We don't have to do this, I tell myself. *Wasn't it enough to drive across the bridge and make a point?* And yet, at the first break in traffic, I yank the wheel and pull a U-turn back to the steep little road that leads under the bridge. You really have to be looking for it, which is why Carl probably liked it down here.

I'm crawling down the road against the force of gravity, wheels crunching the gravel. I park immediately at the bottom but don't open the door. A jungle of concrete pillars and maniacal vegetation stretches out in front of us.

I turn and reach for two white washcloths on the floor of the backseat. Preparation. Paranoia. People fish down here and could remember us. I'm going to drape the fabric over the license plates.

"Don't mess back there." Carl's face is flush and angry. His eyes are darting furiously from the rear window to the pieces of cloth in my hand.

What have you hidden in my backseat, Carl?

My sister's name floats up from my subconscious.

Rachel.

Rachel, Rachel, Rachel. The safe word I used with my trainer although he was rarely close enough to hear.

The scarf suddenly feels like a noose. While Carl watches, I rip it off and cram it in the console between us.

"What are you looking at?" I snipe. "Get out of the car. Let's see what you remember."

TITLE: *THE GRAVE*

From *Time Travel: The Photographs of Carl Louis Feldman*
Waco, 2001
Gelatin silver print

Photographer's note—This mysterious little cross is hidden in the weeds under the old 17th Street bridge in a rundown section of Waco. Every year, I check to make sure it's still there. I always meet a homeless guy or two, fishing in Waco Creek. I like the sneaky shadows under here, the sense of things abandoned and dead. I like that the cross makes people wonder, but they never bother to dig it up.

12

Carl is trudging behind me under the bridge.

I had hoped he would lead. It would make the rest of the trip so much simpler if he ushered me straight to our first spot on my map. To know right away, for sure, that Carl remembers he has been under this bridge plenty of times with the precious camera he famously named George. A camera that spent hard time in an evidence box after an exotic life traveling across Texas.

That was a whole other goose chase for me, trying to find someone in Carl's past named George who might cast significant light on things (not to mention an Allison, the moniker for his old truck).

Every time I stop short, he does. I can't tell if he is messing with me or confused. It was tough enough just to cajole him out of the car. The flirt in the diner has vanished. While I draped washcloths over the license plates, he jumped in the backseat and cooed softly to himself. Anyone watching has already reported the two weirdos under the bridge.

Fishing poles would have been good cover, leaning up on the

trunk of the car. I'm going to need to be much more clever than this. Day Two, and I'm being trailed by Carl under a desolate bridge, certain Mrs. T's advice would have been to frisk him first. But touching him, pulling at his pockets—how much he might enjoy the experience is unthinkable.

"It's just another couple of hundred yards," I say, although inside I'm suddenly certain he knows right where we're heading. The road down here is old, ragged around the edges, but paved and smooth in the center. That means it's still used for something. If Carl flips out at me, someone might hear. Or at least eventually find one of us behind the tall feathery weeds that line the road like Vegas dancers.

I tread carefully in the center of the pavement. Two rusted ribbons of railroad track stretch to my left, reminding me of a particular Pass/Fail day with my trainer. Blindfolded, my foot trapped, the frantic tugging to be free, the train bearing down. It turned out to be the blare of a recording, a track long in disuse, but I didn't know that then.

To our right, quarry limestone tumbles down to a trickling creek bed that streams toward the Brazos a mile or two away. A culvert gapes like a giant empty eye socket, a place for snakes, daring boys, graffiti, things to die. Everywhere, bundles of brush lie in wait, as tangled and cruel as barbed wire. I concentrate on the Mrs Baird's bread factory sign in the distance, the patches of daylight playing on my black running shoes, the clip of Carl's feet behind me.

"We're here." Only three hundred yards, and I'm breathless.

He steps up even with me and stares at the steel cross that rises about a foot and a half out of the ragged weeds.

"I took pictures of that," Carl says. Matter-of-fact.

"Yes. You did." Trying not to sound eager.

I keep my eyes steady on the beams of the cross, which sits half in the shadow of the bridge, the other in sun. Someone has clipped the weeds a little. Rust is bubbling up on its white paint like freckles of blood. A small, empty metal plaque is soldered to the center.

The cross is as stick-straight to the sky and forsaken as it appeared in Carl's photographs. It was freshly parked in his camera, along with the shots he took of Nicole Lakinski and her young son at a park five miles from here, where the cops picked him up for a DUI. That was about ten years ago.

Twenty-seven-year-old Nicole had been missing for three days. Her son, Alex, was found crying on a park bench with an arm hanging at an odd angle. There was a five-dollar bill with her fingerprint and a bit of her DNA on Carl's dashboard, along with a baseball cap in the truck bed. At the trial, Carl admitted being there. He says she offered him the five because she thought he was homeless. He couldn't get her to take it back. The little boy, Alex, only remembered falling off the swing. And a man with a blue cap. Or a green one.

At the time, Carl and George the Camera were on a whiskey bender across Texas in Allison the Truck, with Dylan croaking from the speakers. The backseat had been neatly made up with a blanket and pillow. Not a drop of blood was found there or in the pickup bed. The jury didn't like Carl, but that's what they kept coming back to before they offered a verdict. That, and the only cap they found in his truck was white.

If he kidnapped Nicole, where was a thread of her dyed blond hair? A smear of her spit or sweat? A broken bit of the pink-and-black zebra stripe painted on her artificial nails? The blood-red imprint of the Ruby Woo lipstick she wore? The silver owl ring she wore on her pinky that was always slipping off? There was so little evidence that it took the police a year to officially charge Carl; the judge even set him free on bail before the long march to trial.

For a second, I imagine the scene under the bridge a decade ago—the frenzy after the cops developed Carl's photos and one of them had recognized the spot with the cross.

Regular 17th Street bridge trolls said the cross had been lost in the weeds for years but that didn't stop police from mucking through the gushing creek and the culvert and stomping the wooded area looking for a missing woman.

They picked up nine muddy shoes that didn't go with one another, 208 beer cans and bottles, half of a waterlogged copy of *Bleak House,* a child's B- math test, a biohazard collection of condoms and needles, a litter of tiny animal bones. In the creek, they found four waterlogged guns and three rusty pocketknives. None could be connected to any crimes.

No one thought twice about why people had never questioned the cross if it had been there so long. The cops shoveled up a circle ten feet wide and ten feet deep. After unearthing nothing interesting, the hole was filled in and the cross hammered right back in place. In Texas, whenever a cross shows up, it stays.

The trial judge let the photos in Carl's camera into evidence, no problem. By that time, the media speculation was in full frenzy— reporters, prosecutors, and police officials had been drawing vague lines to crimes and other photographs of Carl's for a long time. It was a journalist who first figured out Carl had photographed this cross more than once, long before Nicole Lakinski's disappearance. A Waco reporter recognized it in Carl's published book.

Carl is running his hand over the metal, admiring it like a carpenter would. It's a serious effort, with beams filched from a construction site or a junkyard, fired together and spray-painted white. Engineered, leaden to carry, brutal to stake into the heart of hard clay.

I think about taking out the small knife on my keychain and scratching *Rachel* in the white space even though I know it isn't her grave. I want her remembered. Whoever went to this much effort to bang it into the ground had a very good reason.

Carl kneels in front of the cross. Closes his eyes. Enacting a ritual? A few inches to his left, a fire ant feels the slight quake of his knee hitting the ground and trickles out of his soil castle. Man on duty. And then another ant, and another, on a bead for Carl's hand. One has crawled to his thumb.

Bite him.

As the ant prepares to set his hand on fire, Carl's eyes flick open. "Smells that pancake syrup," he says. "You know ants have five times

59

more odor receptors than other insects?" He pinches the ant into a crumb. Rises.

"I'm ready to go," Carl says.

This isn't what I planned. Ten minutes of nothing. I wanted to leave here with something tangible. Carl can never be tried again for killing Nicole. Double jeopardy. At this spot, especially, surely he might be careless, unable to resist dropping a detail or two.

"What do you remember happened under this bridge?"

"I remember wanting to write a name on this cross." As if he is reading my mind.

And then I hear it. A tiny, terrified violin. From the creek bed? From deep in the ground under the cross?

"Why you got your fingers plugged in your ears?" Carl's voice tunnels through.

I drop my hands to my sides. Nothing disturbing the air now but the trickle of creek water, the honk of a horn above us.

"Let's go." I turn around.

"You hear that?" Carl asks.

I don't want to. But I do. The sound is thinner now, more desperate. A wobbly bow across a single string. Overhead, the relentless drumbeat of tires thumps the concrete.

Is Carl throwing his voice? Mimicking the sound of someone dying?

He's facing the creek bed, his back to me. I can't see if his throat is vibrating but I know it is.

"You bastard." I snatch at his shoulder but Carl is already tearing away, vanishing into the thicket behind the cross. Red ants seethe over my shoes, desperate for skin. I'm paralyzed. *All that training,* I think. *All that preparation.* Carl is crashing through brush and then, silence. I don't know if there's a way out on the other side. He's gone, maybe for good.

I wait a full minute. Then two.

Carl emerges, bent over by the weight of what he's cradling.

He's stumbling toward me. There's blood on his face, his jeans.

60

I can't help but think of my sister. Of Nicole.

The closer he gets, the more I want to run.

Thirty feet away. Ten.

I have to look at what he's holding.

One of the eyes is stitched shut by infection and crawling with gnats. The appeal from the other, deep and brown, steals my breath.

MISSING GIRLS CONNECTED TO CARL

NICOLE LAKINSKI, AGE 27, WACO

Disappeared: May 8, 2008, between 1 and 5 P.M.

Details: Abducted from park

Last seen by: Son, age 5

Suspects: Husband (alibied), ex-boyfriend (no alibi),
Carl (acquitted)

State of case: Unsolved, no body

Linking photograph by CLF: Titled *The Grave* (a taunt?)

VICKIE HIGGINS, AGE 24, CALVERT

Disappeared: June 9, 2010, time unknown

Details: Reported missing by her husband when he came
home for dinner

Last seen by: 82-year-old neighbor (now deceased) saw her
in yard around 9 A.M.

Suspects: Husband (alibied), FedEx driver (alibied)

State of case: Unsolved, declared dead in absentia

Linking photograph by CLF: Titled *The Bride* (victim about to
celebrate 1st wedding anniversary)

VIOLET SANTANA, AGE 21, GALVESTON,
SAN LUIS PASS BEACH

Disappeared: March 19, 2003, between 10 and 11 P.M.

Last seen by: Friends with her on beach

Details: Alcohol involved, skinny-dipping, very dark

Suspects: None

State of case: Declared accidental drowning with parents'
blessing, no body

Linking photograph by CLF: Titled *The Drowning* (How he
killed her? Has a thing for names that start with V?)

13

 break one of my rules. I use my burner phone under the shadows of the bridge to Google the closest emergency vet. So much for a vow to avoid electronic trails. We end up 1.7 miles away in a clinic in a yellow clapboard house badly in need of paint.

I'd hesitated when I saw the sign: *Budget Holistic Vet: Exotics and Emergencies Welcome.* I almost peeled out of the parking lot for someplace else. But Carl was growling at me to stop the car, insisting the dog had only minutes, like he would know. I imagine the best killers, the ones who stay free, do. I took his word for it.

I also have to accept the unspoken word of the freakishly strong waif of a woman assessing this barely breathing animal that she is a licensed veterinarian. It didn't help that she had greeted us with, *I'm Dr. Kiwi, like the fruit.* When she bent over to scoop the dog off the couch in her packed waiting room, she flashed the tattoo that lined the smooth flat of her back above her Levi's: *Dog whispering is for bullies.* My trainer wasn't a fan of reality star dog trainer Cesar Millan, either. *Dominance does not tame,* he would tell me.

The injured dog lies flat on his side on the exam table, whining through his teeth, lapping in shallow breaths, doing his heartbreaking best to be a good patient while Dr. Kiwi runs hands gently over him, exploring.

I'm working the math on my shrinking budget while staring at tiny cats twisted into yoga poses or in the throes of tantric sex—the wallpaper's too faded to tell. Carl's sitting in the room's only chair, arms crossed, lips crunched.

I'm looking everywhere but at the dog—his gnatted eye, his stomach wound. His whine coils inside me like live electrical wire. I wish the pain were mine instead, a feeling I work hard to control.

This radical empathy of mine extends to things God didn't give a voice—the half-smashed fly wriggling his legs on the windowsill, the fish bleeding from a vicious hook, flapping, puckering his mouth in the air. At three years old, I'd bite into the skin of a peach and wonder if it was silently screaming. My trainer worked on this weakness and got nowhere. He really didn't try that hard. He said it wasn't much of a weakness.

I need to focus on something else. Beyond this door, in the waiting room, people and animals living out unfortunate lives together are packed into claw-scratched folding chairs and old flowered couches. It's biblical out there, a makeshift church waiting to be baptized. Everyone in that church insisted our patient go to the head of the line.

I'm guessing the vet bill is going to be $400–$500, minimum. All Dr. Kiwi has said so far about the dog and our situation is that she offers a forty percent discount "for being heroes." I'm still calling him "the dog" even though Carl named him something ridiculous in the car and the vet is calling him "sweetheart." The dog's whine has shifted down multiple octaves into a moan that reminds me of the eerie sounds my sister used to make while we stared into the lights-off darkness hanging above our twin beds. It was always too easy to scare me.

Dr. Kiwi has to be wondering why I appear uncaring, why my

eyes are focused on her kitty-cat wallpaper like there's some deep message there. Carl has no problem at all keeping his gaze full throttle on the pitiful animal.

"I happen to know the no-kill shelters in a fifty-mile radius are full," Dr. Kiwi is saying, while pulling over an IV pole. "So are my cages in the back. The other shelters . . . well, if he makes it, this guy will be put at the top of the list for execution."

She's already a pitchman for the dog, letting us know he has nowhere to go.

Her eyes roam from my face to Carl's, scratched from the thorny branches that held the dog in their claws. His cheeks and chin look like a toddler took a red ink pen to them. So innocent.

Dr. Kiwi rests her eyes a little longer on my face than is comfortable. It takes a second to remember she is seeing a disguise and not the real me. It took effort to grow my hair to the middle of my back, and three tries to get it the shade of red I wanted.

Three months eating French fries, fettucine alfredo, and cheesecake to add eight pounds to my thin frame. Three hours on Amazon to find comfortable heel lifts to push my height to 5'6" when I want to.

"Where'd you say you found him?" Dr. Kiwi directs the question to me. At the same time, I realize the dog has gone quiet. *Too* quiet.

"We didn't say." I'm trying to think of what lie I want to sell, glancing out of the corner of my eye at the dog. Still breathing.

"Under the damn bridge," Carl mutters.

Dr. Kiwi turns toward Carl. "The 17th Street bridge? A dumping ground. Cats, dogs. Guinea pigs. Rabbits kids got for Easter. They never catch any of these sons of bitches."

She didn't mention the steel cross or the missing Nicole Lakinski, who, like my sister, was never found, or about Nicole's depression, her every affair and mistake held up to searing white light by the defense. *Did she run away with a lover? Kill herself?* While the jury didn't like Carl, they didn't much like Nicole, either.

Nicole's son, Alex, now a skinny teenager, told me three weeks ago that his arm still aches from falling off that swing.

Alex thought I was a reporter looking for his dad, but I'd waited until his father sped off on his evening jog. The boy opened the door after two knocks, like I'm sure he wasn't supposed to. I felt guilty that I gave him a fake name. We sat on the porch steps. He was starving to talk about his mother. Yet the day she disappeared right in front of him isn't burned into his mind. All he can remember now is the cruel snap of bone.

I wanted to hold his still freckly face in two hands and urge him to pursue his mother. Start *now*. I also wanted to order him to forget. *Move on*. Never, ever give in to that tiny devil of obsession growing up in his chest. Instead, I overpromised. As he handed me precious old photographs, I said I'd be back. I didn't say that his mother is only one of the red dots on my map, a few pixels in the big picture.

Dr. Kiwi has leaned into the hall and is yelling for someone named Daisy. Carl has a weird grin or a grimace on his face, either one unsettling.

I find myself standing over the dog, stroking his matted fur. *We might have to change cars before I'd planned.*

A bouncy teenage girl in pink Hello Kitty scrubs has suddenly appeared in the doorframe. Her hand already rests on the IV pole, ready to help roll the dog to surgery. *Daisy.*

There is something about her.

Dr. Kiwi is looking at me strangely. "Are you all right?"

"Your face is puke green." Carl reaches out to steady my frame. I jerk away, heart slamming.

He can't touch me again.

14

For a second, Daisy had reminded me of Rachel. Her perfectly oval face. The lavender shadows under her eyes. Something.

I'd caught myself on the wall of yoga cats and stumbled my way to the waiting room. I didn't let Carl put a hand on me.

Carl suddenly shifts his position on the floor beside me. I have to forcibly stop myself from reacting every time he moves. He's ridiculously agile when he wants to be, I've noticed. An hour ago, we had loaded the dog in the car together. Carl had operated with both his arms, no problem.

I take another slug of Coke and center my attention on the three black tails twitching in and out of the bars of a cat carrier. Think about how to trick Carl into getting back in the damn car before the surgery is over.

The owner of the cats is squished beside me on a couch, tapping on her cellphone, a diamond-chip band barely perceptible on her chubby fingers. It's a poor cousin to the glimmering diamond on the woman at the diner. To our grandmother's square emerald that my mother promised to my sister and now keeps in a drawer.

Primal, those rings. Cavemen twisted grass around women's wrists and ankles and waists to mark their territory. *To control them.*

"I want the dog," Carl announces. "It's a condition." In the weathered face staring up at me, I see a boy, testing his mother. It's hard not to recoil. This is not the relationship I want with Carl. I am not Mrs. T.

"The dog is not going to be a condition," I say as calmly as I can. I won't let Carl have that power over me. He cannot be the better person, not now, not ever—to believe I wouldn't have saved the dog without him.

"Aunt Kiwi says I should register you while the surgery is going on. Are you feeling . . . better?" Daisy is at my elbow, cautiously addressing me, official with an iPad.

Up close, the pieces of Daisy's face don't fit at all like Rachel's. Another thing: Daisy smells like baby powder. She's expertly switching the iPad screen from the cover of a smutty romance novel to a vet registration form.

Rachel liked to read about aliens. Holes into other dimensions. Horror. She left a musky, exotic scent on her sheets.

"Can you spell your dog's name?" Daisy asks.

"It's not our dog," I say automatically.

"B-a-r-f-l-y," Carl spells slowly.

I don't like the way his eyes are traveling over her.

"Barfly?" Daisy giggles, typing.

"You say it Barf-LEE," Carl corrects her.

"Last name?" Daisy asks.

"Smith," I interrupt. "We are the Smiths. We're from out of town so we can skip the rest of your form. I will pay cash."

"Barf-LEE Smith," Daisy says, head down, dutifully tapping.

"Lee is not his middle name," Carl says.

Now Carl is running his eyes boldly over the prosthetic leg of the man next to him. Old military guy, I think. The alert German shepherd beside him looks like he'd kill either of us with a single, sharp snap of the man's fingers.

"My dad had a fake arm," Carl announces to no one in particular. "Got it chopped off in a hay baler at my grandfather's farm. He said the fact that he could still feel his invisible hand fingering chords on his banjo was proof the soul goes on."

"Shut up," I hiss. I throw a silent face of apology toward the man.

I don't remember that chilling detail about his father in trial testimony. *Could Carl's trick arm be psychosomatic? Could a brain tell an arm not to work? Did Carl believe it was OK to kill because his victims floated on some metaphysical plane?*

His grandfather's farm is real, lurking, unmarked on my map. I can put my finger on it blindfolded. It lies hundreds of miles ahead of us in West Texas. In my nightmares, it is an infinite burial ground where I dig and dig like a diligent ant.

The room has gone silent.

Dr. Kiwi.

I focus on her maroon-and-white Texas A&M surgical cap instead of on the thick red splash on her scrubs that makes it look like she just gutted a deer, or on the steel table through the open door behind her where the tip of Barfly's matted tail is so very still.

I'm holding back tears for a dog I don't know. My clothes are smeared with blood. A house full of strangers can't take their eyes off me.

I'm so very far off course, so fast.

15

It's like I'm watching a replay of Carl talking to Rachel for the first time. Charming my sweet, brilliant sister. Fooling her. *How did he do it?* I have to know. I can't pull my eyes away.

While Dr. Kiwi fills me in on the surgery, Carl's across the room, intimately engaged with Daisy. Daisy's smiling up at him, flashing braces with pink bands. The long chocolate-colored braid that had been sloppily wrapped around her head has fallen down her back.

Get your fucking hand off her shoulder. Off those Hello Kittys.

I've finally nailed the elusive thing that Daisy and Rachel have in common. It's the *glow.*

I'm catching only snatches of what Dr. Kiwi is telling me about the surgery. A .22 Long in the hip. No major organs damaged. No ID chip. One night of observation.

"Are you listening?" Dr. Kiwi, impatient. "Daisy will watch your dog tonight for free; she's amassing service hours for her Ivy League campaign."

I nod distractedly. I need to whisk Carl out of Daisy's orbit. My head is fast-forwarding the tape. I'm picturing what he would do with that innocent braid and the prison of wires that clamp her teeth. With Rachel, it was her pierced ears and heart earrings. I dreamed about what happened to Rachel's *ears*.

"Carl." I turn a little more. Raise my voice. *"Carl."*

He shrugs and bows to Daisy. "My master calls."

Outside, alone with Carl, I feel no relief. He's already opening the door to the backseat again. What's with the *fucking backseat*?

I reach around him and slam the door. "Up. Front."

"Daisy says she can't take Barfly because her mom's allergic," Carl says. "And she kicks things."

"We. Aren't. Keeping. The dog."

Daisy, safe in the little yellow house.

In the car, my nose is immediately assaulted by the salty odor of Carl's sweat, or the leftover smell of shot dog, or both. *It's all OK*, I'm telling myself. After the dog's surgery, I'm down to $3,473.43. That includes subtracting Carl's tipping budget. I'd confirmed while counting out the cash that he'd stolen $60 out of my wallet. He has $30 left. Knowing this for sure made me feel better.

I console myself that we will only be a few hundred miles behind schedule by staying overnight. If I leave the dog behind right now, there is a chance that Carl will shut down. So I will use this time practically. Figure out where to dump the car early. Buy a little dog food, plastic sheeting, and a blanket to cover the premium leather backseat. Let Carl lick a Dreamsicle. Talk him into a haircut, shorter, with a little rinse on the gray. If we have to, we can shave him bald.

Carl is oblivious to my internal morale boosting. He's unfolding a homemade pamphlet he must have picked up on the paper-cluttered desk inside the clinic.

From this angle, I make out the spidery shape of a tree, drawn freehand, and a guy's name. *Matthew.* I'm guessing this is a plea from a tree service guy who will be out of business soon if his skill at shaping trees in real life is not better than drawing them. Carl is engrossed by the piece of paper.

I count to three. "Carl. Listen. You have to cut back on all your requests. Your conditions."

He delivers a hard stare. "My preacher always said, *Listen,* at the pulpit right before he read a Bible verse. I've always thought of it as kind of an order."

Carl thrusts the piece of paper to my face so the rest of the words are no longer obscured.

Never forget, it reads.

Matthew 13:42.

Not a man's name—a Bible verse about a blazing furnace. He flips the pamphlet over. He points at the hand-drawn map, to a tiny X off a farm road.

Is that X for Rachel?

"Listen," he says. "New condition. We're going *here.*"

16

Carl is pretending to snap pictures, bringing his hands up to his face, pressing a finger on a button that isn't there. He's like the woman at Mrs. T's knitting nothing. He stands in the middle of a grassy field, weeds up to his knees, about two hundred yards from me. Black clouds are boiling on the horizon. A few buildings are scattered across the property like matchboxes, but otherwise it is all grass and emptiness.

We'd backtracked on this country road once, twice, three times before we found it. It could be any isolated ranch. Any gravel turnoff with a *Keep Out* sign.

Carl insists he's just a tourist, a student of history—that he found the flier on the veterinarian's bulletin board.

There is no remnant of the smoking ruin, the religious compound eight miles out of Waco that was blasted off the earth by the FBI twenty-five years ago, killing more than eighty people, including babies. No trespassers but us—a man pirouetting in a field and a girl with hair being torn apart by the wind. This private field is still owned by the Branch Davidians, and no one is selling tickets.

A developer once had plans to turn the site of the Waco siege into a biblical amusement park, but Waco is very good at cleaning its bloody carpet and forgetting. There is also still no historical marker in town noting that the courthouse hosted one of the most grisly lynchings in U.S. history in 1916. Ten thousand people gawked. The most giddy took fingers and toes of the burned body as souvenirs and mailed manufactured postcards to friends.

I know all of this because Carl read to me from the angry, informative pamphlet on our drive over. Carl has a nice voice for reading aloud, with a lilting inflection. With every word, I imagined him cheerfully reading to my sister, tied up in the backseat of his pickup, while she had no choice but to listen.

Since then, the raised bumps on my arms, the ragged knot in my chest, have settled in. Carl's behavior in the field, like a child at play, is deeply wrong. Yet I don't feel like this is The Place. He is not searching for anything at all out there.

I watch him frolic, and the questions I'm not ready to ask keep pounding. *Did my sister have a flat tire on her bike? Did you offer to throw it in your truck to get it fixed? Did she run across you shooting a photograph on her route? Did she stop to ask about it? What moment did she realize her mistake? Did she say anything at the end?* All these and hundreds more catalogued in my files and journals.

The air is churning, half-hot, half-cool, cream being poured into hot coffee. The disquieting way Texas storms roll in.

I turn back to the small brick memorial by the gate, the only thing that marks the site of the massacre. A litter of rocks and coins stretches across the top of the brick wall. I know the Greek roots of the neatly arranged pennies and nickels and quarters—a myth that the dead need money for passage on the boat that rows them away from the living.

A few more curious tokens are mixed in: a black-and-white die, a large blue button, a single gold earring, a few seashells, a wooden Scrabble piece with the letter X, a green plastic soldier. All of them say, *I was here.*

What would I leave if this were my sister's memorial? The ridged grapefruit spoon we used to fight over? The tiny plastic Buddha that hung from the rearview mirror of the old red Pontiac she took to college? The delicate brass Christmas angel we hung together every year?

My eyes are blurring with tears as they rush across the names, capturing some, missing others. I halt abruptly on Rachel Sylvia, age thirteen.

Rachel. Some would consider my sister's name on this wall as a message from above, a sign that I'm on course. I can't go there. If that were the case, I'd see messages from Rachel every second of the day.

I'd see her in the black-and-white die on the ledge because we played backgammon every Sunday night, in the toy soldier because we made encampments in the dirt, in the earring because my mother was furious when Rachel secretly took me to get my ears pierced, in the Scrabble piece because it was the one game she would never let me win.

Even though I feel her presence sometimes, even deliriously melt into it, believing my dead sister is my partner in crime gets me nowhere good.

I'm completely on my own.

I force my thoughts back to the memorial. The children's names, especially, are such sad, morbid poetry.

STARTLE SUMMERS, AGE 1

ABORTED BABY SUMMERS

SERENITY SEA JONES, AGE 4

LITTLE ONE JONES, AGE 1

PAIGES GENT, AGE 1

DAYLAND L. GENT, AGE 3

ABORTED FETUS GENT

Forgotten memorial. Holy nightmare. Those are the oxymorons my sister would use to describe this place. Rachel used to love to play with words.

Found missing. That's what she'd joke about herself.

Carl's straying farther out, a kid at sea. I'm shouting for him to *come back* and waving my arms at the storm now pulling its curtain over half the sky. Eighty-two young trees are bending in protest in their marching line down the ranch road, one planted for each of the dead Davidians but not a single one for the four dead ATF agents.

I'm still yelling at Carl to no avail. A blast of wind has sucked my words into the waterfall of leaves in the old oak that lurches by the simple brick wall of names. The temperature is dropping fast, too fast.

A couple of hours earlier, the pimply stylist at Supercuts had warned us about the tornado watch as he cropped Carl's hair. So did the Walmart checker, a woman perking up her middle age with red-striped readers, peering through them to admire my new polka-dot clip-on phone case, Carl's large box of Whitman's chocolates and bag of sour gummy worms before dropping them into a plastic bag: "Must literally be Christmas in July at your house." It came out *litterly.*

"What a lucky dog," the checker had said as she swiped the bar codes on the cans of Purina wet food, the jerky treats, and the "extra cushiony comfort" reflective dog collar Carl insisted on. He had fingered the silvery choke chains first.

"How would *you* like a shot in your ass?" Carl had responded.

Click. Click. Click. I swirl around to find Carl and his imaginary camera only a few feet behind me. He's snapping his tongue against the roof of his mouth. How did he get here so fast? He must have run those two hundred yards across the field, yet he's not out of breath.

He's bouncing, kneeling, popping back up, shooting the names carved into polished stones of white, red, pink, brown. Stones the color of skin, blood, and skeleton. Stones dug up from this piece of land, according to the legend on the brick. His eyes are glittering over the coins as if he would like to steal them.

He pauses his frenetic activity and lets the invisible camera drip free off the invisible strap around his neck. His pantomime is so real I almost see it. He points to the field. "My brother stood over there. Watched it burn. Took less than thirty minutes."

A brother. I knew he had one, who'd died of cancer. Surely he was not a cop or a David Koresh follower.

"Norm was part of the volunteer firefighter crew from Axtell," Carl continues. "They were called too late and then forced to stand back. By the time the FBI let them in there with hoses, it was all bones. House bones, people bones. My brother couldn't shut up about it for a year. He liked to watch things burn."

"I wasn't born yet," I stutter. Just conceived. The age of "Fetus Gent," so named on the memorial. I'd learned about this cult stand-off with the FBI in a religious studies class. Two images had stuck, the before and the after. A compound built on the cheap, mass scale of fair-weather apocalyptic architects, and a billowing, tangerine blaze.

"What a politically correct piece of garbage memorial this is." Carl sneers. He nods again to the vacant field where the complex used to stand. "Did you know the FBI cut the power on the fiftieth night of the standoff?"

I shake my head.

"Twenty degrees outside. Thirty-mile-an-hour winds. They ran spotlights on the compound like it was a car sale. Blasted them with recordings of screaming rabbits being slaughtered, dentist drills, Tibetan chants. There were children in there. They used tear gas. God-damn machines of war to ram their home. No wonder these religious nuts thought it was the end of the world. The FBI fulfilled the god-damn prophecy of David Koresh, a dumb-ass bastard named Vernon who came out of a fourteen-year-old mother. If people are not in their right minds, you gotta know better than to push, right? Police don't get this."

Carl appears lucid with an edge of crazy, the man with a graduate degree in art history, the documentarian, hell-bent about his opinion.

Except I think the crazy part of him is making things up. Trying to scare me. *Screaming rabbits.* The first thick drop of rain splashes on my wrist. My hair's slapping across my eyes, sticking to my lips. Carl slowly lifts his hands to his face and snaps a figment of me.

A jagged piece of hail stings my skull. Another hits my neck.

Even in the trial records, Carl's childhood was sketchy. If his brother lived around here once, maybe Carl had, too. Maybe he'd spotted Nicole Lakinski years before the prosecutor even dreamed. I will be sure to put a few of her photos from the green Tupperware container in the mix again tonight. The pinched little face of her son, Alex, is still on top.

"My brother bid on Koresh's 1968 Camaro on the Internet," Carl says. "Too rich for him in the end. Sold at thirty-seven thousand."

"Why did you bring me here, Carl?"

"Wasn't it your idea?"

"You are the one . . ." I catch myself. "Let's head back to the car before it pours. Find a motel."

Carl has stepped aggressively close, his hands up at his face again. He towers over me.

I picture myself in his close-up. Wet clothes clinging to my breasts and hips. The faint white scar between my eyes, more pronounced as the rain filters away my makeup. The one eyebrow that hikes a little higher, the flea of a mole right above my lip, the tiny diamond stud in my left nostril. Hair roots that already need touching up. I shouldn't have chosen the color Cherry Cola for my disguise just because I liked the sound of it.

No one will recognize me in the computer morgue of missing people. My mother could wait for days, maybe forever, to find out what happened to me. Just like she is doing for my sister.

His brother liked to watch things go up in flames.

I think Carl has been here before.

My thoughts churn chaotically. I lurch backward, my hand pressing against my hip for a gun that is still in my suitcase.

Click, click, click goes Carl's tongue.

Mrs. T is right. I shouldn't buy him a camera.

I do not want to be another still life he leaves behind.

Carl drops his hands again, his attention suddenly diverted. "We can't take her with us," he whines, his face twisted in irritation. "No room."

It's getting much easier to play hopscotch with his brain. "I'm glad you agree about . . . Barfly. We'll find a good place."

"I'm not talking about Barfly," he snaps. "Barfly's a condition. Barfly's *a boy*. I'm talking about *her*."

He points behind me to insanity and air.

17

The thunder crack feels like it might split me in two. I shudder, but Carl remains stick-still. I wonder if Carl can see the pulse in my neck pumping like a tiny frog and wants to reach his two fingers over to press the spot still. He continues to point to nothing at all.

"What's her name?" I ask cautiously. Whatever the hell is happening right now, I don't want to screw it up.

"She never says."

"So you've known her . . . a while." *She's not a child from this wall? Not Startle Summers or Serenity Sea or Little One Jones?*

"Sure. I told her five times she couldn't come. She's always soaking wet."

"Has she been standing here . . . long?"

"How the hell do I know? I've been out there in the field. Ask *her.* And tell her to stay in her damn picture."

My clothes are riveted like body armor. Mud is caked up the ankles of my jeans. I remember running in wet clothes, being timed with a stopwatch, and how many precious seconds wet clothes take away when seconds count. I remember one of Carl's most beautiful photographs—a woman fleeing in the rain, her sopping dress draped around her legs, a goddess cut out of marble. Carl titled her *Lady in the Rain*. Does he believe she jumped out of his photo into this field? Did he kill her, too?

I glance past Carl to the property's gravel entry. Little rivers are already running toward the cattle gate, our exit. Carl seems to be waiting for me to speak while water pours off both our faces. "Let's . . . all go to the car," I urge. "It's dangerous by this tree. We're getting drenched."

"That's one of her problems. She never dries herself off or changes clothes. Drips all over everything. Smells like mildew if she hangs out for more than a few days. And there's no room in the car."

"Come on, Carl." I beckon at the emptiness, at his ghost. "You, too."

"Don't even pretend you see her. She's already up there at the gate. When she runs, she's almost impossible to catch."

18

As soon as we get in the car, my body turns on me, teeth clacking like I've been pulled out of ice water. I try three times to grasp the keys in the ignition.

Carl finally reaches over and turns the car on himself, his elbow lingering on my breast. In my shivering panic, I barely feel it. But I *know*. It is a profound line crossed that I can never get back.

Outside, the storm is a maniacal bully, whipping the trees, nudging the car just because it can. Inside, with tight inches between us, I feel the bully beside me deciding. Should he kill me and call it a day? Or is this all just too much fun?

I have one shaking hand on the wheel and one in my pocket, furiously rubbing the black-and-white die. The storm blew it off the ledge right before I ran. It feels slick. Cool. A gift from the Rachel on the wall.

Carl is perfectly composed. No shivering. He's using one of the washcloths from the backseat to towel-dry his hair. He tosses the other one at me from the passenger side. He runs his cloth over the inside of the windshield, begins to fiddle with the buttons on the dash to try to defog the window.

According to Carl, the ghost has slithered into the backseat. Carl's hallucination, so why can I feel her presence? Smell her mustiness? *You have to scoot over,* he'd said to her.

"What the hell's wrong with you?" Carl asks me. "You need me to drive us out of here?"

If I let him, it is over.

Deafening machine-gun hail pounds the car like we're Bonnie and Clyde under fire, an old game of pretend with my sister while we waited out a storm. Under the covers, she once showed me a library book with the old police photo of pretty Bonnie Parker, a bloody rag doll, shot to shreds by the Texas state police in a 1934 Ford V8. She was almost twenty-four, the age I am now. People say she had a death wish, too.

The sky is a giant bruise, a peculiar, apocalyptic shade of yellow-gray.

Carl is reaching for the door handle on his side, impatient, ready to run into the storm, jump in on the driver's side, drive us to a new bloody dot in hell.

It hits me then, how very stupid I am. The very large piece I've been missing.

Carl, opening the door to the backseat every time we get in the car, just *being polite,* he'd said.

Don't mess back there, he'd growled at me by the bridge.

Other odd bits of conversation since we left Mrs. T's chatter away in my head.

Jesus Christ, I'll listen to country crap if you insist. Just shut up about it already.

You're sweating like a pig.

Those times, he wasn't talking to me.

We can't take her with us, he'd insisted a few minutes ago. *No room.*

That's because she isn't our only invisible passenger.

The lady in the rain makes two.

19

I'm on the edge of the bed, drying out, rolling the die between my fingers while Carl talks to his ghosts in the adjoining motel room and the wind howls. The die feels fortuitous. The rain swept it to my feet. It had rolled to a five. My lucky number is three. My sister's was six. I had picked it up anyway.

I put the die back in my pocket and begin to search the contents of the Walmart bags scattered on one of the two double beds. I try not to think about what would show up on the blue-flowered granny bedspreads under ultraviolet light.

I find what I'm looking for in the third bag: the Door Jammer, my most inspired idea of the trip so far, which got a *no comment* from the Walmart checker. *No comment's a comment,* Carl had snapped at her.

Back in the car, while rain whipped, it was like someone reached a hand through the murky windshield and delivered a hard crack across my face.

Stay in the car, I had ordered Carl when we pulled up to the registration office of the first cheap motel that twinkled off an exit. I'd driven straight into blackness to flee that spot in the road with the nuclear sky. The hail eased the farther we traveled back toward Waco, but the rain wouldn't even stop to suck in a breath. The first thing I did when we pulled into the motel parking lot was assess my appearance in the rearview mirror.

Mascara streaked like charcoal tears down my cheeks. I pulled on Carl's new hoodie sweatshirt from Walmart that had been sitting like a dividing line between the two ghosts in the backseat. It neatly covered my Cherry Cola hair, two shades darker because it was wet.

I slumped my shoulders as I entered a lobby decorated with old posters of a beach a thousand miles from here. I slumped because my sister taught me one Halloween that posture reveals everything. Age, beauty, spirit. *You want to be an old witch? Hunch. You want to limp? Drop a few pebbles in your shoe. Tuck a ruler up your pants and tape it to your leg.*

I'd babbled to the skinny Indian kid behind the desk with the Artie name tag that I needed two rooms, one for my husband and me and one for his brother who snores like two pigs full of snot, which is at least half the reason his wife left him last month.

The fact is, the best way to disappear is to blend into the usual, irritating stream of creatures. The silent, frightened girl—she sticks out. She gets carded every time.

So I kept laying it on. I said that we were driving to a funeral for their Aunt Barb in Dallas, that she'd probably died of eating too many sour cream potato chips, that some asshole almost ran us off the road in the rain a little while ago and took us straight to see her. That the men had been arguing for five minutes over who had to get out of the car to book the rooms so I just did it myself.

I thickened my drawl for Artie, apologized for my muddy footprints, watched his big brown eyes begin to gloss over at *asshole*. I think of all those times I watched Rachel command a high school or college stage, all those times I'd watched her spin a teenage lie to my parents.

85

I was surprisingly good at this part, at lying.

I'd signed in with my left hand and a license plate number I made up on the spot, paid $126.42 in cash, and raided the office vending machine for peanut butter crackers, Snickers, and pretzels for our dinner. As for the license plate, I didn't figure the proprietor of Motel Casa Blanco would be out on a rainy night scouring cars in the lot to make sure they matched his registry.

Something brushes against the connecting door between Carl and me. I hadn't officially acknowledged the existence of Carl's other ghost, although he had mumbled about "him." And I'd decided to wait to ask more details about the wet one when I wasn't exhausted and Carl's eyes weren't starting to glaze.

They don't like his weird friends. That's what Mrs. T said about why Carl's fellow boarders avoided him. She didn't find it important to clear that up for me.

The TV, on mute, shows an angry weather map, another red squiggle approaching, and another, abstract art come to life. In the hall outside, an unhinged vending sign clanks mercilessly, metal scraping metal. Inside, in the glow of the TV and 40-watt lamp bulbs, I'm a furtive shadow on the wall.

I dig a pair of scissors into the thick plastic packaging for the heavy fire-engine-red device that is going to slide under the door and barricade me from Carl tonight. I weigh it in my hand. Heavy. Looks like a car jack of sorts. Only $19.95 plus tax, a small price to pay for a good night of sleep. That said, I feel the money slipping away. Another $88.21 dropped at Walmart. In less than forty-eight hours, I've spent almost $800. For now, I slide the Door Jammer under my bed.

I rap on the adjoining door. There is no chain on this one, just the scratched memory in the upper right corner where it used to be. "Carl, did you get your clothes together for me?" I rap again. "Carl?"

The door opens four inches. A hand thrusts out a pair of jeans and a shirt, the day's bloody, filthy clothes. No underwear. For that, I'm grateful.

"Thanks." Almost before I get the word out, Carl's hand disappears and he's clipped the door shut. "Take your pills!" I yell. No response. Sifting through the thin door, the *ding, ding, ding* and chortling laughter of a game show. Probably just as well if Carl and I don't meet again tonight.

I'd divided the vending machine supplies between us already. We'd swiped a Coke and a beer each from the cooler in the trunk, more of our Walmart loot. I don't feel like going through the motions of laying out the snapshots for him tonight. He hasn't said another word about Nicole. I want to crawl into that unforgiving sponge of a bed and drift into black.

But first, the clothes. I'd shed my own on the bathroom floor right before a lukewarm shower. As I retrieve them, I catch myself in the cheap full-length mirror tacked to the back of the door.

I wouldn't be scared of me.

Shoes off, without lifts, 5'2". Stripped of makeup, hair pulled into a messy bun, seventeen, eighteen years old at most. Slightly rounded cheeks. The tiny nose ring that says *just starting to rebel*. A Columbus Zoo T-shirt with a panda because pandas are cute and because I have no ties whatsoever to Columbus, Ohio.

Shorts cut right below the curve of my butt, revealing fading bruises on both knees. Ant bites peppering my ankles.

A vulnerable-looking girl is in that mirror, which is good because it's better if people don't know what's coming at them. Some people would say I'm taunting Carl on purpose. That I should cover up at all times. That I would half-deserve what I got.

Before I go, I wrap my body in a black garbage bag and arm myself with a Ziploc bag of quarters. I feel for the die in my pocket. I grab the pepper spray out of my purse. I leave the gun.

20

It's an uneasy little walk, even though the motel laundromat is only six doors down, in Room 18, just like the clerk said. The slight awning is no protection. On one side of me, rain slaps at my garbage bag raincoat; on the other, room windows gape black and lifeless.

I pass one lonely cell where a lump in bed is watching porn in the dark with the shades pulled tightly up so everyone can see. Only two other vehicles are parked near our rooms—what I'm guessing is the porn freak's old Toyota Camry and a red Audi rental that doesn't belong. The Audi seems vaguely familiar, like we passed it on the highway a couple of times. Or I saw it in a Super Bowl commercial.

I resist the urge to turn around and go back to my room. It's only 7:30 and these are Carl's best jeans. I have to stay on top of every little thing, including bloody clothes.

I twist the knob on Room 18. The proprietor has unlocked it for me as he promised. He didn't bother to turn on the light. In pitch darkness, for a good two minutes, I brush my hands across the wall, finally fingering the switch five feet from the door. The fluorescent light buzzes awake, casting gray light on two old washers, one dryer with a spaceship window, a splotched concrete floor, and no one hiding in the dark.

I throw open the lid of the first washer. The second.

No roaches. No body parts or molding clothes. Scratched metal, spun clean. I let out a breath I didn't realize I was holding. I divide our clothes between the two, let them fill up, punch buttons enough times to figure out that all of the speeds on both washers appear to be slow motion. Whatever, I'm happy not to be doing it by hand in the motel sink, especially after peering into the mud-and-dog-blood soup I'm creating. As an afterthought, I walk over and lock the door, kicking myself for not doing it right away.

While the washers churn, I plug five quarters into the empty dryer and slam the door. Maybe it will make a good space heater for this chill I can't get rid of. It begins its rumble as I slide down to the gritty floor and lean my head back. I imagine Carl's ghosts trapped inside, twirling head over heels.

I open my eyes to complete darkness. The dryer has stopped. My knees are still drawn up to my chest. I have no idea how much time has passed. Cold concrete under my butt, warm metal at my back. Head still clogged with sleep. I was lulled by the heat and thump of the machine, the chatter of rain, the idea of a locked door.

The washers are spinning out of control, like they might explode into a thousand pieces of shrapnel. The air is nauseating, sick with the smell of Tide and smoke.

The light is *out. There is smoke.* These facts unfurl like a pair of black bats, first one, then the other. The possibilities. Someone in here besides me. Something could be on fire. One of these things, or both.

I feel along the floor on both sides of me, desperately seeking the plastic bag with the pepper spray and the quarters I could sling full-force into a cheek, a crotch, a knee. There's nothing but grit, a wad of hard gum, an old dryer sheet.

I begin to crawl quickly toward the door, disoriented, unable to see a thing.

My guess at the exact location of the door is pretty good, not perfect. I find the light switch first, flip it, and turn. The air is hazy but it's easy enough to see Carl, sitting on top of the closest washer, offering me his lazy grin. In his lap, my bag of quarters.

In his hand, the source of the smoke.

"How did you get in here, Carl?" I can barely hold back my fury.

"I twisted the doorknob. The second time, I twisted it harder."

"Why the hell did you turn the light off?"

He waves at a little path of smoke weaving between us. "So we don't get arrested. Don't you sleep better in the dark?" He draws on the roach. "This is good stuff. I'm liking you a little better all the time."

I'd ask him where he got the pot, but I already know. He filched it from my suitcase. He's puffing on the Larry G from the mommyzhelper.com guy at Rice Village who'd provided my driver's licenses and license plates. The freebie sample because I was such a good customer. Larry G turned out to be mellow, all right, just not a jazz CD.

"Come on up," Carl says, patting the other washer. "We've got five minutes left on the spin cycle."

"That is not my pot," I say.

"Of course it isn't."

"You need to stay the hell out of my suitcase, Carl, or we are going to have a big problem."

"Ditto."

Despite his retort, Carl's body language appears docile, un-spooled by the dope. I push myself up onto the other washer. He hands me the roach. I hesitate before taking a deep drag. It's been two years. I'd stopped anything that could affect my focus. But now? Now I think I need to do whatever it takes to bond.

"Who is the other ghost?" I ask. "The one who got in the car at Mrs. T's."

"Who said he's a ghost?" He blows a snaky stream of smoke. "His name is Walt."

"Is he . . . here right now?"

"Walt's back in the room watching *Family Feud*. Refused to change the channel to Discovery. I took a walk."

"How long have you known him?"

"Long time. I shot his picture once in Big Bend. We got drunk a few times."

"What does he look like?"

"Well, he doesn't run marathons. Used to drive a rig. Likes people to buy his beers for him."

I take another puff. Then another. Decide not to ask if Walt's always been invisible, even when bellied up to the bar. If Walt's transparent even in the pictures Carl took of him.

"And . . . the other one?"

"She took off an hour ago. Allergic to dog hair and smoke, who knew? Says *Family Feud* is for morons. She's always pissed off about something." He takes the roach from me and has another drag. "She doesn't like me to talk about her to other people."

"Did you take her photograph, too?"

"Probably. She's a beauty. Pretty lips. Like yours."

"Are you playing with me, Carl?"

"A little," he admits. "I've got a new condition for you."

"How's Barfly doing?" I'm whispering into the phone although I'm not sure why. There is a wall and a Door Jammer between Carl and me, and he was snoring before I left his room at ten. What do I care if Carl knows I'm checking in on the dog?

"He's great. Sleeping like a dog. I stuck my good luck teddy bear in his cage." Daisy is just as chipper at midnight. "We're real happy with his progress. Aunt Kiwi says it's because he's so young. She expects a full recovery."

"OK, then. That's excellent news. I hope you can get some sleep."

"Oh, and tell Mr. Smith thanks again for slipping me the twenty-dollar bill for my Harvard fund. I take the PSAT next week. He didn't have to give me any money. I'm full in love with y'all's dog. I'd take care of him for nothing."

"Mr. Smith." I'm drawing a blank.

"Your father?"

The fake name I gave her.

"Yes, of course. I'll tell him."

Carl's play money, now down to $10. Carl, whose new condition is that he wants to pan for gold with the sauté pan he stole from Mrs. T's.

I want to give Daisy a quick lesson about why Harvard does not choose sunburned girls named Daisy from Waco, Texas, who read smutty romance and love dogs in their spare time, even though they make better people. About how all the stupid reasons that Harvard won't choose her—those are the reasons the Carls of the world *will*. But I don't. Instead, I thank her for tucking her cellphone number into my hand back at the clinic, for letting me call so late.

"Good night, Daisy," I say.

I pry open my laptop lying on the bed beside me. Something Carl said has been niggling at me since we stood in the desolate field of that memorial.

I tap into the motel WiFi. To hell with using my computer only for emergencies. It's taken less than forty-eight hours to convince me that being disconnected from the world would be just as dangerous. I'm going to trust that the encryption tool I downloaded two weeks ago will hide my location.

A few computer strokes, and I have my answer.

I wanted Carl to be lying about the screaming rabbits.

But he wasn't.

DAY THREE

How not to be afraid of falling in
a grave

1. Watch out for holes.

2. Don't step on mushy ground.

3. Carry a loud whistle.

4. Bring Goldfish crackers just in case.

5. Don't talk to the ghosts.

TITLE: *THE BRIDE*

From *Time Travel: The Photographs of Carl Louis Feldman*
Calvert, Texas
Chromogenic print

Photographer's note—I loved her the best of all the girls on the block. I didn't expect to be enticed by all that sexy white lace. I shot her from every angle, every curve. She stared back like the proud bride she was, almost daring me, even when it began to rain. She looked more vulnerable then. I could see the cracks in her makeup. I knew she didn't stand a chance. She'd soon be a skeleton like the rest.

21

For the last half-hour, Barfly's nose has been thoroughly fluffed and pollinated by the wind. He is still roving back and forth between the two backseat windows, sticking his head out, as if there isn't a ghost passenger named Walt to step over or eighteen delicate stitches holding together a hole in his side.

Daisy threw in the teddy bear. No long goodbyes. No chance for Carl to tug playfully at that pretty braid. I don't know why I hadn't thought of this earlier—the likelihood of Carl scouting victims other than me. At the least, seeking cheap thrills.

Carl and I, we're both a little queasy and hungover from the Larry G. We overslept. The bumps on Highway 6 are stirring the pot. Carl's line, not mine. He hasn't been too chatty today after the grumpy acceptance of his budget breakfast: a bruised apple from the Motel Casa Blanco lobby bowl and a generic granola bar. He is insisting that we stop off at some point and pick up quart-size plastic bags as part of his nonsensical plan to pan for gold, which reminds me he didn't return my Ziploc of quarters.

I half-regret sharing the pot. It made Carl open up a little last night but has ramped up my paranoia. It feels like I'm driving ten miles faster than the speedometer says. I've flipped my head around twice because I actually thought I heard someone mutter in the backseat.

"You're in a pissy mood," Carl had grumbled minutes ago.

Maybe that's because I know the bloody mess you made down the road, Carl. We're only a half-mile from the second red dot on the map, a tiny town that is about a sixty-mile shot south of Waco.

I don't know exactly why I call them red dots. It's just better than the coldness of *female victims*. The titillating nature of *dead girls*. I don't want to ever feed the world's ravenous appetite for smooth white skin left to rot. I will never write a book about my sister. None of my files, about any girl, woman, female, *victim*, will ever be public.

I tell myself that people can't help their ghoulish curiosity. They are just too removed. It would take about ten minutes for any normal human being to throw up in my cold, dark cave of a storage unit after just a brief examination of the hard stuff.

Normal people would never be the same if they spent even a little time with a grieving father who hears his daughter scream for him every time he sleeps, in a bar with drunk homicide cops telling jokes to forget, with a serial killer who doesn't seem to care about anything other than where his next sweet tea is coming from.

"Calvert, Texas," Carl says lazily, reading the sign, as I slow my speed. "Pop one-one-oh-oh. This place used to have the largest cotton gin in the world."

I signal, and turn left off the historic main street.

He's talking about a cotton gin in the 1800s. I'm picturing the day in the twenty-first century when news trucks and reporters were crawling all over this town like roaches. The crime scene photos, the ones I bribed a low-level Texas Rangers employee to copy for me. A horror show, and the victim wasn't even in them.

He's wrong about me being in a pissy mood. I'm far, far past that today. "So you know Calvert?" I make it sound casual.

"Bunch of beautiful ladies, barely breathing, almost bones. Jesus, look at your face. I'm talking about the Victorian architecture. It's a cemetery for it. Or a decaying art gallery. Take your pick. Most of Victorian-era Texas is raked over, but not in Calvert."

"Her name was Vickie," I say furiously, pulling up to the curb. "We're here."

"Is this one of your damn red dots?"

I switch off the ignition. Carl is staring at the chaotic explosion of gables, cupolas, wings, and bays that in 1902 was dubbed Queen Anne by its architect. Eight years ago, a caustic media renamed it Bloody Victoria—Bloody Vick for short.

Now Bloody Victoria looks beaten by a lover. Scabbing white paint, plywood-bandaged windows, broken spindles, scratched curlicues, missing scalloped shingles.

"If it makes you happy, I remember this house," Carl announces. "Used to stop off here in Calvert every now and then to document the slow demise of this street of ladies. I called this one The Bride. All that lace and trim. Always my favorite. Got a job off it once. Spent a whole morning shooting it for an old lady in a nursing home who used to live here. She wanted a painting done for her room. Her nephew in California was pestering her to sell the place, give him the dough. Wonder how that turned out."

Not well, Carl. The neighbors remember you, too—the man with the camera peering in these windows just days before Vickie Higgins disappeared. One of them wrote down your license plate. Police tracked you down. They stopped your pickup while you were out on bail before the Nicole Lakinski trial and pummeled you with questions.

Then the prosecutor fired shots at you in depositions. He asked the police to interview your little old lady in the nursing home, but, not surprisingly, she couldn't remember. The judge ended up declaring that any mention of Vickie at Nicole's trial would be prejudicial. So here you are, Carl, still free.

I shut down the speech in my head and remind myself to breathe as

I crack open the car windows. "Barfly, you're going to stay here, OK? I don't want you to pull your stitches." I adjust the teddy bear a little closer to his head and those soft eyes stare at me with more affection than my last boyfriend did. Only Andy had looked at me that way.

Don't get attached, Barfly. I don't know how this is going to end.

"There's a real estate agent on the front porch. We're a half-hour late. Just follow my lead. Whatever I say, nod your head. Whatever you remember, wait until we're back in the car."

"You're the boss. Look, she's waving." Carl cooperatively waves back.

We walk across the bare lawn in silence. I have desperate hope for this red dot. There is a room inside this house that knows terrible things. I'm going to make Carl stand smack in the middle of it. He is going to hear Vickie's screams.

The real estate agent is balancing a floppy straw hat while gingerly walking down the threadbare carpet of moss on the front stoop. A cool cave is visible underneath the rotting porch—a place my sister would have dragged me to play Trolls Under the Bridge. She liked to hear me squeal.

"You're late," the agent says brusquely. "I'm Trudy. Welcome to Calvert. It's a lovely little place to escape suburbia. Not so grand now, but back in the Victorian era, this was the fourth largest city in the state of Texas. *Downton Abbey* had nothing on Calvert but a radically different take on vowels. This home is magnificent, a rare trip back in time. Well worth the investment you will need to put into it."

Not a single word about murder in a town that usually has zero. And just a hint that fixing up this million-dollar mansion could cost at least twice that.

As she delivers her well-rehearsed pitch, I'm thinking for the hundredth time since I started hunting Carl about how much pictures lie.

Trudy appeared a good thirty years younger on her website. Her face is coated with a pinky-tangerine powder that ends at the chin line. Her mouth is outlined in bright red, and when it puckers, as it does now, it's hard not to stare. The collision of white-hot sun and the pandemonium of zebras and pelicans on her blouse makes me a little dizzy.

"Mrs. T liked *Downton*," Carl says. "Had a big thing for Mr. Bates until he started criticizing his wife's cooking."

Trudy smiles at Carl dismissively. I'd told her on the phone that he had dementia and that my husband and I were looking for a place to fix up that would hold his consulting business, my dying father, and a growing family.

I'd pulled out the ring in my nose this morning and threaded two tiny silver cross posts into my ears. My hair is gathered in a long, suburban ponytail and the white Ann Taylor sundress ends primly above the knee. My mother's gold wedding band, which I'd swiped from her jewelry box two months ago, is glinting in the sun.

I can tell Trudy is skeptical anyway; her eyes are focused on the tiny hole in my nose. Now she's glancing past me to check out the car, which she apparently decides is nice enough to proceed.

"Do you have any paranormal devices with you?" Trudy asks.

"No," Carl says.

"Do you work for a newspaper or magazine?"

"I don't," Carl says. "Can't vouch for her."

"We get a lot of lookie-loos," Trudy says. "I don't want to waste my time."

"I understand the house has been on the market for fourteen years," I say smoothly. "We know about the murder. My father . . . believes in ghosts. I want to make sure this house isn't going to spook him before we pour my husband's inheritance into it."

Carl is nodding. "I will need to see the spot."

"Well, that's better than the stories I usually hear," Trudy says, turning to the door. "I'll be able to show you most of the ground floor, which includes an extra-large bedroom that would make a perfect suite for you, sir. On the ground floor, there is also a kitchen, dining room, two living areas, several nice nooks, and the back parlor, where the event occurred. All stains were professionally removed years ago so no need to look around for them. I have a scrapbook in my car with pictures of the second-floor bedrooms and baths and the third-floor servants' quarters, but let's just see if you are still interested after you see the state of things. You will have to sign a liability release to view the rest of the house because none of the stairs are up to code. I can still scoot under an automatic garage door in a pinch but I'm not crazy enough to put a heel through one of those rotting staircases. So it would have to be another day with my boss, who, I'll be honest, is ready to unload this elephant. Murder only sells books and guns, he likes to say."

"I'm very disappointed about a limited tour," Carl says. "Were there a lot of stains?"

Trudy ignores him, punches in the code on the lockbox, and pops it open. She extracts a key, and glances at her watch. "I'm just going to take you straight to the room where the murder occurred. If you're spooked, there's no point in going further."

"I won't be," Carl says.

We enter a foyer that's velvet with darkness and dust. The only daylight streams along the bottom of two front windows where the plywood runs at least three inches short. "Watch where you step," Trudy advises. "The electricity's turned off. We show this one in the daytime."

Two circles of filthy stained glass throw some muted color from the top of an ornate staircase. As my eyes adjust, I can make out an empty sitting room to the right and a fireplace with its mouth bricked up. Trudy is already moving briskly down a long hall that stretches in front of us.

Vickie might have walked this hall to her death. I nudge Carl along like he probably nudged her. Trudy is whipping a flashlight at the walls and ceilings in tour guide fashion. I can't make out her muffled words.

"Did you just say original shit-ass walls?" Carl asks.

We've reached a thick paneled door at the end of the hall. I know this beautifully carved door. In pictures, it was bound with yellow tape. Carl and I are stacked closely behind Trudy while she flashes her light at her keys, finding the one she wants.

"Shiplap walls, sir. *Ship*-lap walls." She throws open the door and ushers us inside a long shallow room that runs all the way along the back of the house. Enough light seeps through the cracks in the outside wall that I can see the raisins of rat feces on cheap linoleum, the broken ribs of two old wooden chairs, the graffiti of a pink fluorescent cross on one of the plywood windows, the letters *ADIH* spray-painted on another.

"What does this mean?" Carl, already at the window, is tracing a finger over the H.

"Another Day in Hell," I translate under my breath.

Trudy has moved deeper into the room. "Teenagers. Have to change the lock on the door once a month. The cops still have to do a nightly swing-by. It's every hour on Halloween."

When she flips her face around, I catch my breath. There's a reason I couldn't hear in the hall. A white mask smothers her nose and mouth. Only her eyes are visible. More concerning, she has lifted her shirt to reveal a triangle of pale stomach fat and a holster with a gun.

"Sorry, didn't mean to startle you. This is a special mask I've had made for my allergies. Who knows about the asbestos in these old places? I used to bring surgical masks for clients, but it got expensive and most are giving me the runaround. I haven't sold a fixer-upper Victorian in five years."

My eye is glued to her hand, now resting on a holster that looks a little like the one in my suitcase. This was not a time when I thought I needed to strap it on.

"My husband insists on the gun. You read the Internet, you know what happens to real estate ladies. There's no need for you to be judgmental. You'd be lucky to have me sitting by you at a movie these days when a semi-automatic comes out of the dark."

"I'm sure real estate . . . is a dangerous occupation," I mumble. Carl is off in a corner, oblivious, in low conversation with a wall. I make out the word *choke*. And *Art*. He wants to choke Art?

"Well, he's found the spot," Trudy says, nodding at Carl. "You can't imagine the weirdos and ghost hunters who've called and emailed. Vickie Higgins was a nice girl. She deserves every respect in death. She had a beautiful life ahead of her. Her husband still lives in the same house, on the next street over. I sold it to him the year before Vickie died. Vickie had fixed it up so cute, then his new wife came in and tore almost every bit of history out of that place. Did you know Vickie vanished on the first anniversary of their marriage? The steak was thawed on the kitchen counter and going gray when he came home for dinner. This house was empty. They didn't find the scene for thirteen days."

"She was stabbed right here, wasn't she?" Carl asks from the far end of the room. "Blood sprayed all over. Sank right in the red wall-paper. It had an artichoke motif. You can see a little bit of it here, in this corner. All this texture would make an interesting photograph." He draws his hands up to his face and clicks his tongue.

"OK, that's it. We're done." Trudy's weapon is out of its home. A Ruger. She's gesturing with it toward the door.

Carl isn't moving, mesmerized by the wall.

On the lawn, the sun splinters the spell of the house. Trudy ushered us out pronto. Now she is back to the practical matters of stripping off her mask and re-holstering the gun like she's done this a hundred times. I turn to Carl. "Why don't you give Barfly a bathroom break? The leash is on the backseat floor. I'll finish up here with Trudy."

Carl makes the cuckoo sign with his index finger and points at Trudy, whose head is down as she fiddles with her holster. "I'll be with you in a minute," she is saying. "Don't want to blow a hole in my lady parts even though I don't use them much."

When she looks up, I'm holding out a fifty-dollar bill. "Please don't be insulted," I say. "We didn't come to waste your time. Maybe you and a friend can have a nice dinner on . . . Dad and me. It's a beautiful house, but I can tell my father would be fantasizing all the time about what happened here."

The money hangs in the air while she considers my motives and her teeth scrape at what's left of her lipstick. Most of it is now a bloody smear inside the mask dangling off her wrist.

I'm sure she doesn't believe me. It's clearly a bribe.

"Oh, why the hell not? My sister and I might go into Marlin for dinner this weekend."

"Terrific. Thank you again."

"Wait. I don't like to let inaccuracies go. There was no red wallpaper in that room. It was blue. And Vickie Higgins was *shot* in this house, not *stabbed*. They dug eight bullets out of the walls. And she wasn't found here, she was never found. There was, however, enough blood to declare her dead pretty much on that alone. And then there was all that business near the Orviss Crypt where her parents put up a fancy stone and buried a coffin that's waiting for a body that has never shown up. But I expect you know all about that."

I nod. Texas ghost websites say Vickie's wedding veil floats over her empty grave, sometimes in the sunshine. Ridiculous.

Trudy's expression switches to pity. "Back there in the house, your dad might have been remembering anything. The time his grandmother lost control of her mixer and red velvet cake batter spattered all over the place. I feel for you, hon. I see all the warning signs. My mother got morbid at the end. Paranoid. Thought someone was following her. She opened a can of French-cut green beans and tried to go after my sister with the lid. My sister *was* a bitch. Never wanted a single dish or a potato peel left in the sink at any hour of the day. Grabbed the glass of tea out of your hand to wash it before you got the last drink out. That doesn't change my advice on your dad. Watch your back."

22

It's a game of chicken, whether the real estate agent or I will drive off from Bloody Victoria first. I pretend to be settling Barfly in the backseat until she waves her hand like a white flag of surrender and pulls away.

I wait another five minutes before maneuvering the same street corner. Trudy's yellow MINI Cooper is nowhere in sight when I park in front of the baby Victorian where Vickie Higgins used to live. One block over and two blocks down from where Vickie Higgins died.

Way too close, I think.

Yet this is still the address of Jon Higgins, once the newlywed husband of Vickie. I'd checked and then checked again. Trudy had basically confirmed it a few minutes ago. Most of the Victorian femininity of this house has been stripped away just like she said. Only a tiny gingerbread detail over the front porch survived. Fog gray siding, aluminum, let-no-scrap-of-air-in windows, a boxy addition—all changes that cheapen it.

There's a Fisher-Price basketball hoop in the driveway and a fancy pink tricycle locked to the porch railing. The pristine St. Augustine yard is outlined with the three-inch-deep edging of an anal-retentive landscaper. Maybe a few blocks, a new wife, and two kids are enough to make Jon Higgins forget his ugly past is a short dog walk away. Or maybe he doesn't want to.

There's nothing to gain by jumping out of the car. Jon Higgins didn't respond to my letters, email pleas, or calls to the secretary in his law office. It doesn't appear that anyone is home anyway. I just want to see again for myself where Vickie left the steak to turn gray. I want to know whether stopping here will inspire Carl to say something. Whether the striking colors of the house when Vickie lived here are imprinted in some corner of his brain.

A year ago in a Dallas diner, Vickie's mother had shown me a photo of her youngest daughter, smiling, right by this porch, perched on a ladder with a paintbrush in her hand. "Vickie was so proud of her Painted Lady," she'd told me. "Painted it green with pimiento-colored shutters and named the house 'Olive.' She wanted every historical detail accurate to 1890s San Francisco. She couldn't make up her mind at first. Should it be purple and peach? Aqua and gold? And on and on. She found California newspaper editorials from back in the old days that warned the trend in violent color clashes was going to incite neighborhoods to madness. Sometimes, I wonder if they were right. If the paint job drove somebody to kill my daughter."

Vickie's mother had revealed these details well into our two-hour conversation, when our eyes were already red. She'd shown me the photo of Vickie's wedding dress that wound up stuffed by its lonely self in a casket in a hole in the earth because Vickie, like my sister, was never found.

Vickie's mother hadn't recognized Carl in a six-picture lineup I laid down on top of a paper placemat with word-cross games and tic-tac-toe.

We'd met fifteen miles from her house. She'd thought this would be a safe way for her to satisfy the strange young woman who dialed up and begged to meet because someone she loved disappeared into the ether, too. Of course, I already knew exactly where she lived: a brick ranch-style home in Plano that fit with her teacher's pension, right next door to her oldest daughter, who had slammed her door in my face two years earlier.

After one cup of coffee, I wasn't worried. Vickie's mother wanted to talk about her daughter, no matter what my motive or how much of a liar I was, at whatever risk to herself.

"Heads up," Carl says.

One of the doors to the detached garage is beginning to scroll up. Someone either coming or going. The answer squeals into the driveway—a green Prius that slams short. A skinny, red-faced woman in black yoga pants and a tight pink top is barreling out of the driver's side toward us. I'm guessing it's DeeDee, Jon's second wife, the woman who took a thoughtless gray eraser to Vickie's house. She'd taken another eraser to the wrinkles on the Facebook profile picture I'd found. Like Trudy.

"Trudy just called to warn me about you," she's screeching. "Get the hell off our property before I phone my husband. Or get the cops."

She's already at my car window, leaning in, providing me intimate knowledge of every rough patch on her unmade face, the skunk of her yoga sweat, and the dutiful boiled egg she had for breakfast.

Several photographs of Vickie, blond and pale and pretty, lay sorted in one of the containers in the trunk. This woman is a lesser Vickie, a poorly sketched reproduction. Vickie's mother told me that she'd met Jon's second wife at the memorial ceremony after her daughter was declared dead in absentia. *Jon deserves that woman,* she told me bitterly. *He always worked too late.* The blame was subtle but furious.

"Technically, we are not on your property," Carl announces to DeeDee. "We're on the street. And we don't know a Trudy."

"You son of a bitch. Trudy told me the kind of car you drive."

DeeDee reaches into the car and clinches my ponytail in a painful hold.

"I'd let go if I were you," Carl warns. "More for your sake. She's tougher than she looks."

The woman maintains her grip on my head. "I'm sick of Vickie being my fucking shadow."

"Did you ever think that you are *Vickie's* fucking shadow?" Carl says coolly. I try to shoot Carl a warning look, but I can't turn my neck. DeeDee's grip is unrelenting.

He is right about one thing. I know how to break her vise. I'm just not ready to do it. Carl's mind has sprung to life again. Maybe he recognizes this house. Remembers Vickie. Maybe he did all along.

"You know that Nicole Lakinski, who went missing in Waco?" Carl asks her. I feel a warm drop of his spittle on my cheek.

"Are you listening to me, old man? *I don't give a shit.*" DeeDee's shriek travels the street, quiet and still except for the merciless humming of air-conditioning units.

"Nicole and Vickie had an interesting personal connection," Carl persists.

"What connection?" DeeDee and I ask almost simultaneously.

"It's a detail not revealed at the Waco trial. My lawyer and the prosecutor didn't seem to think it benefited either side." Carl reaches over and seizes her wrist, still attached to my ponytail. "You might want to ask your husband why."

The muscled knot in his forearm works like a twitchy nerve. He's holding firm.

"I recognize you now," DeeDee says slowly. "You're that photographer who got off. The serial killer. I read that you were homeless. Locked up in some halfway house."

Barfly is beginning to bark—one short yip and then a rapid-fire burst. I don't want him to break open his stitches. I definitely don't want a neighbor to call the cops. DeeDee's eyes dart from me to Carl. She struggles against his clench. Every tiny hair at the top of my scalp is screaming.

"Tell anyone about me and I may pay you another visit," Carl says. "Do you like having your picture taken?"

Enough. I hit the window button and watch it glide up. "Sorry," I mouth as DeeDee yanks her arm free from Carl and stumbles back.

I really am a little bit sorry for her. A dead woman, no matter how sweet she was in life or how very dead now, is a tricky bitch.

DeeDee can paint the outside of her house whatever the hell color she wants, but dead Vickie is still making calls inside. She decides how good DeeDee's sex life is and how often her husband will say *I love you.* How angry DeeDee might get at her kids, how ignored or spoiled they will feel, which toys will be broken and when and why.

Whether DeeDee will stop at one glass of wine or three, will sleep two hours or seven, will bother to put on makeup and make the bed and stack all the mindless pillows. No matter how much yoga DeeDee does, it will be Vickie who decides how deeply she is allowed to breathe.

Maybe DeeDee wasn't always a ponytail-puller. Maybe Vickie wasn't as much of a cherry pie as her mother said she was. The dead are always washed clean.

I don't speak to Carl until DeeDee is a little stick figure in the back window. I'm certain her little stick fingers are dialing trouble, but I halt the car abruptly in the middle of the road anyway.

"Is that true? Is there a connection between these missing women? Did the prosecutor bury evidence?" The Nicole Lakinski case lives and breathes inside me more than any of the others except my sister's. That's because there was so much to devour: depositions, trial transcripts, newspaper and Internet stories. I bought more than a few Shiners for the cops who were the primaries. I flirted and crossed the line with men I shouldn't have. And, still, I may have missed the biggest piece.

"Not that I know of," Carl says. "Remind me. Who else do you think I killed?"

23

The moon is a giant orange ball playing hide-and-seek with a bank of night clouds. Soothing, if driving this pitch-black country road didn't feel like being buried alive, if the tires weren't moaning against the asphalt, if I didn't think there was a serial killer sleeping beside me. I've tried the radio, but it's full of deafening static.

Every now and then, I hit a surprise rut, which jolts my nerves. It's also saving me from nodding off. Barfly is knocked out in the back with his evening painkiller. Carl swallowed his pills or at least pretended to. He's slumped on a feather pillow propped against the door. At his feet, a small pile of rocks and pebbles he "panned" out of a Kohl's parking lot. "Gold," he told me.

He had insisted on buying a 100-percent-down pillow and a 500-thread-count American flag pillowcase, and another pillow and sleeping bag for Walt, which he arranged neatly across the floor of the backseat. "Like a bunk bed," he told Walt. Or Barfly. Or both. Another $310.24, blown.

I think about all those video cameras that recorded Carl and me in the Kohl's home goods department, at the register, in the parking lot, when all I really wanted to do in Bryan, Texas, was quietly retrieve a new rental vehicle and double-check a hotel reservation.

I'd changed clothes at the Whataburger where we stopped for a late lunch. Goodbye to the Ann Taylor sundress. My costume for the next act was a jean skirt that rides high, a tight white tank top, a red push-up bra, and four-inch cheap strappy sandals. I freed my long hair, stuck in the nose ring, circled my eyes with black liner.

At the Avis car center down the road, I had confidently flaunted my second fake driver's license. The hair in the picture was blond and mine was still Cherry Cola but I'd decided it was worth the risk.

I giggled and flirted and lied and asked the cute guy named Mike behind the counter if he'd read the sci-fi thriller where red-haired girls are like Kryptonite to one of the main villains. *My boyfriend loved that book,* I told Mike. *I dyed my hair red because it made him happy. We are going on a hunting trip to Oklahoma, but after that I may break up with him. He is already talking about me getting a boob job, when aren't my breasts nice enough?*

Mike had trouble keeping his eyes up after that. He did bother to make me promise I'd be the only driver, although it was clear he didn't really care. I asked him for a four-door white pickup because there is nothing more ubiquitous on a Texas highway.

My trainer is the one who told me the story about the villain made powerless by red-haired girls. I was pounding boxing gloves into a bag at the time. He was always trying to convince me that my Achilles' heel would be something unexpected, a blow to the mind, not the chest.

I'd paid extra for a pickup with a remote-controlled retractable bed cover and a deep tint on the windows. Play money on the credit card. I couldn't avoid using one for a rental.

Carl stayed out of sight during the truck negotiation, missing another of my performances. They're adding up. Rachel would be proud. For Artie the motel clerk, I'd played an annoyed wife on the way to an aunt's funeral. For the horny car rental guy, I was a red-haired girl with a redneck boyfriend. I practically took my top off and waved it like a Confederate flag.

It was a risk, but I'd had to let Carl drive the Buick and follow me in the truck. It had been Carl's idea to abandon the rental sedan in an enormous long-term parking lot for Texas A&M students. He'd quickly screwed the original rental plates back on and attached another set of fake ones to the pickup while I moved the boxes and suitcases from the trunk to the truck bed.

Because of the long-term rental agreement I'd signed, no one at Avis would be worried about the Buick for three weeks. They certainly wouldn't be looking in that lot.

It was too early in the trip to be switching cars and license plates, too early to be collecting a dog or DeeDee's wrath. It was also too early to be working in such elegant unison with Carl.

When Carl wasn't looking, right before we abandoned the Buick, I had lifted up the console to retrieve Lolita's scarf. It wasn't there.

A shadow is limping across the dark road twenty yards ahead. I slam on the brakes. Carl bolts up. "A raccoon," I say. He whips around to check Barfly, who hadn't let out a peep. "What are those bug eyes behind us?" he demands.

"Is your ghost lady back?" Too flip, I know. The dementia books said to accept hallucinations *because what harm does that do? Don't provoke.*

"Stop calling them ghosts," he says, irritated. "How long has that vehicle been following us?"

I glance in the rearview mirror. "I don't know. They've been way, way back, on and off, for a while. I don't think they are always the same headlights. I'm watching."

"You're going to have to pull over."

"What?"

"When we get over this little hill and they lose our taillights for a second, look for a place to pull over."

We're at the bottom of a hill when he yanks the wheel sharply. "Right here." He has thrown the truck into a half-moon patch of gravel. I squeal on the brakes. The pickup lights illuminate a cattle gate and an old-fashioned metal arch, usually the entrance to expansive family ranchland.

"Cut the lights," he demands. "Pull through the gate, turn around to face the road, and shut the car off."

I don't know whether to be more scared of the bug eyes, Carl, or myself for so robotically obeying him.

We sit there in the dark, facing the road, not saying a word. The only sound is Carl's breath. When the car rushes past, it's a blur of shadow, now going at least eighty.

"You'll get the hang of this." Carl leans his head back against the pillow. "We'll stay here for a while to be sure. They'll pause up ahead and wait for about thirty minutes before they give up. Get some shut-eye."

Inside, I'm protesting. But my neck feels like it can no longer prop up my head, still aching from its encounter with DeeDee. Day Three has been a very long one. I pulled over twice so Carl could pan for gold in the pebbles at the side of the road. And what if Carl's right? The possibility of being tailed is the paranoid reason I chose to drive in circles for a while on the back roads. I know what *I'm* worried about. I know the laws I've broken, the snakes I've poked. But who does Carl think is following us?

Carl's breathing is even again, his head snuggled back on the pillow. It takes everything in me not to steal the one out from under Walt's head for myself.

The seat glides back easily when I press the button.

I feel my sister's presence. The first time this happened was three days after she disappeared. My scalp tickled, like Rachel was back to French-braid my hair like she'd promised. Of course, when I stole a look in the mirror, my hair was still a ratty mess, full of tears and snot.

Rachel's presence is not at all like one of Carl's ghosts. And there's no angel on my shoulder. No angel would agree to what I'm willing to do. I think about the Glock. Whether, after all that training, I'll still have the guts to use it.

I lie back and stare at the moon eyeing me through the sunroof.

It's no longer fun and games up there.

The clouds have gathered into an ocean of rushing waves. The moon is fighting the inevitable, sinking into the depths of things no one can see.

Bright and shining, and then swallowed whole.

Like my sister.

24

I was twelve when my sister disappeared, the exact age she was when she stood laughing in that grave, reaching her hand up to me. It was the summer of Rachel's sophomore year in college, so she was home, my family complete, what my mother referred to as "blessed chaos." When my sister was at school, I felt like a leg on our table for four was missing. Now that table is firewood.

Despite our seven-year age difference, we had always shared a room. So when the cops asked, while my mother was inconsolable, I could name Rachel's precise measurements (32–25–34), her dress size (4), her shoe size (7), weight (108), number of piercings (three: one in nose, two hidden), her drug use (pot, occasional), the three-quarter-inch scar on her knee from a softball slide.

I could tell them that on the morning of her disappearance, Rachel left for her summer babysitting job at exactly 8:14 A.M., a little earlier than usual. She ate Cheerios with Almond Breeze for breakfast, brushed her teeth with a purple toothbrush and Crest Whitening, dressed in jeans, a blue T-shirt, and silver heart earrings that an old boyfriend had given her.

The last thing she said to me as she was going out the door was, "Sorry, I finished off the strawberries." She was grinning. We both loved them, and she'd already eaten her half, so I was mad. I never bit into another strawberry again, but my late-night reading included searching for them in the stomach content listings of coroners' reports.

When Rachel disappeared, it had been years since my twin playmates were taped to the back wall of my closet. I vaguely thought of the picture, of the naive, silly little girl I was, when I began attaching new photographs to the pine paneling. This time, my secret gallery was devoted to suspects.

When I divided the clothes in the middle, between my sister's sky-blue prom dress and her candy-cane Christmas robe, there was Mr. Eversley, her old English teacher, frowning in a picture clipped from one of my sister's old yearbooks. He gave my sister A's when she was a B student at best. In the beginning, that was plenty to make my suspect list.

To the right, between my favorite jeans and a rose print sweater, I'd pasted up a spread on the two boyfriends Rachel tossed back and forth in summer and winter—one at home, the other in college, where she was a theater major.

The back corner was dedicated to pictures of the three men within a mile radius of our house listed on the Texas sex offenders' registry. I had snapped surreptitious shots of them in their yards and through their windows. One of them had chased me away with a hose. I was lucky. He was too used to a rabid group called Mothers Against Molesters bugging the crap out of him to report me.

By the time I was a junior in high school, every inch of space on my closet wall was layered with maps, notes, photos, headlines. There was an ugly beauty to the display on the days my parents were out of the house and I swept all the clothes out of the closet and laid it bare.

I was careful about my obsession. I hid things. Under the red lining of my violin case, I tucked a timeline of Rachel's movements during her last week on earth.

By the time I was fourteen, I had stored a black T-shirt, black sneakers, a flashlight, and one of my father's pistols under the floorboard by the window. I found a heady power in roaming at night— what predators must feel when they stare at sleeping houses.

My dad knew all about the weapon in my room. That's where he wanted it after Rachel went missing. I practiced with him at the range twice a month. He didn't want me to hesitate to shoot in self-defense. He bought me the holster I'm wearing. More than once, I almost told him everything. If I had, I wonder if I would be different. If he would have tried harder to stay alive for me, instead of letting his heart stop.

Inside the lining of the pillow where my sister used to lay her head, I stashed the notebook with a list of girls and women from ages eighteen to twenty-eight, women who had vanished in Texas the ten years before and all the years after my sister did. I've never stopped adding names to the list. I used to say them in bed silently with my eyes closed, like other people count sheep. Now there are way too many to memorize.

While my mother thought I slaved over AP history at the library, I tangentially linked cases to my sister's and eliminated others. After I got my driver's license, I followed people. I retired suspects and added more.

For example, I eventually had Mr. Eversley for class myself.

Rachel wasn't special to him, it turned out. Mr. Eversley gave everyone A's.

Two of the men I suspected on the sex offenders' registry had simply been guilty of slightly underage sex with women they married. I felt guilty for bothering them. I made oatmeal cookies and left them on their doorsteps with an anonymous note as an apology.

That was rare. A lot of the men I stalked were guilty of something. I watched them slap their wives, cheat in their own homes, sell pot and painkillers to neighborhood kids. Occasionally, I'd leave a different kind of note on the windshields of their BMWs and Toyotas. I wanted them to know someone was watching.

The nice cop who sat at my kitchen table and wrote down my sister's measurements retired to run his father-in-law's concrete company. After that, when I showed up at the police station once a year with my investigative collection, I was passed around. Someone always called my mother afterward and told on me.

I became smarter, leaner, sneakier. I let my hope continue to beat against all the statistics.

Still, it got harder to brace myself to meet other sad families in secret so my mother wouldn't find out. To be hung up on and have front doors slammed on me.

To awkwardly ask families for spare copies of snapshot after snapshot so I could scour and compare every face in the background, thinking that one day I'd see a connection. I never did.

It was pure luck that I found the link to Carl, even though it had been in the back of my closet all along.

DAY FOUR

How not to be afraid of the dark when
I go to bed (things Rachel says)

1. Our curtains do not turn into witches.

2. The floor won't fall away and take me
   to hell when I get up to go to the
   bathroom.

3. Rachel is still breathing. Do **NOT** put
   my hand under her nose to be sure,
   and wake her up.

25

I pull into the parking lot of a small-town dollar store after a fitful night sleeping in the truck. Carl's still snoring like a horse. We're in Magnolia. Or Bellville. I'm not sure. I've stayed off my phone, taken a few iffy turns. The last time I looked at the map was with a flash-light.

I free Barfly from the back and lead him over to a grassy patch of dandelions to do his business. He's barely limping.

If Barfly keeps improving at this rate, it's more of a reason to in-sist we find a no-kill shelter. Practically speaking, he needs to go. People are more likely to remember a couple of people with a scruffy dog. More of a problem, Barfly makes me feel. Once that well opens, it will overflow. I have no idea what I'd do to Carl. At the back of the truck, I crank open a can of dog food and pour some bottled water into a shiny metal bowl.

Barfly and I are resettled in the truck at 8:36 A.M. when a pimply teenager drives up in a beat-up green Camry to unlock the store. The place doesn't open until 9 but he waves me in after I show up at the door with my knees squeezed together, holding a magazine in front of my crotch.

I tell him I'm on a desperate early-morning hunt for tampons, which is part of the truth. He waits patiently at the register, where I figure he is also keeping a careful watch on the security screens as I roam the aisles.

My hair is tucked into the *Hollywood, U.S.A.* baseball cap Carl picked up at a gas station. My eyes are concealed behind a pair of pilot Ray-Bans. That's really not so weird at 8:30 in the morning, because Texas sunrises are blinding, Texas hangovers are a bitch, and Texas women spend freely on good sunglasses.

They're out of tampons. When I show up at the register with my basket of goodies, he seems disinterested in what I do purchase: four mini-packages of powdered-sugar donuts, two single-serving-size milks, a twenty-count box of quart-size Ziploc freezer bags, and three different shades of hair dye. It had occurred to me on Aisle Three that I shouldn't be advertising to the dollar store cameras that I might be going blond next, so I bought a variety pack.

Carl is wide-awake when I get back to the truck.

"Everything you buy at the dollar store causes cancer," he announces as I open the door.

I fling him a package of donuts, followed by the box of Ziplocs. He catches both, one at a time, like someone who knows how to catch.

"You remembered. Thank you." He seems genuinely touched that I bought him the plastic bags he requested for his gold-panning enterprise.

"Where we headed?" He's tearing open the donuts.

"Houston," I say. "Then Galveston."

"Which one did I kill there? Is this your last dot? Are you running out?" The powdered sugar has dusted his lips and chin.

"Violet," I say, while the ocean drums in my ears.

26

Carl and I funnel into the fast, smoky churn of Houston.

The traffic feels gritty and forgetful of Harvey, of the deep rivers that raged on the highways, swallowed homes, and churned up heroes who transformed Houston into one of the bravest, most famous cities in the world.

Ahead, the skyline stands untouched, no holes, no missing towers. The dark clouds scudding outside the windshield are the only reminder that everything is on a timer.

A reminder that, for the next forty-eight hours, *I* am on a timer.

Right now, I'm just trying to deal with Carl. For the last ten minutes, he's been waving out the passenger window at a kid in a Honda Civic, no matter how many times I tell him to *please stop.*

If the kid waves back at his current rate of seventy miles an hour, we might collide. He's steering solely with his knees. His hands are gripped tightly to a rope over his head that loops through the windows and prevents the rug balanced on top from flying off. Meanwhile, eighteen-wheelers flirt with me, crossing back and forth over the line, ready to kiss.

When Carl says, "Get off at this exit," I don't resist, because my nerves need a break even though we only abandoned the back roads two hours ago. On the service drive, Carl gestures for me to turn about a block down in to a mostly abandoned strip mall. I immediately have second thoughts. I was thinking we got off here to feed his Whataburger addiction.

Only two out of five storefronts appear active: The Eyes of Texas and Frisky Business Rentals. Both places borrow parking spaces from the back corner of an old Luby's cafeteria lot.

All three businesses are giving it their best Las Vegas effort at staying alive in the cracked, concrete landscape Harvey left behind: The window of The Eyes of Texas blinks with two orange-and-blue eyes; Frisky Business flashes a salacious pink neon tongue; Luby's is offering an all-you-can-eat chicken-fried-steak and shrimp special with unlimited pecan pie and sweet tea for $7.99.

Carl waves me over to a space about a hundred feet from the strip center. Before I can say anything, he hops out of the car and heads straight for the blinking eyes. Now I'm wondering if they are animated boobs.

I roll down the window. "You are bringing porn back to this truck over my dead body!" I yell. Half the time, I feel like Carl is only pretending to have dementia; the other half, he is a child, bagging gold, needing a leash.

I instantly wish I could take back the part where I'm a dead body lying in a pile on the asphalt. Carl doesn't even turn his head. Barfly stands up shakily in the backseat of the cab, leaning over to swipe my bare shoulder with his rough tongue.

Carl disappears behind the opaque glass door of The Eyes of Texas. I imagine lurid takes on Georgia O'Keeffe, chocolate-flavored plastic, my sandals sticking to God knows what on the floor.

I glance around the parking lot. No sign of life. It seems as good a time as any for a Chevy-truck quick change. I need to upscale my look for our next hotel stop, a temporary graduation from the dumps where we've been staying.

I lock the doors, climb over the seat, assure Barfly everything is OK, and strip down to my underwear. I pull a pair of expensive jeans out of my backpack, yank a pretty, if wrinkled, peach cotton top over my head that hangs just the right amount of loose to cover the holster, the one my dad gave me.

I leave in the nose ring, add a delicate silver chain around my neck and three expensive silver rings to my right hand. The ring circling my forefinger feels heaviest but not because of weight. It was my sister's favorite—a sea-blue turquoise nugget with veins like a spider's web. The rings make holding a gun a little harder, but they are good for a punch. I still don't completely buy what my trainer said—that it's more useful to know how to take a punch than to throw one.

Back in the front seat, I clean off my raccoon eyes with a makeup remover wipe from my purse, pencil a finer line for my eyebrows, and delicately apply mascara. As I smear a nude gloss on my lips, I think about how much this constant costuming calms me down. And the comfort I feel the second I let my fingers roll over the die from the wall. I've begun to return to it again and again, counting the dots on its six faces like it is my own secret Braille.

I'm worried about DeeDee back in Calvert. *DeeDee DeeDee DeeDee.* Her silly little name trills in my ears. DeeDee recognized Carl. Of course, she doesn't know who I am or my aliases or that we are now driving a ubiquitous white truck instead of a granddaddy Buick.

I stare out the dirty windshield at the door that swallowed Carl. His absence is making me antsy. "OK, Barfly," I say. "We're going in." I dig my gun out of the console and slide it into the holster. Girls might walk in that door every week and disappear. *Human trafficking is a bigger network than drugs,* a cop used to tell me. No matter what he said, I never thought that's what happened to Rachel. So why am I thinking about it now?

As soon as I open the door, I'm overcome with the sensation of falling. The wall in front of me is papered top to bottom with a photograph swooning from the top of a skyscraper—the suicide jumper's perspective.

I have to look at a spot on the dirty carpet to win my equilibrium back. When I lift my eyes, I'm alone in a tiny, fluorescent-lighted room. A black curtain is slung shut over the room's only other door.

Voices murmur behind it, one of them Carl's. My fingers wrap around the gun at my hip.

On every side, on every glass shelf, one-eyed things peer at me.

Cameras. A hundred, maybe more. Used cameras that know things they'll never tell. Old instamatics and high-tech aliens. Some with lenses that appear as heavy as tanks; others that are the size of a box of kitchen matches. None of them feel friendly.

Carl hadn't brought up his No. 1 condition for miles, and neither had I. But he certainly hadn't forgotten. He was here for a camera. As I try to make out the muffled, intimate conversation, I think he might also be here for something else.

"Sit, Barfly," I whisper. I regret not leaving him in the truck. I don't want him to get hurt.

The narrow curtain puffs and floats. A Hispanic man whips out from behind, laughing hoarsely, about forty-five, wearing a black Willie Nelson T-shirt that says *Outlaw*. His hair is Willie-like, too, tucked into a man bun with a few scraggly gray pieces hanging over his eyes.

Suddenly, he's not laughing. He's staring at my right hand and reaching behind a wooden podium in the corner. A rifle is pointed at my face before I realize why. He thinks I'm going to rob him. I hadn't remembered taking my gun out of the holster, but it is clutched in my fingers, pointed at the floor.

Carl is right behind him. "They're with me, Angel. Put the gun away."

"You don't need a camera," I say to Carl, not moving.

128

"You don't need a gun," Carl replies. He steps forward and pushes down the nose of Angel's rifle. "Relax, Angel. I said she's OK."

Carl is cradling a Nikon. A yellowed paper tag dangles off it like it's been sitting in a morgue. I continue to aim the gun at the floor. My uneasiness lingers. Not because of Angel, who is now on his knees, sweet-talking Barfly.

A camera is Carl's weapon. It gives him power. When he points the camera, people either do exactly what he says or throw their hands up to their faces for cover. *Don't move,* he says, and they don't. *Was that Rachel's mistake?*

Carl shoots, and everything bleeds black and white. The ordinary transforms into the profound, the beautiful, the sinister.

I don't know for sure all that Carl has done. Not yet. But his documentary photographs, which I've examined a hundred, a thousand times, make me see everything in terms of something else. They beg dark questions.

What made the black stains on that mattress by the curb?

Will the stitches leave a scar over that old man's eye?

What if the shiny penny wishes in that fountain didn't come true?

Is the cat curled in the cardboard box dead or sleeping?

Is the man with his hand raised high about to strike that child knee-deep in a river or baptize his soul?

You can't turn away from Carl's pictures. You can't help wondering about the way his camera is manipulating you. About what happened to these people and objects long before the shutter clicked, and after.

I'm certain it is the mystical creepiness of his photographs that made a jury with very little evidence take two days instead of ten minutes to set him free. The bit of DNA could be explained away. The little boy witness was a joke.

Angel is now cross-legged on the floor, scratching behind Barfly's ears. "The lady's too young for you, Carl."

"They're always too young," Carl says.

"What happened to this dog?" Angel asks grimly.

"He was shot," I say. "Dumped. We picked him up."

"He's going to be a real good dog," Angel says. "I can tell." I don't like the way his arm is now curling around Barfly. Possessive.

Carl hooks the camera's strap around his neck. "My friend here is giving me this Nikon. He knows I'm good for it."

Angel's eyes are roving over me. I can't tell if it's sexual or an assessment of my mental health. "If you feel bad about Carl not paying," he says to me, "I'll trade you for the dog."

"I'll give you cash for the camera," I say immediately. "How much?"

"More than Carl can afford."

I pull six fifty-dollar bills from my back pocket and put them on the counter. "Please don't mention us, OK?"

"I've never seen you before in my life," Angel says. "Next time I don't see you, leave your gun in the truck." He pulls a package off a rack and tosses it to Carl. "Take a memory card for the road."

We are back in the truck and I'm twisting the key in the ignition when Carl remarks slyly, "You didn't give him Barfly."

"We're not keeping him," I reply.

As we feed back into the traffic, I think how I just blew another three hundred bucks when I already have what Carl really wants.

George, the camera he mourned on the witness stand with actual tears, is riding along in a box in the bed of the truck.

Carl thinks his beloved Hasselblad is missing. Lost forever. That's because I stole it out of an evidence box. In the end, it may be all I have to barter.

TITLE: *LADY IN THE RAIN*

From *Time Travel: The Photographs of Carl Louis Feldman*
Gelatin silver print

Photographer's note—She came out of nowhere in the rain, running ahead of me, fleeing on a street that shone like wet mirror. She was mist and moonlight. Liquid silver. Cinderella. A girl in a time machine, chasing her other life. She held a small black umbrella high, like it had floated her to earth. I found her shoes up ahead by a tree. I wanted to follow. To see her face. But I knew that would break the spell.

27

Two days of my life are always running back to back like a double feature.

The day my sister disappeared.

And the day I knew Carl took her.

It was my senior year. I was sitting in an empty classroom before school, waiting to ask my art teacher a question.

At that point, I'd been obsessing over suspects for almost six years. The back of my closet was a maze that even I was beginning to have trouble following.

The book, titled *Time Travel: The Photographs of Carl Louis Feldman,* was lying on my teacher's chair. A student had just returned it, and walked out.

This particular book had become so morbidly popular that it required its own special sign-out sheet and an overnight return. Three parents had protested to the principal that it should be censored despite its complete absence of obscenity. The year before, the same parents had tried to ban any mention of Robert Mapplethorpe and the picture of the naked *Napalm Girl*.

The teacher was late. I was curious. My name was at least a dozen down on the waiting list to check it out. Carl's name was somewhere on one of my suspect lists at home, but it was really just a chicken-scratch question mark. He'd been acquitted. During the recent trial, he had become the most famous photographer in Texas, maybe the whole country.

I flipped from one page to another and another, thinking how dark and transcendental his photos were, like haunting poems. I decided someone so talented had to be innocent. Maybe I should cross him off the list entirely. The eleventh time I turned a page, I moved him to the very top.

I knew this picture by heart. I was staring at two little girls in white veils standing in a forest. The same little girls I hid and played with in the back of my closet. The same white dresses, the same scraggly blond hair, the same lovely faces, the same blur of motion. In this book, Carl called them *The Marys*. In the artist's note on the opposite page, he said he stumbled across them by accident.

I sat in that classroom, stunned. There were no windows. A prison architect had designed the high school where I spent four lightless years, so I couldn't see the rain but I could hear it pounding like rubber hammers on the roof. I didn't understand my connection to this photograph, just that it meant something terrible.

My hands stumbled and fell to the back flap of the book where a much younger Carl stared out of a self-portrait. Handsome. Jeans. Boots. Cowboy rugged. And he was ominously, nauseatingly *familiar*—that relentless itch I still can't scratch even though Carl now sleeps in my passenger seat and I can stare in his flesh-and-blood face whenever I want.

When the teacher walked in, I'd already shut the book and was fumbling with her tissue box.

I remember her name, Alegra with one *l*, because that's what she made us call her instead of Mrs. Bukowski, and that her glasses were sharp black squares with an aqua edge that made her eyes piercing and invasive. Her hug that day was stiff, maybe because neither of us had enough fat to melt into the other or because we were both stand-offish huggers.

I don't know how much she knew about me during that awkward embrace, but enough. My Greek tragedy family was pretty famous, too.

Alegra and I may have had a whole conversation. All I remember is that she dropped her arms and backed up when I mumbled, *"He killed my sister."*

While she called my parents, I tried to remember elusive details about the trial in Waco but couldn't. There was something about one of Carl's photographs in that case, too.

Questions were thumping my brain, relentless.

Did Carl Louis Feldman, an accused serial killer, slip one of his photographs under our attic staircase? Why?

Could I really have seen him before?

28

Carl is snapping off shots of me from the passenger seat. Real ones this time, digitally recorded. We left the photography store two hours ago, yet we're still crammed in Houston traffic, a mile from the hotel. We've traveled six miles.

Every minute we sit here, I'm a minute angrier. Not once has Carl stopped fiddling with his new toy, the one I paid for with blackmail money so a man in a Willie Nelson shirt wouldn't snatch my dog.

"I don't know if I killed anyone," Carl is saying, "but I've always considered every picture I take to be a little murder. My Hasselblad sounded like a gunshot when I fired it. A solid, *good* sound. That, and it's inevitable that my subjects will be dead someday when someone looks at their pictures."

"How about you give it a rest with the camera." I can't keep the edge out of my voice. "The traffic's tough. It's very distracting."

He adjusts the lens and shifts it back up to his eye. Snaps off another shot. "The traffic is standing still," he says. "All you have to do is keep your foot on the brake. But all right. How about a game of Twenty Questions?"

"Whatever makes you stop."

He presses the shutter. Three more rapid-fire shots. "You're very hard to resist. Your face has intriguing angles. Forgive me, but I haven't had a camera in my hand for over a year."

"I don't like my picture taken." *Forgiveness does not apply to you, Carl.*

"That's why you take a good picture. It's a myth that traditional beauties make the best photographs. You, you're real. Hurting. Hell-bent. My camera appreciates that kind of honesty."

"That's some irony—that you think I'm honest." I press lightly on the gas and inch forward two feet.

"My camera is deaf. It's not listening to the lies coming out of your mouth. When I look through this little hole, I see a sweet, ordinary girl. I see the soft heart beating away. The taut muscle on your arms and legs that is a layer of pretend. A brain that is quick but frankly maybe not quite quick enough."

"You can't analyze me like those women in the diner. You have no idea who I am."

"It's . . . animal."

I turn my head sharply. "What?" *You're the freaking animal.*

"Animal, vegetable, or mineral. The game. I'm giving you the first answer for free. It's animal."

I swallow hard. "Can I see it with my little eye?" I hope the sarcasm hides the fact that he is once again drilling into my nerves. "Is it Barfly?"

"No. And no. You just wasted two questions."

"Is it furry?"

"No."

"Scaly?"

"No."

"Does it have smooth skin?"

"Yes. Fifteen questions left."

"Does it have a tail?"

"No."

"Is it fast?"

"Dumb question. Everything is fast when it's scared."

"Is it something found in the sea?"

"Yes, it could be found in the sea."

"Is it that octopus with the weird ears that you liked on Discovery Channel?"

"That's nine questions, and you're way off track. Think more broadly. Animal was a very broad category when my brother and I played. Didn't you ever have a brother or sister to play this game with?"

I slam on the brakes as a blue Toyota whips in front of me.

"Jesus, watch out. *Now* you seem distracted. Maybe we should stop playing."

"I'm fine." I'm beginning to have an uneasy feeling about Carl's game, a game I've never been good at. "Does it have wings?"

"No, it does not have wings."

"Eight legs?"

"No."

"Six?"

"No."

"Four?"

"No."

"Two?"

"Two?" Carl echoes.

"Two legs. Carl, is this *animal* a human being?"

"Yes. Good job. You are thinking broadly."

"Is this person . . . female?"

"Yes. You've got four questions left."

"Is she . . . dead?"

"Yes. Dead people are allowed in this game. People from the past. Historical figures. Dead celebrities. People you know."

"Does her name start with an *N*?" I stutter.

"No."

Not Nicole.

"Does her name start with a *V*?"

"Nope."

Not Vickie. Not Violet.

"One question left and there are twenty-four more letters of the alphabet," Carl says. "Your odds aren't good if this is the route you are taking."

"An *R*? *Did her name start with* R?" I can't bear to say my sister's name to him.

"You're out of questions," Carl says. "And you're barking at me. You lose."

29

I apologize to Carl for barking at him. How crazy is that? I apologize to a killer who is dangling a dead female, possibly my sister, in a game of Twenty Questions. *Smooth skin. Could be found in the sea.*

Did he drive all his victims to the ocean?

His arm is trembling again. I don't think he is faking. *Tremors,* Mrs. T called them. *Part of the disease.* I have to get Carl in good enough shape to pretend to be my father when we hit the boutique hotel where I'd made reservations. Mellow enough for an appointment tomorrow that Carl doesn't have a clue about. It has nothing to do with Violet. It was a long shot I'd been working for days.

An hour later, when we pull up in the wide celebrity drive, Carl is back in a decent mood. I almost cheer when I see six other late-model white pickups parked along the entryway. I plan to let our truck get lost in this herd of white ponies for the next two nights.

"Now you're talking," Carl says, as a bellman pulls open his door.

"Don't get used to it," I reply.

The Hotel ZaZa lobby is spacious and dark with deep red undertones, low-lying modern couches, and complicated oriental rugs. Carl has already declared the art on the walls "pure crap"—black-and-white photos of sleek hipsters and skillfully painted murals with cartoonish, distorted people who seem only part human and a lot angry about their career in a hotel lobby.

Two young women are efficiently operating behind the front desk, comfortable in their prettiness. I choose the one with the ultra-black bob, Lady Gaga pale skin, and "Harriet" name tag. Carl, directly behind me, slumps on the luggage cart that displays our cooler, two suitcases, Carl's patriotic pillow, Walt's sleeping bag, a brown sack with Barfly's food and bowls, and my backpack. At my instruction, Carl has posed Barfly with his best side showing.

"I'm Meredith Lane," I say, so that I match the name on the credit card with the red-haired ID that I've laid down on the desk. "I have a reservation for my father and me."

Harriet isn't concerned about my ID or the credit card. Her attention has turned to Carl and Barfly. "Are they both with you?"

I'm hoping Barfly's soft golden nose and brown eyes are very hard for her to resist. His coat is already a little fluffier. Right now he's performing his role better than Carl, who's sneering at the blown-up oceanfront photo of a muscled, chest-bared man with an adorable shaggy blond toddler on his shoulders. *The life you want.*

"Yes, they're with me."

"I'm sorry. We don't take dogs." She really does look sorry, so I think I picked the right reception clerk.

"He's an ESA," I say smoothly. "Your website says you have no problem with that." In fact, the website says nothing about this at all.

Harriet glances toward her colleague, who is busily changing rooms for a businessman who wants to know why his *fucking TV does not face the bed*. I silently thank him for being an asshole, so Harriet has to deal with me on her own.

"An emotional support animal," I explain softly, "for my father. E.S.A. He's here to visit a specialist tomorrow morning in the medical district. We brought Barfly all the way from Phoenix. My father really struggles without him." Casually, I drop my hand with its many-splendored rings to the driver's license still lying on the counter. The license does, indeed, say Phoenix, even though I've never stepped foot in the state.

"I like your rings. Barfly . . . is the dog?" Harriet asks. I had only two choices about Barfly. I could have tried to sneak him in, but then there would be the maid to deal with. Instead, I am banking on the proven fact that people are far more likely to buy a lie if there is a cute animal like Barfly advertising it.

Carl waves at Harriet. She cheerfully waves back.

"Yes, the dog is Barfly. My dad named him."

"Is he well trained?"

I don't hesitate. "Oh, the dog. Yes. By the best—a former Iraq War veteran who takes in strays and turns their lives around so they can help the elderly. He's part Cherokee. He's been on *60 Minutes*. He might get a reality show."

"That's awesome. Your dad is cute." She's lowered her voice. "My aunt has Alzheimer's."

"Lung cancer," I lie.

Harriet's fingers are busily working the computer. "I'm so sorry. MD Anderson is amazing. Maybe you know that Hermann Park is just outside the hotel. It's gorgeous. You won't even know you're in Houston. You can walk him there. Not your dad. The dog. Also, we have a free shuttle service that runs every twenty minutes in the morning to the hospital district, which is super easy. Oh, I see here that you already booked for the medical rate. I'll take another ten percent off for AARP. I don't need to see a card."

I feel a firm nudge at my leg. Barfly has wandered over with his leash hanging free and his bandage in full view. I flip around, and Carl is nowhere in sight.

"Hi, there." Harriet leans over the desk, gushing down at Barfly. "What happened to you, sweetie?"

I grab the leash. "He just had a suspicious knot removed. We're hoping for the best. My father is bonding with him more than ever now, of course."

I can see her mind working, I just don't know if it's in my favor. I'm already loading up the truck again and sleeping on sandpaper sheets, searching for pubic hairs on pillowcases before I put my head down.

"You know what," she says, returning to her screen, "we have a larger suite available on one of the high floors. A bridal party just backed out. I heard the groom was hooking up with a bridesmaid." She rolls her eyes. "OK, here we go. You'll love this suite. And I won't charge you extra. It will just be sitting empty anyway for the next few days. One of the bathrooms is bigger than my kitchen. It's perfect for your dog. The windows have crazy gorgeous views of the skyline, the museum district, and the fountains in the park. When you look down, it feels like you're falling, you know?"

I certainly do.

30

I let Carl order New Zealand Lamb Lollipops and Volcano Salt Fries off the room service menu. I feel reckless. Not like counting at all. Not money, not days, not how many times Carl says Walt has farted. We pick out a couple of craft beers apiece. I go for the Southern Star Bombshell Blonde and he picks the Buffalo Bayou More Cowbell IPA. I'm wondering how drunk you have to be to name any of the things we ordered.

The two-room suite spreads out before us with eclectic grandeur: Three deep couches, a dining table with six chairs, a lovely private bedroom with a plushy white comforter, two big-screen TVs. The hotel's signature red has dripped its way from the lobby into lamp-shade fringe and paintings of dancing poppies.

I keep catching unnerving glimpses of Carl and me in the antique-framed mirrors. It would be hell to be pimply or plump in here, and I say that not to be snotty but because I've been both at one point or another. I know the purpose of all this reflection—to pouf bridal

tulle and adjust cleavage and paint pouty lips and snap drunken self-
ies. But every time I move and see myself before I know who I am,
my heart bangs.

Of course, the first thing I did was check for a solid lock on the
door between the bedroom and the living area. Otherwise, I'd be
spending the night on the marble floor of the locked master bath
curled up with Barfly on top of Walt's sleeping bag, and that would
have meant another fight with Carl.

The bedroom lock plus the Door Jammer is going to be good
enough, though. Carl is oddly amenable to sleeping in the living
room on a foldout couch as long as Walt can stretch out on the other
one across the room. Walt's snoring has started to keep Carl awake.
I say it as a fact, because no matter how utterly coherent, even ratio-
nal, Carl has been at times, there is one thing I absolutely believe at
this point: Carl sees and hears his ghosts.

"Glad you're loosening up." Carl pokes the last fry in his mouth.
"Not worrying so much about your budget. I can help if I need to. I
have a little tucked away." This announcement makes me immediately want to count my cash, $2,000 of which I wisely or unwisely
left locked in a box in the bed of the pickup after moving it from the
spare tire in the Buick.

As far as I know, another $500 is still in the suitcase with my un-
derwear, ready to replenish my wallet, pretty decimated at this point.
The wallet sits in the hotel safe in the walk-in closet that Barfly has
already adopted as his private quarters.

Carl is in a mellow mood. After I'd hurriedly finished checking in,
I found him seated at the restaurant bar with an empty shot glass
and several stacks of quarters. Now he's halfway through a second
beer.

While I set the room service dishes outside the door, Carl flips on
a rerun of *Family Feud*. "For Walt," he informs me, and then sug-
gests a trip to the balcony to finish off the Larry G.

On TV, it's a storm of neon and an ebullient Steve Harvey in an
electric green suit asking a fat contestant in a Hawaiian shirt littered

144

with pink flowers, "What is a word that follows *pork*?" The man replies, "Upine." The audience laughter is like a porch full of tuneless wind chimes.

"Come on," Carl urges. "If someone smells pot, we can always say it's medicinal. For my lung cancer."

"No," I respond firmly. "I didn't know you heard that."

Ten minutes of Carl whining and Steve Harvey's exaggerated facial contortions make me change my mind. I dig the little bag out of my purse and roll a tiny joint over the bathroom sink. In minutes, Carl's seated on a cushioned outdoor chair on the balcony and I'm standing in the open French doorway, leaning against the frame.

Houston stretches out before us, a modern goddess, bruised but not defeated.

Carl gestures toward the other balcony chair, but I won't be taking him up on it. There isn't a move he could make I haven't taken into account. That includes tossing me down eleven stories into the circular lighted fountains that glow at night like landing pads for flying saucers.

The heat easily snuffs the chilly air-conditioning escaping out the door. Sweat trickles down my back while Carl is flicking a lighter, turning Larry G into a tiny firefly.

Surprise. In the brief spurt of flame, I see the lighter is the silver one with the N I'd found hidden in his suitcase at Mrs. T's. He snaps it shut. "This was my father's. Pretty thing, isn't it? Can't tell if it's for a girl or a boy."

"What was his name? Your father."

Carl travels his finger over the N. "Everybody called him Cutter. He told me it was a high school nickname because he was real good with a hunting knife, not because he got his arm cut off. Not sure what this N stood for, either. He'd never say."

He takes a hard drag and tilts his head. His profile in shadow is like sculpture against the abstract edges of the skyline. I'm reminded again that Carl is, and was, a good-looking man, especially in the dark. I can't control a shiver as his lips pucker and the vapor swims lazily over the edge of the balcony.

Claire in *House of Cards* sucks a drag like that, like Carl. The utterly ruthless way she treats a cigarette, the intimate one that she and Frank pass back and forth like Russian roulette, is the thing that finally convinced me she is the more evil of the two.

"Walt's got a crazy laugh, doesn't he?" Carl asks. "He gets a kick out of the sexual innuendo. Steve Harvey saying *badonkadonk. Baloney pony. Going to pound town.*"

Suddenly, he's scooting the chair around, harsh metal scraping concrete. I take a quick step back across the threshold.

"Relax, kiddo." He holds out the joint. I shake my head.

I want the thudding in my chest to stop. I want to ask Carl whether his female ghost has joined us for the finer accommodations and if she's steaming up the mirrors and leaving damp, curvy prints of her behind on the cushions. I want to ask about those beautiful, spirited twin girls who kept me company as a child and now feel so worrisome.

I want to put my Glock to his head and ask why in the hell that photograph of them was stored under my staircase like a secret long before my sister disappeared.

I want to know everyone he killed and when and how and why because I don't know which case will be the one to trap him into admitting he's a monster.

Rachel vanished into vapor. She was here, and then she was not, just like Nicole and Vickie and Violet. I had no choice but to follow their cases. In Nicole's, at least there was a bit of her DNA on a five-dollar bill and a trial. In Vickie's, there was a crime scene, her blood spattered on the walls. In Violet's, there was a frightening stretch of water and a best friend who maybe hadn't told the police everything.

I want to provoke a driving, productive conversation, instead of waiting passively for Carl's memory to uncurl from a fetal position on its own. I want to find my sister, whatever it takes.

Right now, I have to refrain. I have to leave my gun where it is. I can't throw too much at him at once. My trainer was a stickler on negotiating strategies.

Use comfortable surroundings. Interrogators are fourteen times more likely to get information quickly if they are nonconfrontational and establish rapport first. A confession is four times more likely if you strike a neutral and respectful tone.

But something in my gut is howling that I'm not going to get six more days to parlay this out—that the shadows pounding in the sand behind us are catching up. So I move a knight instead of a pawn.

"I saw a ghost once," I say.

"Oh, yeah? How'd that go?"

"I was fourteen. I walked in the kitchen at our house. She was at the microwave, making macaroni and cheese out of a box."

"Did she say anything?"

"She said, 'Fooled ya, didn't I?' And then she was gone."

"Ghosts are like that. Kind of funny." Carl, giving nothing. Asking *nothing*.

"My school counselor told me it wasn't that unusual," I persist carefully. "She called it a bereavement hallucination. She said half the people in the world who lose someone think they hear or see them again at least once. She told me one student saw his friend's face for a month if he looked up high and to the right. Just a tiny head floating in the upper corner of his vision. He went to three optometrists."

Carl's silence is painful.

"The ghost I saw was my sister," I say.

Carl drops the joint and crushes it with his heel. He's up on his feet, this part of the night over.

"My mother said I just made it up to feel better. That's what I think, too." There's a desperate edge to my voice. I hope he's too high to notice.

"They can explain ghosts any way they like," Carl says. "But no one has a clue."

31

After I opened that book of photographs in my teacher's classroom, I did all of the obvious things. I sat my mother and father down at our kitchen table and asked why one of Carl Louis Feldman's photographs was hidden under our attic staircase. I reminded them who he was, a suspected serial killer. I explained exactly when I found the twins and who they were to me. Playmates. *Sisters.*

Rachel was so busy.

My words were frantic, garbled. The despairing look they exchanged felt like they'd picked up the crumby butter knife on the table and stabbed it in my chest. Their faces were frightened, not by my story, but by *me.*

Both of them said they had no idea what I was talking about. They asked me to retrieve the photograph. I was on my knees in the dark, searching the closet floor, when they came up behind me. My mother made a terrible sound, an animal strangling for air.

In my panic to find the photo, I'd piled most of the hanging clothes on the bed. My pathological crazy quilt of suspects plastered on the back of the closet wall was in full, raw view.

My mother fell on my sister's bed, wailing. My father just put a hand on my shoulder. He helped me sweep every scrap out of my closet, down to the brown petal dust of one of my sister's old homecoming mums. The twins were gone. Had I thrown them out?

I showed them exactly where I found the envelope, halfway up, underneath the tenth attic step from the bottom. There was a piece of yellowed tape hanging loose, which I eagerly pointed to as proof.

My father, still wearing his work uniform, a blue starched shirt and a tie with red stripes, retrieved a flashlight. He crept into the crawl space that stored the upstairs furnace and shined it up to make sure nothing else was there but fluffy streamers of spider silk. He beamed the light on every single step that was visible.

That was a Friday. On Monday morning, he arranged two appointments—one with the young FBI agent who'd been newly assigned to my sister's cold case. The second I saw him—tall, strong, energetic—I'd felt better, like something would *happen*.

He smiled at me with white, perfect teeth. His physique had bullied an inexpensive pilled blue suit into hanging like Armani. Rachel always said she wouldn't marry anyone without good teeth or a six-pack. My dad teased her that she'd never get married. I'm sure he regretted that.

It felt like my sister was approving her investigator, too.

It wasn't just his looks. He'd stuck out a handshake that felt genuine and firm. "I'm DeAndre, but you can call me Andy if you don't tell my mother." I didn't care how many times he'd used that line—it made my parents smile. Instead of stashing us in a refrigerated interview room, he had arranged three desk chairs neatly around his cubicle.

He talked directly to me instead of at my parents, even when they were the ones asking the questions. I later learned this is a technique that neurologists use when their patients have dementia, to make them feel worth something. *I'm listening to you, not them, even though you are out of your mind.*

He scribbled notes. He told me he was officially adding Carl Feldman to my sister's suspect pool. That came with a warning not to hope too much for quick answers. Carl had vanished not long after being acquitted in the Nicole Lakinski trial. No one knew where he was.

Andy politely wrote down the name of Carl's book so he could see the photograph of the twins for himself. The whole time, his computer was open to a picture of my sister. It was the only way he was insensitive. My parents and I couldn't bear to look at it. At that time, we were all parked somewhere on the ladder of grief. My father was locked in at anger, which produced calves carved from treadmill running and a lawn scraped bald by ruthless mowing. My mother hunkered down at depression with an endless, golden glass of "iced tea" that smelled like varnish.

I was still foundering on guilt. For instance, I knew Rachel would blame me for the fact that the picture she hated most represented her on every FBI computer and missing persons poster.

Andy didn't know that his picture of reference, this senior class portrait, had produced a screaming match between my mother and sister. It was the one time my mother put her foot down on my sister's love affair with blue hair dye and nose rings.

So, for the first time in her life, my sister was documented as ordinary and cookie-cutter as everyone else, an immortalized Texas girl in jeans, boots, and a crisp white shirt.

The weathered red barn she'd leaned against would forever loom like a blood-spattered premonition. My mother limited her to one necklace and her favorite turquoise ring, the one that is tight on my finger right now, turning it a little pink. Her hair had been dyed dirty blond, back to its estimated natural color.

The second appointment my dad had made was with my art teacher, Alegra-with-one-*l*. In the way that one page turns another, my father struck up an affair with her two months later while my mother drank from her icy glass. But I didn't know that then, and I thought my teacher was nice to murmur sympathy and spend an hour with us thumbing through Carl Feldman's book.

She'd sworn she was going to burn it in her gas fireplace that night even though it was 70 degrees outside. As the pictures bled into one another and my mother murmured *these photos are sick,* I was surprised that something inside me had protested. Even as a teenager scared out of my mind, I knew there was something important about Carl's work.

While my parents finished up with the teacher, I'd slid the book into my backpack. Everyone watched me do it. No one said a word. I was realizing that none of them really believed that the photograph from under the staircase and the one printed in Carl's book were the same.

It was grief intruding on imagination. Maybe the photograph in my closet never even existed. Right then I decided not to tell them about the weird feeling I got when I looked into Carl Feldman's charismatic face on paper.

My mother suggested therapy. After ten forced sessions of that, I'd shut up about Carl, about the twins. If I could point back to a moment in time, this would be the one where I began to act more like my sister, to tell a few necessary lies and begin to enjoy it.

I felt fractured, like the light that fell through the amber glass in my mother's hand and splintered on the wall. I thought that when I had daughters, I would be more interested in their secrets.

I ripped everything off my closet wall. Carl became Suspect No. 1. I tried desperately to find a trace of him using the limited resources of a seventeen-year-old girl.

When that went nowhere, I decided to eliminate other possibilities. I hunted down the two previous owners of our house. The first owners were a dead end, literally—a couple who died right after each other in their seventies, twenty years before we moved in.

The second owner was Mrs. Zito, the widow of an Italian immigrant, who sold us the house with all her carefully placed instructions. She had settled in a nursing home forty-five minutes away. I traced her son first. His name, Nixon, had been penciled at the top of a height chart on the frame of our kitchen door.

I was the one who painted over it because my mother said the kitchen smelled like a lasagna factory. I felt bad about getting rid of his name and the tiny specks of tomato sauce, like I was erasing somebody's history. I had brushed Nixon's name with only the slightest of coats so I could still see it if I looked hard enough.

How many Nixon Zitos could there be?

One, it turned out.

32

Carl had abruptly left me on the balcony. I sat in his chair for a long while, watching Houston go to sleep and the stars wake up.

Peaceful, if I didn't still picture it drowning.

When I walked back into the suite, Carl was not interested in me laying out snapshots from my Tupperware container like a game of memory solitaire, or sticking out his tongue to show me he'd swallowed his meds, or discussing the metaphysical abilities of my sister.

So once again, Carl is on one side of a door, and I am in bed on the other. I'm propped up with Carl's well-thumbed book of photographs, something of a nightly ritual since I was eighteen, as if it holds all the answers. I hear the faint hee-haw sounds of *Family Feud,* a marathon that may go on all night. He knows nothing about our little detour tomorrow. I've told him to be dressed and ready to go at 8, and he didn't ask why.

The stack of four pillows I'm leaning against is so dangerously plush that I wonder how many geese had to die for them. The Door

Jammer is firmly lodged in place, an ugly artifact in a room trying so very hard to soothe me.

A little while ago, I'd removed Barfly's bandage as instructed on the sheet from the vet clinic and popped a pill down his throat. The closet door is cracked about six inches, enough that I can hear his sleep sighs and piggy snorts. It took ten minutes of watching his stitches rise and fall to assure myself he was dreaming and not sucking in a last breath.

One of my father's extra-large white T-shirts is falling loose around me, hitting me mid-thigh. It is thin and worn and soft from the sweat of all of his labor and worry—the one possession I asked for specifically when he died of a heart attack after mowing the lawn in August heat during my junior year of college.

I used to be revolted by the idea of people wearing a dead person's clothes or rolling in bedsheets like a dog for a whiff of someone they love. I didn't understand why my grandfather's dark suits and golf shirts were still neatly hung in his closet for fifteen years after he was buried.

My grandmother stored her tank of an Electrolux behind his dress pants, so whenever she asked me to go get the vacuum, my heart would pound. It was like opening the door to a tiny haunted house with Old Spice air freshener. Rachel said it was like getting a vacuum out of a coffin. She never minded like I did, though.

I understood later. Later, I'd sit in the dark of our closet and let Rachel's dresses tickle my head. I'd breathe in dust and her perfume like sweet cigarettes.

I'd remember just how sweet she could be. Every day I had chicken pox, she waited outside our house for the ice-cream truck so she could buy me a rainbow Popsicle. She spent a whole summer coaching me for middle school volleyball tryouts. She started a rumor about a boy who'd started one about me.

I flip a page in Carl's book and then another. It seems like I've spent most of the last six years of my life with people on paper. The spine is loose and cooperative at this point.

I stop at *Lady in the Rain* and wonder again if she is Carl's wet ghost. A victim who won't let him go. It's such an evocative, surreal photograph. In the artist's note, he calls his elegant subject "Cinderella."

I want to flatten myself and enter the photograph, feel the slap of the rain, yell at her to stop, ask if she is dead or alive. Is her face beautiful or ordinary? Is she running home or for her life?

I turn two more pages. I'm back in my childhood closet, parting the clothes. The twins. The Marys, as Carl calls them.

There's a dull thud in my stomach. It always hurts to look at them now. I could never ferret out their last names or track them to a missing persons' list. I could only wonder.

I flick to the next picture, an empty old swing, with its rusted chains and slats splintered like rotting teeth, an abandoned object Carl's camera has brought back to imaginative life. On this swing, minds wandered, girls kissed boys, babies rocked, people talked low, sweat dried, fevers cooled.

The river of life. Where did the twins fit into it? Rachel? Me?

Carl's pictures never stop talking, they just don't say what I need to hear.

The explosion of sound from the next room is so loud that my hand involuntarily slings the book into the wall. I watch the spine crack, the book split cleanly in two as if hit by an ax. And then silence.

I'm already across the room, aware of a chill through the threadbare T-shirt, my trembling legs, Barfly's high whine from the closet. I'm wondering if somebody's face got kicked in—Steve Harvey's on the TV, Walt's chubby one in the mirror. Worse—if Carl kissed the flame of his lighter to something he shouldn't have.

Barfly is still whimpering.

I don't want to go out there. Neither do I want my only option to be jumping off an eleven-story balcony with a dog in my arms. My sister loved the exhilaration of heights. I always stayed on the ground, staring up.

No smoke is filtering under the inch gap between the bottom of the door and the carpet. I bend over to smell only the potpourri of fiber, dirt, a flowery carpet deodorizer.

When I press my ear to the door, I hear Carl. He's reciting. Counting. Sliding gravelly objects across a hard surface, one at a time.

"Everything will be OK," I assure Barfly. I dig a pair of shorts out of my suitcase and slide them on before I crack the door.

Carl has dumped the bag of rocks he collected onto the shiny maple dining table.

He's counting his gold.

"You came out of your fortress," Carl says congenially. His head is down, focused on his task. The rocks have scratched thin, jagged lines on the table. They join the faint ghostly rings of champagne bottles. "Thirty-two," Carls says. "Thirty-three. Thirty-four."

The Tupperware container of snapshots that he'd refused to consider an hour earlier is on the floor in the middle of the room, empty. Victims and their families, people I'd collected and obsessed over for years, are a tornado of debris across the carpet, the brocade couches and high-backed chairs.

One photo has been propped up against the lamp on the end table behind him. I think how pretty she is. How the barn is another pop of red accent in the room. How the toasted glow falls through the lampshade fringe in a way that makes her seem more alive, light arranged by someone who knows how.

"Your sister," Carl says.

"And how do you know that?" My breath is skipping, uneven.

"Thirty-eight," he says. "Thirty-nine." His finger draws another rock across the table, a ragged claw down my spine.

I clear my throat.

"Fifty," he says. "Fifty-two."

"How do you know that's my sister?"

"How do you think? She looks like you." He points to my finger. "And you are wearing her ring."

TITLE: *THE MARYS*

From *Time Travel: The Photographs of Carl Louis Feldman*
East Texas, 1992
Gelatin silver print

Photographer's note—I stumbled across these twin girls the day of my uncle's funeral in East Texas. He was a potato farmer all his life until skin cancer got him. The mortician left the dirt stains under his fingernails. He said he could bleach them but my aunt said no, that's who he was. After we put him in the ground, we went back to their cabin for the usual gorging on grief and Southern food. At some point, I escaped with my camera and went out for a shoot in the woods. I snuck up on these little fairies about a quarter of a mile in. I don't know where they came from or why they were trekking in the mud in their Holy Communion dresses. I photographed them for twenty minutes before they saw me. *Who are you?* one of them yelled. *You scared us.*

   I'm Carl, I told her.
   I'm Mary, she replied.
   I'm Mary, too, said the other, with a grin.

DAY FIVE

How not to be afraid my sister's *Scream* poster will come to life at night

1. Keep tapping it three times before I go to sleep.

2. Try not tapping it.

33

"OK, young man, let's get started. What is today's date?"

"July something," Carl replies cooperatively.

The woman, who actually *is* young, has identified herself as "Dr. Amy, a neurology fellow, the doctor appetizer before you get the main course." She's officious, pretty, smiling like the sun, and the epitome of that patronizing-old-people thing I hate. Carl seems to be getting a kick out of the way her white lab coat is cracking open at her bare knee.

Last night, I'd picked up the photographs littered across the hotel room. I hesitated, then left the one of my sister in place under the lamp. I stayed awake half the night in my plushy ZaZa bed in a frantic state of mind, worried about how to break the news to Carl that the first half of the day would be spent in a famous neurologist's office, an appointment I had to lie and raise hell to confirm.

Carl had surprised me. "I'm in," he'd said amenably this morning. "Maybe the doc can get this arm to stop jumping around. Also,

I want to order the Brioche Toad in the Hole French Toast from room service. Read here: It's got orange vanilla soak, warm balsamic strawberry preserve, pickled rhubarb, whipped basil-mint butter, goat cheese, and sorghum molasses drizzle."

Carl got his fantastical breakfast, and the ZaZa shuttle gave us a free ride because the office was within its four-mile radius, and now Dr. Amy is making marks on her clipboard. She flashes her eyes back to Carl.

"Who's the president?"

"An idiot."

Another mark.

"You can't count that one wrong," Carl says.

"You just worry about answering the questions as best you can, sir. Can you please repeat: 'Dog, fork, leg.' "

"Cat, spoon, arm." Without a beat.

"Spell the word *world* backward."

"K-C-U-F."

"Let's try that again. *World*." She says it slowly, with a blowing, sexy *wh* sound at the beginning. It indicates why she was able to skirt her way into one of the most experimental dementia research programs in the country.

"U-O-Y," Carl replies, with a *wh* sound on the *y*. He puffs out enough air that it tickles the blond strand dripping down her cheek.

"Perfect. Now, please take this piece of paper in your hand, fold it in half, and put it on the floor."

Carl does exactly that.

"Perfect." She picks up the piece of paper and hands it back to him.

"Now close your eyes," she purrs.

"If you insist, sweetheart."

He puckers his lips. She ignores him.

"Take the pencil from my hand. Write a sentence on the piece of paper. Here, use the back of my clipboard. Sorry, I'm a little out of sync. Long day already." She sucks in a breath of fake exhaustion.

"This is a simple three-step command: Close your eyes, take the pencil, write a sentence." I'm sure she wasn't supposed to say *simple*.

"Write anything?" Carl asks innocently.

"Anything at all."

Eyes squeezed shut, he scribbles for a few seconds, then folds the paper along its creased line and hands it back.

"Perfect," she says. "You can open your eyes."

She unfolds the paper and sticks it under the clip on her board without looking at it, busily writing. When she does digest what it says, the blush spreads down her neck like a bad burn.

"The doctor will be in shortly," she says brusquely. Dr. Amy is done.

"How much are you paying for this?" Carl wants to know as soon as the door clicks shut. "Did you give them one of your fake names and credit cards? What am I supposed to call you today anyway?"

"Try harder," I say. "This is part of the process that you agreed to back at Mrs. T's. And I've told you not to use my name at all when we are with other people. It's easier that way."

"I don't remember agreeing to this. I don't trust anyone who uses the word *perfect*."

"I get it, Carl. Move on. She's not the doctor we're here for." *Just the appetizer.*

"*You're* here for," he corrects. "I'm a veteran of these so-called Blessed tests, based on the Blessed dementia scale, dreamed up by some guy named Blessed. If the Virgin Mary's got something to do with this, and if this is the best stuff they've got, our brains are screwed."

With every mile, every minute, Carl has transformed from the mute at Mrs. T's who wore the Christmas tie and appeared unmoved by my recitation of Walt Whitman's "Song of the Open Road." He's off-and-on smart, funny, cruising on multiple levels at once.

And yet, sometime in the night, Carl had removed every red poppy print and mirror from its hook in the hotel suite, placed them carefully on the floor, and turned their faces to the wall like naughty children. Without the dancing reflections, the grandness of the room disappeared. It became small, one-dimensional—as anonymous and flat as the brown paper backing on the mirrors. When I asked Carl about it, he couldn't say why.

"The doctor we're waiting for—she knows who you are," I say.

"I don't know what that means. Does she know who *you* are? Because you are damn sure *not* my daughter."

I feel a small measure of panic, which is exactly what he wants. "You don't need to get into that. In public, in front of other people, *don't say a personal word about me.* Unless you want to go back to Mrs. T's."

Carl just grins.

I hope that the controversial Dr. Lucy Blumstein lives up to her hype. Coming here was a big risk on my long list of them. *You're fumbling in the dark,* she'd told me on the phone. *This is an unusual circumstance so I'll agree to fit him in, but you can't expect the kind of instant assessment you're seeking. I won't be able to tell you if he's a murderer.* She was intrigued, though, I could tell.

Carl and I turn at a brief knock at the door. A tiny woman enters the room *not* smiling like the sun. According to my research, she was adopted from a Korean orphanage forty-six years ago and attended both Princeton and Johns Hopkins on a full ride.

Now horseshoe bags puff out under her eyes. Her blue scrubs are wrinkled, hanging on a form that reflects a daily diet of tasteless bars that fit in her hand, and workdays without end. There's no jewelry, no phone at her waist or on her wrist, no clipboard, no iPad. The only thing she is bringing is her brain.

"Hello, Mr. Feldman. And you must be his daughter." I nod.

"I'm Dr. Blumstein. Call me Lucy." To my relief, no mention that we've spoken on the phone, although she bluntly, almost rudely, told me she doesn't keep secrets from patients if they are able to comprehend at all. "Mr. Feldman, come over and sit in the chair opposite mine, if you don't mind."

Carl's mood has shifted. I can tell by the stiff way he gets off the table, lets his boots clunk to the floor.

As instructed, he takes a seat.

The doctor rolls her chair so it directly faces him. "Mr. Feldman, I want you to use your hands to push against mine as hard as you can."

I watch Carl bring up his palms slowly. I stare at four planted feet. Birkenstock clogs vs. snakeskin boots. It's a duel that I'm certain will shoot the doctor's chair flying across the room into a brightly colored plastic model of the brain sitting on the desk. Carl had named it Mr. Potato Head as soon as we walked in the room.

I have to warn her.

"I'm not sure that's a good idea," I interject. "He . . ."

Carl's hands are already pushing against hers, the knot in his forearm pulsing.

But I've misjudged this woman. Her chair scoots just a few inches before she releases the hold.

"Not bad," she says.

Carl's face glows. Not with exertion. Anger. "I want my *daughter* out of the room for the rest of this."

Lucy nods toward the door. *Get out,* she's telling me.

I worry about what's in Carl's pockets, about the things I still can't find. The small knife. The red rubber exercise band. He wouldn't let me check this morning.

I worry about what he'll tell her. Carl alone with anyone wasn't in the plan.

I say, "Of course," and close the door tightly behind me.

34

Forty-five minutes have passed in the waiting room while Lucy and Carl get to know each other. Forty-six. Forty-seven.

Dr. Lucy Blumstein spends almost every waking hour of her life with a murderer. It was naive of me to think for a second that she can't physically handle Carl or that her beautiful brain hasn't been pushed around before. Lucy's primary world is not this office where her name is etched with a stack of partners on the door. It's the wing of a federal prison.

She agreed to this interruption to her routine because I lied and pled my case as the long-lost daughter of possible serial killer Carl Louis Feldman. As the kill shot, I'd emailed her a selfie of Carl and me hanging out on the crumbling steps at Mrs. T's. I knew it would be a hard combination to resist: Carl's celebrity, my youthful vulnerability, her own dark backstory. And I knew she'd be forced to keep us confidential.

The same adoptive father who had loved Lucy before he saw her face, who had determinedly pulled her across the ocean at two years old like he was dragging a fishing line, shot her mother one morning in bed. By that time, Lucy was out of the house, a college freshman at Princeton. He was a victim of Alzheimer's and his aim, luckily, not so good. Her mother survived but endured a long rehabilitative struggle and refused to ever see him again.

A scroll through the Dark Web for *neurologists murderers dementia* is the way I learned all about the brilliant Lucy and her weekends spent cramming for the MCAT in a motel. It was five miles from the un-air-conditioned Texas prison where her father endured a military routine equivalent to setting an Alzheimer's patient's brain on fire.

After medical school, she'd convinced a rich Texas conservative to fund a prison program that separates dementia patients in their own unit, away from predators, so they can chew a piece of cold toast as long as they like and wake up at their leisure instead of in terror because a man they don't remember with a gun and a uniform is dragging them out of bed.

She blazed a way for a cheap, and, it turned out, humanizing solution to the care of felons with dementia: a work program using fellow inmates to change their diapers, feed them, coax them into showers. Killers caring for killers.

So even though she wasn't that nice to me on the phone, I know that Lucy's nice. Somewhere inside me, I'm still nice, too, just no longer the shy little sister of that wild girl down the street.

Fifty-two minutes now.

The glass is sliding open at the receptionist's desk and a mop of curly black hair leans out. "Miss Feldman?"

It takes a second to remember she means me.

"Yes. Yes." I'm out of the chair.

"Lucy wants you to meet her in her office. I'll buzz you in. Go left, and it's the second to last door on the right past the bathroom. Your father is being taken for a quick brain scan."

Quick. Perfect. Simple.

Lucy has already changed into slim jeans and a blue T-shirt that says *Girls Are Not for Sale*. She's replaced her clogs with white slip-on Keds and has strapped on a blue Apple Watch. Her office is windowless, claustrophobic, neglected. Nothing on the walls except a few scratches.

It's basically a storage closet for a lonely desk, old papers, thick medical journals, awards and degrees that must mean zero to her, except as a means to an end. I'm guessing she thinks of this room as more of a cell than the ones she visits.

She's shrunk a couple of inches by taking off the Birkenstocks but seems no less intimidating. I imagine killers listening for her rubber-soled Keds squeaking on shiny prison linoleum.

"Take a seat." She tosses a stack of papers from a chair to the floor. "I met Walt."

"I didn't know Walt came along."

Lucy's not biting. She doesn't think I'm funny. She might not think anything is funny.

"The hallucinations possibly suggest LBD—dementia with Lewy bodies. It's caused by abnormal protein deposits in the brain. It affects thinking, behavior, mood. Seeing things that aren't there is one symptom. Hallucinations present early only in a very small percentage." She shrugs. "I'm guessing he has a little psychosis as well."

I shake my head. "All I know is that he was diagnosed with dementia after the police picked him up for vagrancy. He claimed he couldn't remember where he'd been or who he was."

"That could be the result of a fall or a transient ischemic attack, a ministroke. I told you: It's impossible for me to make a judgment in this short amount of time. I won't charge for the brain scan. He's agreed to let me use any information I gather on him in my research. He signed a release."

"I don't know if I'm comfortable with him . . . signing things with me not there."

She shrugs again. "His call, don't you think?"

"Do you think he's lying to me?"

"About?"

"Do you think he could be pretending about the ghosts? All the forgetting?"

"He's not making up the hallucinations. Yes, he probably lies about some of the forgetting. There are no great answers here. My research into the brains and DNA of killers with dementia is in its fetal stage. Killers already have something mental going on. Carl may seem in bad shape to you, but I'm about to meet with a prisoner who keeps begging me to get his wife out of his cell toilet. He sees her face in there every time he pees. The same wife he can't remember beating to death with his son's baseball bat. He *does* remember that once upon a time he nicknamed his wife Little Dumbo. *Please get Little Dumbo out of the toilet*. It's his constant refrain."

"Carl also sees what isn't there," I say.

"The patient I'm talking about wears a diaper," she snaps. "He doesn't bathe. Mr. Feldman is functional with some memory loss. He wasn't convicted of anything. And you and I don't know whether he is a killer. You wouldn't be here asking questions otherwise."

"There must be something else you can tell me."

She's quiet for a long time. Too long. "I appreciate your time," I say. "Really."

"The truth is," she says slowly, "I think you'd get more definitive answers with Carl by trying a more creative approach, like interviewing Walt and delving into whatever interesting layer that is. But I want to be sure you understand the ramifications."

"What do you mean?"

"You're out there on your own playing guessing games with a smart, highly unpredictable man. When you hit just the right spot, there will be no guards to rush in and remove his hands from your throat. And when he hits *your* raw spots—and he will—are you ready for it?"

I fight to keep the mask on my face. "What about the scan . . . when can you tell me about it?"

"That's up to Carl. I let you forgo the usual paperwork because you said you didn't have access to all of his records. I can't waive the records permission form when he is not a regular patient of mine."

"He told you I'm not his daughter." I say it flatly, a statement.

"It seems to be the one thing he's a hundred percent sure of." She holds up her hand. "Don't say anything. I don't know what's motivating you. It doesn't matter to me. If I haven't made it clear, I'm a person way past making moral judgments. And you look to be in great shape physically. Just never look away too long. For God's sake, *be alert*."

35

"Windows and mirrors," Carl is muttering.

He's back at the hotel, sorting his gold into the small sauté pan he stole from Mrs. T. Carl seems especially off after his visit with the doctor. Barfly's camped out underneath the table, his nose resting on Carl's boot, which is becoming a habit.

"*I am not cruel, only truthful,*" Carl quotes. "Sylvia Plath. Talking in the voice of a mirror."

I watch him silently, not sure if he expects my participation. The crisscross of scratches on the table stick out like a manic game of tic-tac-toe. I plan to attack them later with the Cherry Oak touch-up furniture marker I found at a drugstore in the hospital district while Carl hunted for Mountain Dew.

The sun is climbing down outside the wall of windows.

"I'm not putting the mirrors back up until we leave in the morning," I assure him. "I can close the curtains if the windows are bothering you."

Carl has barely said a word in the last two hours, except a disparaging remark to the over-pixelated image of Frank Sinatra tipping his hat in the elevator. I asked him about his visit with the doctor and he seemed genuinely vague, as if the brain scan and the examination were fragments of a dream.

"I'm talking about photographs," Carl says. "They are both mirrors and windows. The story the photographer tells and the infinite interpretations of strangers. The perfect shot lives. Breathes. *Expands*. People think music is the universal language. It's photography."

This is almost a direct quote from the preamble of his book of photographs. *Do I tell him that I know this? That I've spent countless nights in bed freefalling into his black-and-white worlds? That I've bobbed with Violet in the sadistic gray waves of Galveston? That I played with his little Marys shut up inside a closet?* It makes me sound as unhinged as he is.

The picture of Rachel is still propped against the lamp. I will myself to pick it up and lay it flat on the table in front of him. "Tell me about this."

"I didn't shoot it."

"Just tell me what story *she* tells."

"That girl wishes like hell she was somewhere else."

"What does Walt say about her?"

"Walt says it's too bad she died. He says set-up shots like this are for the birds."

With one furious movement of his arm, Carl sweeps his loot onto the floor. Barfly raises his head and decides it's better to stay put.

I walk over to the lamp a little unsteadily and prop my sister back up. I bend to pick up the rocks so he can't see my tears, then change my mind. Open my fist. Deliberately let the rocks trickle out of my hand and fall to the floor.

"Pick up your own gold, Carl. Order room service. Don't bother me for the rest of the night. Come on, Barfly." Once I'm behind the bedroom door, I work steadily to even my breath, to stop the flow of tears. I pull the die out of my pocket and roll it across the carpet as many times as it takes until it lands on my lucky number, three. On Rachel's lucky number, six.

In ten minutes, like always, I am better. It never takes longer than that for me anymore. I have even trained my grief.

Carl's book of photographs, in two pieces, is lying on the dresser.

The bed and pillows are still tossed like a snowdrift. No maid service today. I'd hung the *Catching Some Zs* sign on the door.

I walk over and scratch on the hotel pad by the nightstand. *Newspaper, $1.25. Cafeteria lunch, $10.12. Furn markers, $8.37.*

In the closet, I unzip the hidden pocket inside my backpack. My fingers graze the wad of nylon rope first, slick as a snake, before I hook my finger into the silver duct tape and pull it out. Carl has turned on *Family Feud* again, although I only hear the occasional spurt of raucous laughter. It is now and forever the soundtrack of crazy.

Walt said my sister was dead. No one had ever said that aloud to me.

I lay Carl's book on the bed and carefully tape its broken spine.

DAY SIX

How not to be afraid of a roller coaster

1. Imagine you are riding rainbows.

2. Pull lap bar as tight as possible.

3. Tell yourself the chances of dying are
   1 in 300 billion (fact).

4. Scream and breathe, scream and breathe.

36

I was eighteen when I tracked Edna Zito, the previous owner of our house, to a nursing home. She was the master hider of envelopes with appliance instructions, and I couldn't just dismiss the possibility that she was the one who placed the twins under the staircase.

Her son, Nixon, thought there was a chance. "She hid crap everywhere," he'd said when I called him. He described his mother as "forgetful." When I told him I had lived in his old childhood home, secretly saved his measurements on the wall, and found an "interesting" photograph of little ghost girls under the attic staircase, he'd described me as a born romantic.

Still, he'd arranged the first meeting with his mother rather reluctantly and didn't bother to show up himself. He didn't ask too many questions, either, which was good. I was still working to limit any tattletale calls to my mother at that point.

The first time I saw Edna, she was crumpled in a wheelchair in a red polka-dot shirt and black pants, a shriveled ladybug. She was part of a tight circle of five elderly women grouped around a game table, all confined to metal devices. They called themselves the Roly Polies and shot marbles like professional gamblers.

They remembered playfully torturing roly-poly doodlebugs in their tiny palms; Beatrix Potter's roly-poly pudding; every word of the "Roly Poly" song where *Daddy's little fatty* ate corn and taters.

Just not so much what year it was.

Her son warned me to go slowly, so I had waited until my second visit to place a photocopy of the little girls in Edna's hands. *Look at their faces,* I urged her. *Do you know them? Are you related?* I thought I saw a flicker of recognition. She muttered, *Little devils, aren't they?* before she shook her head *no* and passed the picture to Ida, and Ida to Gertie, and Gertie to Hazel, and Hazel to Opal.

That glimmer in Edna's eyes kept me going back. Edna was my earliest trainer for Carl, even if she never knew it. She made me patient, able to coexist with invisible things. In her cozy room at the nursing home, we lived in her colorful hallucinations.

We ate lunch with Audrey Hepburn, sped along a treacherous sea coast with our hair flying, watched the harrowing birth of her own stillborn daughter, only this time, she lived. Once, she whispered in my ear: *Fantasy is just an alternative to reality, dear.*

Edna is why I dragged myself out of ZaZa's bed of clouds this morning with renewed hope. Edna had starred in my dreams last night. She dyed my hair blue and we danced barefoot in the sand.

The Edna of my dream had assured me that Violet Santana, the third red dot on my map, would crack Carl wide open.

The Galveston beach where Violet disappeared fifteen years ago is only an hour away from the hotel. I'm dressed and packed by 8 A.M. Carl and I won't be coming back here.

Instead of coloring my hair as planned, I pack the dyes. When I venture out of my room, the door to the half-bath in the living area is shut. I can hear Carl running the sink.

The TV, on all night, is low-talking about the orchid mantis, a pretty, pink-petaled insect that captures its prey by pretending to be a flower. On-screen, the bug looks like a stem fresh from the florist. Carl must have won a battle with Walt for some Discovery Channel time.

An encouraging sign: Carl has picked up everything but the mirrors, including the rocks scattered across the floor. Whatever room service tray I heard him clanking around last night is gone.

I snap off the TV. Carl has folded the newspaper that was covering the table and laid it by the trash can. My finger snags as it runs over the scratches he made, deeper rivers than I thought. I glance around, but I can't find the package with the new furniture marker anywhere to color them in. I'll have to ask Carl. I tackle the rehanging of all of the mirrors instead. It's a blinding task; when I'm done, halos of light hover in my vision.

Carl is still camped in the bathroom. It's been a long time, even for him. I knock lightly. "Carl, are you good in there? Did you eat breakfast?"

No answer. Carl pretends to be a little deaf, or he actually is. I wander over to the mini-fridge to hunt for some $4 orange juice. It's an easy search because half of the shelf is bare. The fairy-size bottles of Tito's, Jack Daniel's, and Don Julio, the cheap single-serve wine-glasses with the rip-off tops, the Stellas, the Buds, the Sam Adams—all missing. I'd memorized every label so I'd know what he drank.

My eyes whip back to the closed bathroom door. Carl could be drunk. Passed out. Dead, if he combined all that alcohol at once with his medication.

I bang with my fist this time. "Carl, are you OK?"

No answer.

The knob twists easily.

The room is empty.

The faucet is running.

So, I realize, is Carl.

37

The panic doesn't begin to set in until I hit the lobby and see the disco show of cop car lights bouncing through the revolving door.

I pick the youngest of the three valets on duty, the one whose eyes are already focused on the smooth white ribbon of belly peeking between my tank top and jeans.

"What's going on?" I ask sweetly.

"Someone stole the longhorn skull that was wired to the hood of our guest shuttle," he says. "Nothing for our guests to worry about. Our manager is real ticked. Hard to lose horns ten feet long."

He nods to a woman animatedly accosting the two police officers at the end of the drive. The cops appear sexist and bored.

"I'd like the keys to my truck," I tell the valet. "Here's my ticket."

"If you give me a minute, I'll bring it right down for you. Yours is the white Chevy with the Warrior Wheels, right? I explained our retrieval policy to your father when I helped him out last night. We like to bring up the vehicles ourselves. I'm sorry about his brain tumor. He asked me to pray for him. Gave me a super sweet tip."

Brain tumor? A lie or the truth? Did Carl get bad news I didn't know about yesterday? "You pulled the truck up for my father? Last night?"

"Yeah, he wanted to make sure his remote was working. Thought it might need a battery. Then I took the truck back to the garage, where it is safe and sound."

He must have stolen the extra remote from my makeup bag. Carl could be turning the ignition as we speak.

My eyes are glued to the perfectly square yellow soul patch on the valet's chin, definitely bleached, and his perfectly hip name tag with the Z.

Warrior Wheels, he'd said. This guy had eyes. He could probably recognize my belly in a lineup. Not good.

"It's Harry, right? Give me my keys."

"It isn't our policy." Harry's grumbling, but he turns to the over-loaded hooks behind him. "Here. Space 317 in the garage over there." He points right. "Third floor. You'll have to walk up the stairs. Elevator's broken today. I'll have to let my boss know you're going in there."

"You do that."

I fly down the drive and up the three flights to the truck. I open the stairwell door, then stop abruptly. Fifty yards away, Carl is on a tear inside the truck bed, throwing open my boxes and Tupperware containers. When he sees something he wants, he drops it directly into a hotel dry-cleaning bag with a large Z on it. Now he's counting out bills from my $2,000 stash. He glances up when he hears my footsteps. A quirk of his lips, but he doesn't seem all that surprised to see me.

"I thought we had a deal," I say.

"I did, too, until your little science experiment yesterday. And your nasty mood last night."

"I'm sorry. I should have told you about the appointment. Do you . . . have a brain tumor?"

"Where'd you get that? Are you trying to scare me?"

"How about this, Carl: You go with me to Galveston. After that, you pick any condition off your list. *Any* of them."

"Walt doesn't like Galveston beach. Hot. Depresses him."

"You two can wait in the truck . . . while I meet someone."

"Any condition at all? You'll do anything."

"Yes."

"I'll need time to think about it." He eyes me meaningfully as he finishes tucking a little more cash into the ZaZa bag and zips it up. "Why is your hand always in your pocket?"

TITLE: *THE DROWNING*

From *Time Travel: The Photographs of Carl Louis Feldman*
Galveston Beach, 2002.
Gelatin silver print

Photographer's note—I can't step on this stretch of bossy
Gulf shore without being soaked in humidity and dread,
even though it's been more than a hundred years since the
Great Galveston Hurricane. Children are building sandcas-
tles where bodies are buried. The storm wiped out more
than six thousand people in Galveston; estimates range up
to twelve thousand casualties for the entire island. Many
of the dead were weighted and dropped to the bottom of
the sea, burned in city pyres, entombed in the sand where
they were found. Housing contractors still run across their
bones. I shot this photograph in front of the historic Hotel
Galvez, where ghosts are known to roam the beach, including a suicidal bride and a saintly nun. In 1900, as the storm
roiled, the sisters of St. Mary's orphanage tethered themselves to the children with clotheslines. Some of them
were still roped together when their bodies were found. A
century later, I discovered this dress swirling in the seaweed where so many souls were sucked away. I didn't see
the face until I printed it in the darkroom.

38

Barfly and I are dipping our toes into the murky water of San Luis Pass on Galveston's west end, where Violet is supposed to have slipped under in the dark. In old police photographs, a yellow stream of crime tape blocked off the beach behind us and beer cans and empty bottles stuck up in the sand like shipwrecked pirate trash.

Violet. Girl No. 3. The final red dot. It's OK to call her a girl today, I decide, because she *was* a girl to her parents. Only twenty-one.

I'd wanted to meet Gretchen Mullins, Violet's old college roommate, for more than a year. She was the closest thing I had to an adult witness in any of my cases. She said no, no, *no*. On the fourth try, I gave her a new fake name. I made up a better story. It worked.

I wanted to ram Carl with this memory, so it wasn't my first choice that he is hanging back in the truck with the air-conditioning and The Who blasting. On the plus side, now there's no chance he will uncloak my identity in front of Gretchen. She thinks I'm a reporter hoping to get more warning signs posted on the beaches by posthumously profiling a few past victims of rip currents.

Our rendezvous is taking place on a high-risk beach about twenty miles from the stretch of sand where Carl shot his most profitable and haunting image of a scrap of fabric that he titled *The Drowning*.

In his book, in interviews, he claimed the piece of fabric was a dress, some kind of ghostly ode to the lives lost in the great Galveston hurricane.

I shiver, staring at the lapping Gulf, a monster at sleep. So little warning in 1900, unlike now. No technology. The day before it struck, the wind prowled. The sea swelled. The paper ran a one-paragraph alarm bell. Twenty-four hours later, the city swam with bodies.

Carl says he let the dress in his photograph wash back out to sea. So who knows? It will forever be as he and his picture imagine it.

I wonder now if it was a scarf. If Carl has a thing for scarves, like the one he stole at Mrs. T's and curled up in my suitcase, then stole back. He could pull it out like a diabolical magician at any minute. Try to tighten those pink-and-white snails around my neck until I am a flat, airless balloon.

The two of us left the Hotel ZaZa and its mirrors for good about an hour ago with an apology and a $300 donation on the credit card to repair the table. The hotel manager was distracted enough about the stolen longhorns that she probably would have let it go. I just didn't want her rethinking things later.

I originally suggested that Gretchen and I meet at a more famous spot in front of the Galvez, an old hotel nestled behind the seawall in a daring and tenuous love affair with the Gulf. It would make sense. Gretchen and Violet had stayed there once. So did Carl, at least twice a year.

But Gretchen picked this spot, where she last saw Violet alive. She wanted to toss a bouquet of violets in the water in memory of her friend, claiming it was a yearly ritual. I didn't believe her.

How many florists sell violets? Could anybody even grow this delicate flower in Texas? And who actually follows through on this kind of good intention? Melodrama, I figured, in her hopes to make a better story for the newspaper I didn't really work for.

Today, San Luis Pass is scattered with just a few tan-seekers. It's well-known as one of the trickiest places to swim in Galveston, an end piece on the long baguette of shore, where swimmers can drop off into uncharted nothing.

No warnings have ever stopped college partiers like Violet and Gretchen from showing up, or from doing all the wrong things if they get trapped in a current.

Even an Olympic swimmer can't beat the time of a fast riptide.

Don't flail. Give in. It won't pull you under; you'll die from exhaustion while fighting it. Trust. Let nature bring you back to shore.

My trainer shared his rulebook for everything, just in case. He had no idea about my motivations for hiring him or whether I would end up in the mountains or the sea. He knew nothing about my sister's disappearance. We might have liked each other better if he did.

I try not to imagine this churning water dragging me out while people turn to colorful polka dots on the shore.

I glance at my cheap little watch and wonder if it and Carl's bandaged book of photographs under my arm can withstand the spitting of the ocean. Only five more minutes before Gretchen is supposed to arrive.

I told her I'd be wearing a red baseball cap and walking a brown dog. She told me she'd be wearing a yellow dress and bringing her little blond-haired boy, Gus.

Violet Santana had blond hair, too, and a sweet, bare face that made my stomach hurt when her old case had popped up in one of my random searches two years ago. I'd missed it in earlier Internet hunts because her death was never declared a homicide.

I opened up that terrible possibility to Violet's parents on the phone: *Could Violet possibly have been the victim of a killer?* They wouldn't consider it. Their daughter's death was God's will, a baptism of sorts. As part of the Master Plan, she stepped into the water and disappeared forever. *It was written down before she was born.*

I had a better idea after communicating with them why their daughter liked to get drunk. When talking to police, the spring break partiers that Violet spent her last night with admitted to being so loaded up on

Bud and Jack Daniel's, switching rooms and partners nightly, they didn't even miss her until a group breakfast at the Hotel Galvez two days later.

Everyone had just assumed Violet had walked out of the ocean that night. I think she did, too. I think she dried off, put her clothes back on, and traveled a different path, one that led to Carl.

Barfly is dancing along the waterline, claws biting the sand. His wound is still worrying me, even though I'd bought a waterproof bandage at Walgreens for the occasion. I pull a little overprotectively on his leash.

I shade my eyes and glance back at the truck parked in the distance beyond the seawall. Maybe Carl's gazing at me, a polka dot, wondering how much I know about that night. Maybe he's mesmerized by the rippling Gulf, thinking about Violet and his famous picture of the drowning dress. I turn my back to him.

Fabric and water, that's what that picture is. Except what people see is a pretty face of terror in its folds, a spirit that knows it is being sucked under—a classier, spookier, artier version of Jesus in a piece of toast or Elvis in a potato chip.

A framed copy of *The Drowning* photo hangs in one of the most ghost-infested suites at the Galvez. Shops on the historic Strand still hawk postcards of it. It's one ghost and a thousand ghosts that walk this precarious slot of land. I wonder if Carl still collects royalties or if he just doesn't remember where the check goes.

During one of my Dark Web crawls, I stumbled across an original signed print of *The Drowning* for sale on a site that mostly specializes in ultra-gruesome serial killer trading cards. How does that kind of collecting even work? *I'll give you a Jeffrey Dahmer and a Ted Bundy for your Green River Killer?* How would Carl rank if everyone knew the truth?

A salty breeze rolls off the water, shivering over me. I feel more afraid of Carl right now when he is hundreds of feet away.

I glance back. There's a woman up in the dunes, shading her eyes, zoning in on me. A little boy with blond hair, carrying a white rose, is already running for the water.

39

"Do you mind if I tape this?" I hold up a small recorder, hoping to look reporter-like, while Gretchen's eyes rove over my jeans, loose white top, Nikes, Ray-Bans, red baseball cap. From what I know of journalists, my fashion isn't that far off the mark.

Gretchen is still lovely in her thirties, with auburn hair dyed two shades lighter than mine, freckled skin, and twenty pounds of extra weight that, if she lost it, would make her less attractive. Her beauty is all in fresh appeal—soft, rounded edges, a light drawl rolling over me like a massage.

"I'd rather you didn't." Gretchen's eyes are laser-pointed on her son. A Superman cape billows off his small shoulders. He's tossing the white rose about a yard into the water with every ounce of his miniature might, only to have the water roll it back to his feet every time. This constant rejection doesn't seem to be bothering him in the slightest. I've already counted five throws. Now six.

"You said this is about where Violet went in?"

"As best I can remember. I always use the bridge as a marker. Gus! Come and try over here!"

"What's the very last thing you remember about that night?"

"The round white moon of her butt going in the water. She was tan everywhere else. I was going to tease her about it later because it was funny. Fourteen kids were skinny-dipping and no one has the least idea what happened to her. She was with Fred and Marco, one on either side. They are good guys. You'd think they'd all stay together, right? But no."

"You changed your mind about going in the water?"

"I never really planned to. Earlier that day, a lifeguard asked me out for a drink called Pop My Cherry. That kind of low quality opening line is all it took for me in those days. I left the beach early to meet him. I didn't come back to the room for a couple of days."

Her shame is still a slow and steady burn. I smile sympathetically although I'm certain this is part of a ceaseless confession she tells everyone. I decide to divert for a second. "Your little boy is really cute. Determined."

"Yeah, he's my youngest. My hair used to look like that on the beach. Like the sun had set it on fire. This is his second trip here with me. He understands Mommy lost somebody. The fifteenth anniversary, but I guess you know that. I don't want to say too much to Gus, or he'll never go in the water. His dad has big plans to make him a sailing buddy. That rose isn't cooperating, is it? The violets tend to melt into the seaweed right away and disappear. My own patch looked like crap this late in the season so we stopped off at the grocery store and got this white rose. Like Violet cares about a flower I buy out of a plastic bin near the bananas. It's more about me. Gus! Try over here!"

"How long were you and Violet in Galveston on your break?"

"Six days at the Galvez. A present from my parents for being on track to graduate on time. They paid for the room. I talked Violet into coming with me. She couldn't have afforded it otherwise. It's a gorgeous old hotel. I'm glad Harvey didn't take it."

Gus's scream is so sudden and shrill it easily rises above the pitch of the gushing waves.

Gus is chugging toward his mother at the fastest speed he can, little feet stumbling through the sand. Carl is close behind him, jeans rolled to the knees, barefoot. He's wearing the Hollywood hat. His shirt is off, the necklace with the key glinting in the sun. A large white scar runs diagonally down his chest, like the beginning of an X in tic-tac-toe.

"Gus!" Gretchen kneels and opens her arms protectively for her child, while I check that Carl has nothing in his hands.

"Mom, this man says that when baby sharks wake up, they eat their brothers and sisters! He said one shark is called the Cookie Cutter, and if I go in the ocean, it will take a round bite out of my butt like I'm a chocolate chip cookie."

"Don't say *butt*," Gretchen says automatically.

Carl grins at me. "Reruns of Shark Week."

What now? Should I introduce them? Apologize?

Carl takes care of the dilemma for me. He tips his cap. "I'm going to head out now, ladies. Just didn't think the little guy should be dipping his toes in the water without adult supervision. Things happen." He hands me Barfly's leash. I hadn't even noticed I'd dropped it. "You might want to take care of your dog, too."

Carl meanders away, while Gretchen fumes. "What is wrong with me? I almost let a homeless man touch my child. Maybe he did." I think her face is red with fury for Carl and his homeless brethren. Then I realize that the fury is for me.

"Let's stop this sentimental charade right here, OK? I was wondering how far you'd go. I know you're not a reporter at the *Chronicle*. I checked. My husband told me not to come, that you were just some Internet weirdo. He doesn't know I'm here, or he'd be pissed. I was up there watching you for the last twenty minutes, deciding. I figure either you lost somebody in the ocean, too, and if so, God bless and I'm so sorry. *Or* you know something new about Violet. If you have answers about Violet, I deserve to hear them. Have they found her?"

While his mother rails, Gus focuses on poking the rose stem into the beach so it is stick-straight, the beginning of an unlikely garden. Now he's plopping beside Barfly, burying his front paws in the sand.

Gretchen isn't going to believe anything I make up.

"Did you ever see a photographer hanging around your group or Violet in particular?" I ask quietly. "A man? Anyone familiar?" It was unlikely she would recognize Carl after fifteen years, and her eyes were probably mostly wandering that freaky scar, but who knows. He had been standing only inches away.

"It's Galveston," she sputters. "It's the *beach*. There are always a million cameras and a million guys gawking. It's a goddamn free *strip club*. You didn't answer me. Who the hell are you?"

Barfly is swiping Gus's hair with his tongue like it's delicious. Gus, giggling, has managed to get three paws buried.

Not much time with Gretchen left, I think. I abruptly drop the leash and open up the book of Carl's photographs I've been protecting under my arm. I struggle to keep the pages still as another breeze skirts off the water, whipping at the hem of Gretchen's thin yellow dress. "Have you ever seen this photograph of fabric floating in the Gulf? That people say is a ghost?"

Gretchen leans in, reluctantly curious. "I've seen it. Supposedly the drowning face of one of the nuns who walks the beach during a storm."

"Do you think this . . . item of clothing could have belonged to Violet? That maybe she was wearing it the day she disappeared?"

Awareness is creeping into her face, shading her freckles. "Wasn't this photograph taken by that serial killer who got off in Waco?"

"Please, Gretchen, just look at the picture. It's important."

Her eyes graze over it quickly, as if she can't bear it, as if I'm asking her to stare directly at her friend's decaying corpse. "I don't know. How can I know? Vi had this cute cover-up thing that she wore over her bathing suit. I think it was blue. This picture is black and white. You're scaring me."

Still, Gretchen can't resist the page. I move it a little closer to her face. Her mouth relaxes, transforms to relief, the joke on me. She taps the picture vigorously with her finger.

"Look at the date. This was shot sixteen years ago. We were here *fifteen* years ago." Her tone says that I'm an idiot. It also says that as much as she wants to know about her friend's last night on earth, an equal part of her doesn't want to know at all. She must not know about the hotel records. Carl had stayed in the Galvez two of the six nights that she and Violet did, one floor down. I found it buried in a police report, a detail that never begged enough attention back then.

"Gus, throw the flower in the water. Then we'll get some ice cream on the Strand."

"Thank you for coming," I say. "I didn't mean to upset you."

"Like hell you didn't," she snaps. "I hate when my husband's right."

Gretchen's already losing venom, though, I can tell. She wants to ask me something. She almost does, and then Gus tugs at her dress. Her hand runs lightly over his hair. She checks the shoreline for Carl. "Everything's OK now, Gus. Go ahead. Pull the rose out of the sand and throw it in for Violet. I saw a mermaid flip her tail way, way out there by the bridge. She'll swim in to get it."

Gretchen waits until the boy's out of earshot before demanding: "Take off your cap. And your sunglasses." She squeezes my shoulder. *"Take them off."*

I don't know why, but I obey. Her fingers dig into my arm. My eyes are unprepared. Watering in the sun.

"You really are just a baby." She searches my face before releasing me to check on Gus, a little too close to the edge again. I slide my cap and glasses on while she heads for her son.

I'm picking up Barfly's leash when she stops abruptly and turns her head. "Don't call me again. Get your shit together."

I nod. She's the third person since I put Carl in the car to utter some kind of warning.

"All right, then," she says, a little more kindly. "God bless."

The two are about halfway up the beach—Gretchen bending down to carry Gus the rest of the way—when the rose tumbles back to shore. I pick up the stem and run my finger down its smooth surface, every thorn blunted.

I think about stealing it, pressing it between the pages of Carl's book. Except I've always found something very wrong about a faded, disintegrating flower representing a memory. I fling the rose as far as I can into the waves. This time, the petals separate, surfing like tiny chips of bone before being sucked under.

Gretchen doesn't want to believe the date in this book is a lie. It's right there, printed in black and white.

I want to scream at her that *this is Carl*.

There could be a lie on every page.

40

I'm relieved to see the truck still parked along the seawall. I took a risk and didn't bug Carl to return the extra set of keys. Carl, however, is not in the truck.

I slide Barfly from my arms into the backseat and release an avalanche of wet sand. Our combined dog and person smell is overwhelming: fishy ocean, wet fur, sample perfume from the ZaZa bathroom.

Carl has opened the Texas map wide and stuck it in the windshield as a sunshade. Not a bad idea. I wonder where he's gone. I flip on the air conditioner to combat the hot, sticky humidity, lie back against the seat, and try not to feel discouraged. Six days in, just a little more than halfway. I don't know where he's run off to, but my gut after seeing him on the beach is that he didn't crack wide open like Edna Zito promised in my dream.

I can't get discouraged. It's a process. I always have a Plan B. And C and D and E and F, all the way to Z. The problem this time is, I have less than four days left.

Plan B is East Texas. My research, the trial transcripts, his photographs—Carl haunted and stalked those woods. His camera transformed tree roots into scaly monster toes, sunshine into fairies dancing on a dirt floor, the faces of dirt-poor people into something profound and dignified.

Everything, even the light, somehow doomed by his lens. Every picture, a little murder.

Carl mentioned in a deposition that his family used to "keep a place."

When pressed, Carl had clammed up, refusing to reveal a location. The prosecutor asked for a local police search of the area, but what a joke. There are private land patches in Texas the size of Rhode Island. You'd need a very personal guide, and that's exactly what I'm going to convince Carl to be.

Where the hell *is* he? I yank the map out of the windshield and try to refold it. That's when I see.

In Cherry Oak furniture marker, Carl has drawn his own line on the map, a crooked scar that ends at least six hundred miles west in scorching desert. *New Conditions* is scrawled at the top, covering up the Panhandle. His line snakes in the opposite direction of the Piney Woods.

Instead of dots, he's marked three X's, the first one squarely over the city of Austin, along with the words *Invisible Girl*.

My head is buried in the back of the truck. Carl's casual destruction in the hotel garage of my meticulous filing system fills me with wrath. Papers, photos, magazine articles, research printed off the Internet—everything about his life I had labeled and deconstructed is scattered to all four corners of the truck bed.

I turn out to be lucky. The magazine article I'm searching for is still sitting in one of the few boxes Carl left untouched. It's tucked in a file titled "Austin" marked *NR*—my code letters for Not Relevant.

I *knew* I remembered Carl's *Invisible Girl*. She was part of a paid assignment for a *Texas Monthly* pictorial on the homeless teenagers who rove Guadalupe Street near the University of Texas. It made some industry and media noise because Carl shot the whole thing with four disposable cameras, his not-so-subtle way of saying society considered his subjects just as disposable.

In the magazine photo, she's sitting with her back against a brick wall, reading a battered physics textbook. An empty Starbucks cup has a one-dollar bill sticking out of it. A hand-lettered sign in angry black marker announces *I am invisible.* She's brittle, thin, but pretty. Her dirty clothes and matted hair are all that differentiate her from the two girls in sorority T-shirts walking by, eyes averted.

Invisible. Not Relevant. She didn't make any of my lists. I don't know whether she died or ran back to a home she hated. Nobody would have spent much time looking for her. Certainly not me.

I've had to draw lines over the years. At one point, I was so tangled up in the hidden meaning of photographs, so infected with the grief of other families, that I couldn't pull myself out of bed.

Even with just three cases, my head is so full I mix up details: *Was it Violet who played cello? Vickie who was addicted to orange jellybeans? Nicole whose eyes were two colors?*

The *Invisible Girl* is tugging on me now, though. *I'm still relevant to Carl.*

I quickly stuff everything else back in the boxes and scan the seawall and the beach below.

After walking two blocks, I don't find Carl, just where he's been. A group of homeless men are camped around a bench eating hamburgers and counting cash that I assume used to belong to me.

When I describe Carl, one of them shrugs. "He said that if a cute white girl with a nose diamond came asking about him, tell her he was gone."

Back at the truck, I reopen the bed, climb up, and begin to shove things around with calm fury.

I find the box quickly, at the back. Carl hasn't disturbed it. I yank

George out of the secret little nest I made for him. He's a beauty, an old Hasselblad, with a lovely hand crank on the side. The Rolls-Royce of cameras.

I think of all that George has seen and done.

Across the road, the seawall stands, seemingly impenetrable, built way back before hurricanes were christened with nerdy boy-next-door names like Harvey.

I feel like a reckless storm myself, dodging cars across the busy road, camera swinging around my neck. The drivers probably think I'm a stupid tourist crossing traffic, risking my life to snap a shot of the Gulf that will be lost in thousands of other vacation shots on a computer.

When I make it to the wall, breathless, I stare down into the viewfinder. That's the way the Hasselblad works. You see the world in front of you by looking down.

All I see is concrete wall. Did Carl ever find my sister's face in this hole? Was she smiling? Angry? Alive?

I press the button. Carl's right. It's a very solid, satisfying sound. A gunshot.

I lift the strap from around my neck.

I'm so frustrated, so full of rage. I don't care how stupid this is.

I slam the camera against the seawall, again and again, watching it crack and shatter.

A little murder, Carl.

It feels good.

For the next several hours I drive, scanning the side of the highway for a scarred, shirtless man with a dry-cleaning bag stuffed with belongings. There's only one logical road out of Galveston, and Carl isn't on it. A tiny fear is wriggling its way out—could he be skipping his way back to Daisy?

I find an alternative station and let Cricket Blue's lyric harmonies about myth and the ends of things blast everything else out of my head. I croon along. *The wasps that live inside my chest build paper nests.*

The sun is sinking when Barfly and I land in Austin at a Motel 6. It isn't the ZaZa but the rooms surprisingly take a few of the same eclectic cues. Bright sage walls and bedspread. Furniture with clean, modern edges. A warm laminate wood on the floor and a sleek photograph of Austin-proud Willie Nelson Boulevard on the wall.

For twenty-four minutes, I lie flat, staring up at a blinking smoke detector and imagine Carl out there doing the same thing. Making plans.

I change tops and strap on the gun. It's almost dark. I stroll the half-filled parking lot.

No dark sedans. Lots of bumper stickers. *Atheism Is Myth-Understood. Don't Frack With My Water. Keep Austin Weird.* Carl must be loving Austin right now. In Austin, natives are liberal, tacos are for breakfast, music is like breathing, and a million freaky bats fly at sunset. Hate is a devil you can smoke away with enough weed.

When I push open the lobby door, the assistant manager is missing from his post. It wasn't hard to surmise he was both gay and intelligent from our encounter at check-in. A rainbow flag wrapped his personal laptop. The intense hieroglyphics of math problems had lit up his screen.

Never carry any accessories that aren't the story you want to tell.

Only one man sits in a chair in the lonely lobby—about sixty, in boots and a custom cowboy hat with the Gus crease, made famous by Robert Duvall in *Lonesome Dove*.

There are immutable rules to wearing a cowboy hat in Texas. The kind of crease in the hat tells you a lot about the man. My grandfather wore the Telescope crease, a low crown and wide brim, which makes it easier to take the Texas sun.

I'm guessing this man, intently listening to the chatter of CNBC, owns a closetful of creased cowboy hats and chose this low-end motel because he spends his money on blue stocks instead of cushy beds.

He's as genuine as it gets, so I decide to ask. Normally, I wouldn't want to leave a trail. Carl has changed the rules. I *want* him to find me. "Sir, can you suggest a place close by where I can get a drink and something to eat?"

"The Black Pony," he says, without glancing up. "Ten minutes if you've got a vehicle. Good music. Taco truck across the street. Whiskey on tap."

"I'd call a cab." The assistant manager is sliding back into his rolling chair. "And don't use the bathroom there unless it is an emergency."

While I wait, I call Daisy's cellphone. There's no answer, just a never-ending ring.

41

I'm sandwiched tightly between two strange men at the bar. Their bodies are radiating like space heaters. They've taken turns, each buying me two golden fingers of the Knob Creek that drools out of the tap in front of us. It would have been rude to refuse.

A puke smell slammed me when I pushed open the door of the Black Pony but that has evaporated so quickly I wonder if I imagined it. The gray-haired fellow to my left is an age I'd call near-death; the one to my right is no more than twenty-five, clean-cut, with short, straight-edged sideburns and rounded biceps, characteristics that always bode danger for me.

The band is loud and good and raunchy, playing no-holds-barred get-up-and-dance country. On the crowded dance floor, hipsters are gyrating solo while mated-for-life couples two-step and twirl like conjoined twins. All of my disguises could melt in here. Carl could be melting in here.

Beside me, danger is drumming his fingers, a sure sign he is going to ask either me or the wisp of a girl twirling on the barstool on his other side to dance. Onstage, The Beaumonts are singing a love song about an East Texas girl who still has her own teeth and a car "that don't break down too much."

The guy's hand on my shoulder, possessive and warm, says he's chosen.

So, now *I* have to choose. One is to make an enemy out of a drunk. The other is to lose a barstool in a place I will never get it back. He leans in closer, all breath and Jack Daniel's and expensive cologne, intoxicating even though I don't want it to be. One dance won't hurt.

He pulls me to the center of the dance floor, where polite space opens up for us. He checks me out, a honky-tonk pro, swinging my body away long and slow and then back in so tight and close I don't know if it's his heart or the drummer jarring my bones. He has to know two things at once while he holds me still against him, his hand commanding my waist. I'm carrying a gun. And this isn't my first dance.

Then I'm lost—in the pulsing of music, the rhythm of a hundred bodies, the comfort of being led.

Four dances in, he breathes in my ear, "What's your name?"

After two Buds and several rounds of partner switching, apparently a friendly tradition at the Black Pony, I've lost him. This seems like a good thing since I can't remember what name I gave him or whether he ever told me his. Also, because I'm furious with myself. Too many of my body parts intimately grazed his.

This is how my frustration usually reveals itself, in some act of bad behavior. The Buds are sloshing with the whiskey and the chorizo-pineapple-cilantro Bomb Taco that I bought from the food truck out front two hours ago. I'm considering throwing up every bit of it into a toilet. I start for the bathroom and then remember the warning of the Motel 6 manager.

A couple whose tongues are marrying lets me push by them

toward a dim exit light. As soon as the monster metal door chunks shut behind me, I realize my mistake. I reach back for the knob. Locked. *Not an Entrance* is sloppily hand-lettered in fluorescent white on the door.

I'm stuck in the back parking lot with an army of stinking trash cans, a fence lined with scraggly bushes, and a single bulb above the outside door that barely illuminates either.

Two shadows are taking long, aggressive strides out of a dark patch along the fence. Coming for *me*.

Muggers. Rapists. Rednecks.

It takes a split drunk second to decide to run, not toward them, because they seem determined, but the other direction, into the gloom behind the building. I want to get my bearings. Maybe I can go around the other side. Maybe I'm overreacting.

"Jesus," one of them whines as I take off.

Halfway around the building, I realize there is no exit.

I'm kneeling behind a dumpster, the very first place they'll look. My options are climbing a ten-foot wooden fence or pulling out my gun. Neither appeals to me.

Bad things happen when you point a gun. Three-fourths of the decision is already made. There has to be another option. Still, my hand falls back to the holster.

I remember the day my father presented me with my own Glock. His agony that he didn't save his other daughter. I don't want to disappoint him, even dead. I pull out the gun.

Where are they?

Music is leaking out of the bricks behind me. The Beaumonts are crooning about jumping in the hay.

The men should be on top of me by now.

I slowly edge back to the corner of the building and peer around. Now there are three shapes in the dark. Two to one. The new guy swings a sharp punch, and one of the men falls to his knees. The other one instantly raises his arms in surrender and backs away, dragging his injured companion with him. All of this happens in deep silhouette, like I'm watching a violent cartoon.

I hear the chirp of a remote. See the brief flash of headlights.

The third man watches until he's sure they've pulled out.

Then he turns back. He stares so intently into the dark that I think he must see me. And then he's gone.

I'd only heard one clear word since that door slammed shut behind me. *Jesus.* I'm thinking, maybe Jesus heard.

42

Carl stole my sister's picture. The senior portrait posed by the red barn. This sudden realization floats up while I steam myself to death in a hot shower at the Motel 6 and try to forget the entire night at the bar.

Last night, I left my sister's picture under the lamp in the ZaZa hotel suite. When I got up this morning, I was so distracted searching for an escaped Carl, I forgot about it. It bothers me, even though I can find it online in a hundred places with a few simple clicks on my keyboard.

I lean my face into the hot water and strip it nude. After an hour-and-twenty-minute hike back to the motel, this fiberglass rectangle feels more luxurious than the two-seater stone waterfall in the ZaZa bathroom.

I'd waited by the dumpster for half an hour before easing my way out of the parking lot to the front of the building.

"You sober?" the bouncer had yelled out as soon as he saw me round the corner. "Need a ride?"

I said yes. I had wanted to ask him where the hell he was when I needed him. He was way too tall and wide to be my savior in the parking lot.

While he was distracted, calling me a cab, I'd slipped away. I'd needed to walk fast, to filter the whiskey and fear out of my pores. It wasn't hard to remember the route back, which was an unpleasant hike near a buzzing, chaotic highway. I clung to all the ruts and dark places. I'd had plenty of time to think about those men in the alley—all three of them.

I'm toweling off my hair, dressed in shorts and my panda T-shirt, when there's a sharp rap on the door. I'm almost expecting it. Barfly's ears have perked up; he's lying on the bathroom mat beside me. I pick up my gun from the counter by the sink. Maybe my hero wants to be rewarded. Maybe the men who gave up want to finish what they started.

"Everything's OK, Barfly. You stay here." He's up on four legs now, but I shut him in the bathroom and cross to the door. The blinds are tightly closed.

I stare through the peephole. It's a blur, greased on the other side with Vaseline. Probably done a long time ago, the trick of teenagers who like to tilt side mirrors on cars and replace Oreo filling with toothpaste.

When I open the door, my gun is pointed.

It's not my dance partner from the bar. Not Carl. Not the aggressors from the alley. Not my trainer, testing me because he's an insane nutjob.

In many ways, the man standing in front of me is the one I fear most.

He's also the third man.

He pushes his way in, disarms me, and slams the door.

"I thought your dad taught you better than that." He releases the magazine and ejects the round from the chamber. He sets them on the bedside table.

I'm glaring at him, not thinking clearly, still in shock. I'd hurt this man. It's been more than a year.

My hair is red now instead of brown; his head is shaved bald instead of like fine black sandpaper. I don't like it shaved. It makes him look a little mean. Relentless. His costume is the same as the last time: black polo, black Nikes, black jeans, a badge, gun attached to his waist. Everything about Andy is true.

I've felt his shadow for months and yet I'm still wondering where the hell he came from. What mistakes did I make with my quick-changes, fake-IDing, car-switching? Which one did me in?

He was the hero in the dark, and the realization suddenly pisses me off.

"Why in the hell are you following me?" I spit out.

"Where's Carl Feldman?"

"Are you here to arrest me?" The conversation is beginning to feel like the ones late at night with Carl, where every next question spins us deeper into a dark hole.

Andy shoots me a look of incredulity.

"I'm sorry," I say. The words hardly cover the things I've done. "Please, sit down." I gesture to the side of the bed. He flips the desk chair around and sits. I can't bear to see exactly how much he despises me, so I perch myself on the corner of the bed and focus on his shoes, size 11. I know the size of everything on him.

The first time I saw Andy, I was seventeen. He was a twenty-four-year-old up-and-coming cold case detective with a cheap suit and hope that coursed through his veins and into mine like sugar water. My sister's face had smiled off his computer screen while she leaned against that dumb red barn.

The last time I saw him, he wasn't wearing anything.

We slept together for the first time when I was nineteen, almost twenty. It stretched on for a month, on picnic blankets and his old leather couch, in the back of the five-year-old Lexus SUV that my parents bought to keep me safe.

It began with a covert kiss in a parking garage. He was politely escorting me back from his FBI office in Dallas after dark. When we arrived at my car, I reached up. He lifted me off the ground. I was a broken bird, rescued. Seconds later, he'd declared the kiss a slip. *Slip.* I was a feathery four-letter word, not even big enough to be a mistake.

That was back when we officially met every year on two significant dates to discuss my sister's case: the anniversary of her disappearance, and her birthday. Regular briefings turned out to be too painful for my parents, so I'd arrived each time by myself, with fresh questions and my obsessive research jumbled with college textbooks in my backpack. I never told him everything, of course. He would have thought I was crazy.

Andy updated me on any little blip in my sister's case; plugged in headphones for me so I could listen over and over to recorded phone call tips; compared Rachel's disappearance to other, more current ones; assured me there was still an ongoing effort to track the whereabouts of Carl Louis Feldman and link him or his photographs to my sister or other girls who vanished.

Every visit grew more personal. The fourth time, I noticed that the picture of the twins was his screensaver. I knew he believed me.

Andy was finishing his master's in English, a promise to his grandmother, a former teacher, who was terrified he'd die in a gun battle he didn't see coming. We would collaborate in the interview room over ugly files until he'd force me to take a break. Sometimes he'd recite poetry to dilute the horror.

Angelou and Frost, Hughes and Dickinson. He said it kept him sane in a job like his to be reminded of all the joy and sorrow of the lives before us, to know we are knitted into a beautiful, flawed pattern that never ends. For a long time, Andy and a bunch of poets were the best therapy I got.

He had been otherwise kind the day in the garage that he declared me a slip, while I'd tried to cover my embarrassment. He'd named every reason why we were a terrible idea, like I hadn't thought of those before I reached up.

He had a girlfriend. I was too young. It was unprofessional and could end horribly. He would lose perspective on the case. Hurt me. Get fired. My parents would feel betrayed. He was black and I was white and his own mother would kill him if a redneck, cop-hating asshole didn't first. The last reason he meant as a joke, to make me laugh, but I didn't, because it wasn't funny.

We met again, as scheduled, six months later. I remember thinking my sister would have been twenty-six, plenty old enough to kiss him.

I remember dressing carefully that day. He didn't want me, but I wanted to appear worth wanting. So it was thin lace and bare legs, loose hair and musky shampoo, a blue line around the smoke-and-mirror eyes that either drew people in or shuttered them out.

I didn't feel nineteen and naive. Around him, I felt electric. I had leaned in and put my fingers on his shoulder just once that day. He flinched. I loved that bit of power.

The poem he'd shared at our break was sexless and lovely and full of hope—Walt Whitman on miracles. *Every cubic inch of space is a miracle.* In return, I recited a poem I wrote about the twins long before my sister disappeared. *Two little girls play in the dark. There are monsters.*

This time, when he walked me to my car, he jumped behind the wheel and drove us to his apartment. We didn't speak all the way, just held hands tightly, knowing exactly what would happen when we got there.

Each time, afterward, it chewed at him. He thought he was ruining my life. I was the selfish one, though. My life felt pretty ruined already. I didn't make it easy for him to end it. When I was wrapped in his body like an eternal poem and he was urging me to let my sister go and get on with my life—those are the only moments I ever thought I might.

After twenty-seven days of this, he stopped calling. He didn't have to tell me why. He'd told me a hundred times. I let him go. I didn't want to ruin him.

Last July, after more than three years of silence, he called out of nowhere and asked to meet at a restaurant. The man with all the reasons didn't give me a good reason why. I showed up anyway and ordered a potent Lemon Drop martini. He seemed worried that day. Asked a lot of questions about my life, my Sister Quest (as he called it), the bruise on my right knee.

Later, he kissed that bruise.

While he was sleeping, I'd scoured his phone for passwords and codes that would get me access to more of what I wanted. I discovered a file on his laptop about my sister. The sight of the little icon with my sister's name made me ache. He hadn't given up. It had been opened only three days before. I copied that on a thumb drive, too.

He was still sleeping when I walked out the hotel room door.

An hour later, he'd changed every password I'd stolen.

I didn't get much more than I already knew, and I lost a lot.

I can appreciate that right now when he's real and present, four feet away, so livid and beautiful that I can't breathe.

43

Barfly is raking his paws across the back of the bathroom door, a steady scratch-scratch rhythm. Andy has wheeled around, his weapon drawn and aimed.

This is fear—the thought of bullets ripping and splintering through that door. I grab Andy's arm. "That's my dog on the other side, not Carl. Put your gun away. Please. I'm the only one here."

"Show me." He shakes me off.

"It's my dog," I repeat, twisting the knob. Barfly bounds out, jumping on Andy's legs, tail wagging, as if his scar is drawn on with a marker. I whistle Barfly over and listen to Andy slide open the shower door, making sure. Trained.

"Where is Carl Feldman?" he repeats, as soon as he reappears.

"I don't know."

"I'm not messing around. I know you are together." And then he says my name. It spreads like a warm burn through my chest. The name that will be permanently etched on my grave, just like Sophronia's and Jimmie Elizabeth's on those stones at the cemetery where my sister and I used to roam. My mother picked my name out of a novel when she was a child herself.

"Carl and I were together for a few days," I admit. "He took off."

"You don't know where he is." Flat. Disbelief.

"No." I'm trying to remember where I left the map that I had no interest in showing him. In the glove compartment? In full view on the passenger seat?

"I never thought you'd go this far." He's pacing the narrow patch between the double beds. My trainer said pacing was a good technique to use on the other guy. *It's like a player on first base toying with the pitcher.* Barfly, sitting perfectly still beside me, begins to pant. I rest a hand on his head.

"Meaning . . ."

"Meaning, taking whatever delusional, dangerous path you're on. You don't understand what you're stirring up."

"I do. And I'm prepared."

"Oh, good God, you only think so." He's stops abruptly. "What do you expect to gain from this? Do you really believe Carl Feldman will lead you to Rachel's body?"

Harsh. He knows the soft spots so well.

"The day we first met, I should have shut you down. Convinced you that a picture you accidentally found in your house had absolutely nothing to do with your sister. *Nothing.* That it was a coincidence or your mind made a connection that wasn't there. I should have never let you consider for a second that Carl Feldman was a possibility. I should have gotten you some . . . help."

After all this time, he's finally implying what he never would.

"Don't you understand?" I strain to ask the question calmly. "I would have arrived at this place, in this motel room, with or without you. You always blame yourself, Andy—it drives me crazy. I'm not a kid. I was *never* a kid."

"Are you positive Carl's responsible for your sister's death?" he snaps. "Because I'm not."

"We don't know for sure she's dead." It's like releasing a breath

I've held since the very first night her bed was empty beside mine, the sheets tangled the way she left them.

But it's true. No one has ever handed me a single piece of evidence. No one has shown me a sharp sliver of my sister's bone or a microscopic spot of her blood, which always ran a little darker than mine. No one has played me a confession.

That leaves one percent hope. Or ninety-nine percent despair. It depends on whether my glass is filled with whiskey or tea.

There is such weight and pain in my name. He's saying it again. He needs to *stop saying it*.

I'm trying to think. *Did Andy put a tracker in my suitcase?*
Was he in my apartment? Has he been on my tail since Mrs. T's?
How much does he know?

"How long have you been keeping tabs on me?" I fume out loud. "Since we last met? Since Carl popped up on the radar. Longer? Have you been tracking me *longer*?"

"Go home. Or to London, where you've convinced your mother you are having the time of your life. Let us do our jobs."

But you won't, Andy. Not like I will.

He's talked to my mother.

"Who is *us*?" I ask softly. "Do you have a partner with you?" My head pivots toward the window. The idea of someone else, anyone else, on the other side of those blinds feels like a betrayal.

The *us* was always Andy and me.

"Are you wearing some kind of wire? Go ahead, take me in." I hold out my wrists. Daring him. I need to know how far he will go. Why he's here. "I've done plenty of things I can be arrested for. I've stalked people. Bribed people. I stole Carl's camera out of evidence."

"Stop. Talking."

"If you aren't arresting me, then please leave. Carl is gone. That's the truth, Andy. My Sister Quest is a failure. That should make you happy. I appreciate that you took care of those creeps at the bar, but you need to understand something. I would have gotten out of that myself. And you? You would not be in this room unless I *let* you in."

My wrists still hang in the air.

I can't let him stop me.

Andy takes a purposeful step forward. It's a mistake.

Grade: B- Lovely imagery but did not follow assignment

Paper Ghosts

Two little girls
In pretty white dresses
And floating veils
Play in the dark
There are monsters
In my closet
In their forest
Don't be scared!
When I step into their picture
Do I look frozen still?
Turned to stone?
Invisible?
Can anyone hear me?
I climb, dance
Run, hide
Whisper
Cry
I was meant to find
My secret sisters
To make me brave

44

It was my fourteenth visit to Edna Zito, two days before I graduated from high school. She leaned over and whispered, "I'm not supposed to talk about those little girls in the forest."

We were sitting alone together in the nursing home's little garden. A brightly hued shawl was tossed around my shoulders, a graduation gift crocheted back and forth between Edna and the Roly Polies. They had presented it to me an hour earlier, wrapped in creased, reused wrapping paper decorated with Christmas bells.

I couldn't believe it. Edna had been disappearing a little more every week. I'd decided weeks ago that she knew nothing. I'd stopped showing her pictures. I was only still visiting because I'd grown fond of her. "It's OK to tell," I cajole. "What do you know, Edna?"

Edna had placed her veined, papery hand on my knee. "Do you think it is Opal or Gertie who is spraying Windex on my blue Jell-O? The blue Windex wouldn't show up. It'd be a clever way to get me."

"Windex sprays on clear," I'd reminded her impatiently. "It

wouldn't show up on red Jell-O, either. Tell me what you know about the twins."

"What twins? I don't know any twins. I thought we were talking about blue poisons."

Then I had impatiently yanked two pictures of Carl from my backpack—a copy of the portrait in his book and a newer one, of him maneuvering his way through the media at the courthouse during his trial.

"Is that a movie star?" Edna frowned.

"Please, Edna. You've seen these pictures before. *Focus.*"

"I think it's time for Chips Ahoy and fruit cup." Her face was a little pale, her breathing more rapid.

I was eighteen. Untrained.

I shut up and wheeled her in for the afternoon snack.

A week later, Nixon Zito stood in front of his mother's door, arms crossed, waiting for me. "I think it's better for everyone if you don't come anymore."

45

While Andy's fingers touch my throat, I'm thinking about Carl. Whether he will break down the door and kill us while I am naked, and put me out of my misery.

While Andy's hands hold me down, I'm picturing his partner outside in an unmarked car, perhaps a woman secretly crushing on him, who has already imagined their pretty babies.

I'm wondering if she will be the one to enter and finish me off with her words. While I close my eyes and spin wildly into black, I'm thinking about how nothing but Andy has ever felt this painful, infinite, and profound.

When Andy had reached for my wrists, we could have done what we trained to do. We could have hurt each other.

Instead, I let Andy yank me to him. His warm hands ran under my T-shirt, then his lips. I'd involuntarily winced as his fingers roved over an old bruise on my back, a souvenir from the final training exercise. He's always touching my bruises.

The attack at the bar was beginning to seem like a dream, a photo wavering, half-developed.

Andy had misinterpreted my flinch. Stepped back. Stared at me with eyes glazed with lust or hurt, hard to know. "This has to be your call."

I didn't even have to think. I'd curved a hand around his cheek just like the very first time in the parking garage.

He'd searched my eyes while removing his gun—a purposeful interval, a chance to change my mind.

And then we fell back on the bed, bouncing a little awkwardly on the hard mattress, laughing. We'd stripped away everything. His jeans and shirt, my bra and patch of underwear, every bit of armor, until we were naked and equal.

Now Andy's slowing down, balancing his weight on his hands, nuzzling my ear. I imagine myself as a bird, perched and spinning on the ceiling fan, watching. I'm the soulful nightingale flown from Andy's favorite Keats poem, or maybe something darker and less easily missed—a scribbled crow from Van Gogh's wheat field.

How much time has passed since he kissed me? Two minutes? Fifteen?

I'm arching my back. Andy's mumbling something I can't understand.

Whoever bursts in the door will have to kill us, or wait.

I want to deserve Andy's forgiveness. When this is over, I want him to love me again.

"This was never wrong," I whisper.

DAY SEVEN

How not to be afraid of ghosts

1. Don't watch *Poltergeist* anymore with Rachel.

2. Don't play Ouija board with Rachel.

3. Don't believe in them.

4. Don't eat lemons because Rachel says they like the smell.

46

When I wake up, Andy is gone, which seems more than fair. There were no promises, no free verse, no conversations about his role at the bar or about me going home, no questions about what I stole from him the last time or about what either of us plan as our endgame.

Before drifting off beside him, I'd decided he could steal everything while I slept—the map, my phone, the boxes in the truck. My life, if he wanted it. Instead, he chose to simply leave, which seems even colder.

I raise myself on an elbow. Barfly, at the foot of the bed, lifts his head. Last night, after a couple of rounds, Andy had found him hiding out in the bathroom. He'd scooped him up, thanked him for his discretion, and laid him down with us. It appears that Barfly hasn't budged.

Andy had left the magazine he took out of my gun on the bedside table. The motel pad next to it is a blank, hurtful thing. No note. Andy is always bursting with words. I've saved every one of them.

An envelope in one of my boxes is stuffed with twenty-seven days' worth of the notes and funny little drawings he would leave on a pillow, tuck by the dollar bills in my wallet, clip under a windshield wiper, place as bookmarks in my textbooks, tape inside the toilet paper.

My keys are positioned exactly the way I left them on the desk. The one to my safety deposit box points north and the ignition key to the truck points west. My phone is still flipped on its back in the bathroom with a nearly invisible hair still in the same place.

I didn't know Andy was coming but these little paranoid quirks are now a force of habit. A quick inventory shows that he's swiped nothing from the room. I find the die under the bed, knocked off of the bedside table.

Except for that, it was like he was never here.

I know better. *Trained*.

I start my search in earnest, to see what he's left behind. I discover a tiny tracker in the bottom of a plastic dental-floss box that looks almost exactly like the dental floss I brought with me, and another one under the sole of my Nikes.

The black rubber is sliced and glued back together so perfectly I can barely see a line. The trackers crunch under my feet, their little body parts exploded on the white tile like roaches murdered after crawling out of the cheap walls.

I throw on sweats and my panda T-shirt and go outside. The motel lot is still dark and crowded with parked vehicles. Someone could be watching me from any of them. I drop to my knees and rove the flashlight around the undercarriage of the truck and into the wheel wells.

I find what I'm looking for under the back bumper—a little box that wasn't there yesterday. I examine it closely. Nothing special. The magnetic case holds the kind of GPS tracking device that is an online click away. The one designed for life's ordinary spying, so parents can simultaneously check on their alcoholic teenagers and watch

Netflix, so divorcing husbands and wives can gather evidence to more efficiently slice their children in two.

I attach the device in exactly the same place to the vehicle parked next to mine, which is, fortuitously, also a white pickup.

I return to my room, throw the chain, set the alarm for eight. In case the one on the bumper was a decoy, I plan to check for trackers hard-wired into the car in the morning—under the hood and dashboard, near the sunroof, below the seats, in the carpets, all the usual places. This won't be the only time I've checked, but I'm clearly not doing it often enough. I'd already removed the one installed by the rental car agency.

I feel only moderately sure that I found all of the trackers. I feel even less sure that I know exactly who left them.

I have to wonder if all the time I was making my plan about Carl, other people were making plans about me.

I've called Daisy's cellphone thirteen times, every call now dropped directly into voicemail. The veterinary office is letting the answering machine pick up. I leave the same message on both. *If you see my father, please call the police immediately. He's lost. He has dementia. A tendency to get violent.*

Fear for Daisy is grinding away in my gut. If she dies with all that sappy hope, all those Harvard dreams, it's on me.

I want to leave the motel room but it still smells like Andy. I keep going back to that empty pad by the bed like it is mistaken. I hold it up to the window and search for any imprint in case Andy jotted off a note and ripped it away after changing his mind. That happened once. The phantom message had said *I love you.*

So why did Andy return? Why now? How long has he been following me? Could it be since I was nineteen and we broke up? Wouldn't I have noticed? If true, wouldn't his obsession be even scarier than my own? It's been a year since his surprise call and re-

225

quest to see me. I've thought back often to that day at the café and what I revealed.

While he'd drilled me about my sister and my latest research, I'd hidden myself in short answers, licked the sugar rim on my martini, and drifted into a pleasant alcoholic haze. He'd commented on the new muscle tone in my legs and arms, stirring both desire and a paranoia that he knew about my trainer and about how far gone I was into my plan. I simply said I'd joined a new fitness club.

Are you finally moving on? he'd asked. *Close,* I replied. I didn't tell him that the clock was ticking down, not because I was giving up on my sister, but because I wasn't ever going to.

I didn't say that I sometimes holed up in my concrete cave at Uncle Fred's Self Storage Units, where bright color-coded plastic containers sit with white IKEA file cabinets. The four walls are an exploded version of my old closet gallery.

Two years earlier, I'd moved a desk in there from my apartment. A tattered lounger. A good floor lamp. A small refrigerator. The five guns I'd inherited from my dad. My sister's things that my mother dumped in cardboard boxes, tossed in the attic, and never touched again. I even studied within those tight four walls for my master's degree.

I try to force Andy out of my head. I fill Barfly's food bowl, pack up my clothes, brush on mascara. The questions pound on. Was Andy planning to arrest me but just couldn't bring himself to do it? What would he arrest me for? Stealing Carl's camera out of evidence? Sneaking into an FBI file on his computer? Kidnapping a dementia patient from the state welfare system?

Not for the first time, I wonder if he left his laptop and phone wide open to me that day at the hotel on purpose, as a test of my willpower. I only gleaned a little new information before he'd snatched his passwords back—that Carl's case was active. The FBI suspected Carl in the cases of Nicole, Vickie, Violet, and four other missing women, all on my list, too.

Andy could be using me to get to Carl.

TITLE: *INVISIBLE GIRL*

From *Time Travel: The Photographs of Carl Louis Feldman*
Guadalupe Street, Austin, 2002
Kodak disposable camera

Photographer's note—Amanda K., homeless at seventeen, told me she wrote *I am invisible* on a cardboard sign after no one on Guadalupe Street spoke to her for two weeks. "Maybe people think they can't really change anything for me with a dollar, so they just ignore that I exist. They could change everything about my day by just saying hello."

47

I have to dial in on finding Carl. Focus on his map.

If *Invisible Girl* is his next clue, she's the one I need to follow, even if he shot the picture more than fifteen years ago, even if I have doubts that he would remember which bare brick wall on Guadalupe Street held her up.

Barfly and I are wandering along hip shops and college eateries with a parade of granola students, sorority girls, and ragged people speaking and gesturing to the air. No sign of Carl and Walt, but the two of them would fit right in. The loneliness and desperation that lurk in the shadows of affluence along this university drag force me to once again appreciate Mrs. T's corrupt little care system and burned Eggos.

Carl had snapped a number of homeless photos here. Not just *Invisible Girl* but another renowned series of tight, unflinching black-and-white portraits, so textured they could be charcoal drawings. Carl captured hollow, insane eyes, toothless smiles, angelic light on molten, sun-beaten skin. He captured *humanity*. With that lens, he fooled everyone.

It was in Carl's heyday, when critics were predicting fame and legacy. He titled the series *Guadalupe's People*. He was referring to more than the street. Our Lady of Guadalupe, the patron saint of Mexico and the blessed virgin, had appeared first to a peasant.

Someone snatches my arm, digging in nails painfully. It isn't Carl. The man appears to be a street fixture. It's impossible to tell his age from the rough leather of his skin. Forty? Seventy? He's wearing filthy jeans and old sandals. One toe is missing on his right foot and two on the left. He points to the empty space beside him and asks, "Isn't she pretty?"

"Yes," I say. "Very. She's beautiful." I dig for some money and tug on the leash as Barfly tries to lick his feet. "Why don't you buy her dinner?"

He tucks the bills I offer in his pocket and drifts into the crowd. *Walt, are you here?*

What if we could suddenly see all the invisible companions on Guadalupe Street? If we could stick our hands through these ghosts of the homeless, and they'd smile? The dead lovers who curl up with them in grimy sleeping bags; the childhood friends who once split their peanut butter sandwiches; the war comrades who died by their sides; the long-buried fathers who picked at every flaw; the articulate, funny characters who have sprung to life from the battered novels they haul around.

Elvis, Marilyn Monroe, Mark Twain, the Lady of Guadalupe herself. If we could see for ourselves their imaginary world and the real one side by side, maybe we would be changed. No cup would be empty.

I'm invisible, too. I could have been any summer college student strolling along with a dog. At least six of me passed us on the sidewalk. Oversize sunglasses, jean shorts, backpack, tank top, Birkenstocks. Bait for Carl, I can't help thinking.

Twice, I tap men on the back, hoping for Carl. As I apologize to the second one, it strikes me how anonymous Carl's body really is, a slender, boots-and-jeans Texas stereotype—how he must have used this cloak and his camera to subtle and frightening advantage.

After a couple of hours, I give up looking at walls and graffiti and stray onto the University of Texas campus.

I blend in for a while, then duck into trees along the shady edge of Waller Creek. Judge Lamar Waller designed the downtown grid of this city in the 1830s, naming the north-south streets for rivers in exactly the order they were listed on the state map.

Almost two hundred years later, Austin is the new Brooklyn and an explosion of construction, congested traffic, and narrow streets, seemingly impossible to fix.

Would Lamar Waller be upset by his shortsightedness?

He'd certainly be horrified at what happened where I am now standing, at the creek named in his honor, where a girl who liked to leap and fly in the air was murdered in 2016.

She had nothing to do with Carl. Her name was Haruka, and her suspected killer was caught almost immediately. She'd made my memorial list like all of the women since I started keeping count. Young. A first-year dance major recruited from Oregon. One night, she called her roommate at the dorm to say she was on her way from the theater building. She never showed up.

In the minutes after that call, police say that Haruka was attacked and murdered by a homeless teenage boy as she walked by the creek, hope and hopelessness intersecting in a random, brutal moment.

The suspect was a seventeen-year-old runaway from foster care named Meechaiel. I wondered that he once had a mother who cared enough to think up that name and then let him go. His shadowy figure had been captured on a nearby street camera with a woman's bicycle and an unidentified object he pulled out of his pocket.

Haruka's parents released paper bird lanterns into the sky at her vigil. I'd memorized their beautiful statement right after the young man was arrested, at a homeless shelter.

We remain steadfast in our desire to honor Haruka's memory through kindness and love, not violence. To the police officers, the UT community and all who have been impacted by this, we just ask that you hug your children, hug your parents TWICE, one from you and one from us.

I want to be like them. Everyone should be like them. But we're not.

48

might find Carl through his nutty list of conditions.

That's my sugar-rush epiphany as I down a caramel, cream-cheese-stuffed, peanut-sprinkled donut called Salty Balls under a red umbrella at a decadent food truck called Gourdough's.

At noon, most of the college couples at the outdoor tables around me are ending their night, nursing hangovers, starting to think about unfinished papers. I'm thinking about how Guadalupe Street was a dead end, about the places on my body where I can still feel Andy's touch, about those insidious GPS trackers.

Carl didn't plant the trackers. At no point on our journey together had he been out of my sight long enough to buy a device like that. Until he took off, he didn't even have the hundred-plus dollars needed to purchase one of them, much less three.

Andy wouldn't use the very common GPS device I'd found on the truck. I'd seen the sophisticated devices casually strewn in the drawers of his apartment; he'd be the shoe-and-dental-floss guy. So who, then?

My donut, half-finished and melting on its cheap, floppy paper plate, looks like something I threw up. I turn on my phone.

This time, there's a message. My throat constricts. I recognize the number. Daisy's. My fingers fumble to find voicemail. It feels like a fifty-fifty shot that I will hear Daisy's voice. I expect Carl's. He might tell me he's taking Daisy out for a Whataburger. He might tell me she's already buried.

I think she would have fought.

When Daisy begins her cheerful ramble, the pounding in my ears is so loud I have to replay the message. She's at Disney World. A family reunion. Sorry she didn't get back to me sooner. She sure hopes I find Mr. Smith soon. *How's Barfly?*

Solace, but it's fleeting. Already I'm picturing other, faceless girls straying into Carl's path. Red dots I put into play as soon as I walked into Mrs. T's and told a lie.

The physical warning signs are sudden, like always. The dread gathering like a biker gang in the center of my chest. The deep, surging flush. My right temple, pounding. It's been happening at least three times a year since I was fourteen.

Every table around me is full. No one looking my way. No one cares. Just Barfly knows. He is whining softly at my knee. "It's OK," I whisper.

My high school counselor, the stupid therapist, my mother, my trainer, Andy, know-it-all Google—they all offer a comforting, scientific explanation.

As for me, I'm certain that for a few minutes, four tops, I live Rachel's terror.

We breathe together, shiver together, sweat together. When it's over, I almost wish it weren't.

The interlude with my sister took three minutes and five seconds.

Barfly and I begin the trek back to the side street where I'd had to park the truck. A hundred feet away, I see pieces of paper fluttering under the windshield wipers.

My heart begins an idiotic dance. I think of Andy, deciding to leave a goodbye note after all, or Carl, laying out a more specific route after deciding I was a less agile opponent in our game than he'd thought, or maybe someone else.

I pull Barfly's leash a little tighter and sweep my gaze. Aging fences lean on both sides of the street. Big teeth gaps to wriggle through and hide. Knotholes for spying. Beater cars are parked nose to butt on the curbs. I feel for my gun before I remember I left it in the console.

The only thing moving is a lithe figure in UT burnt orange running steadily away from me. Alone in broad daylight, just like my sister on the day she was taken. Bright sun, every corner exposed, is never a comfort to me.

"Stay," I order Barfly. I have to stand on the running board to reach the first piece of paper. It tells me that a local band is debuting tonight at a bar on Sixth Street. I stretch for the other—a flier for a three-legged fat black cat named Baloney who is "free to takers, declawed, and hits the cat box."

The papers are just windshield litter. Ironic for a town that outlaws plastic grocery bags and wants to fine anyone who won't compost.

I don't know what I'm feeling more—relief or disappointment—as I settle Barfly in the back and slip into the driver's seat. At straight-up noon, the truck is broiling. Once more, I flip the air conditioner to full blast.

Perspiration sticks like apple juice behind my knees and stains the back of my shirt. Like always, my sister left me soaked, with the slightest of headaches. Carl liked to keep his conditions in the glove compartment, within easy reach. I pull them out. The single piece of yellow legal paper is folded, creased many times. At various intervals, Carl had manipulated it into a paper airplane, a paper football, and a little yellow sailor hat, which he had managed to balance on his head once for two hours while he napped in the car.

It concerns me that he left something so freakishly important to him behind. I have to gamble that Carl's brain hasn't erased this. I know by now that the things he cares about remain in his head on a loop. He'd bugged me relentlessly about his conditions—new ones, old ones—at least ten times a day.

The black leather seat is still so angry from a persistent beam of sun that I've slid down so my bare thighs hang off the edge.

How many minutes does it take on a 90-degree day for the temperature in a car to reach 160 degrees? a) two hours b) forty minutes c) less than ten minutes.

C, less than ten minutes. I'd aced my trainer's written final.

The electronic readout on the dashboard declares today's temp close to 100. I turn to check Barfly. He's perfectly happy, his nose inches from a vent, ears blowing.

I mindlessly flatten and smooth the list on the steering wheel. I stare at the collection of words, numbers, and letters that tumbled out of Carl's brain, and try to decide the best way to approach it.

I remind myself that everybody's lists are inscrutable. We all have a personal shorthand. It was almost impossible to decipher my mother's grocery lists unless you knew things like *t.p.* meant toilet paper and *b.p.* meant big potatoes and *d.p.* meant dill pickles. No one would ever figure out some of the lists filed tidily in my storage unit at Fred's.

Lightly, I cross off all of Carl's conditions I've already met: *Camera, sweet tea, Dairy Queen, Whataburger, new nail clippers, 100 percent feather pillow,* and *CFS. CFS* was chicken-fried steak, and he'd eaten it twice.

I run another line through *Bible.* Carl had snatched one from the drawer in one of the motels.

The New York Times. A near-impossible find at a Texas truck stop.

I mark through almost everything that can be eaten or swallowed. I pause at *1015s.*

A 1015, I'm sure, is not a tax form. It refers to the popular super sweet Texas onion, named for its planting date of October 15. Most Texans don't know this. Carl, being a farmer's grandson, probably does. And Ruby Red is not a stripper; it's a grapefruit.

The three books——*11/22/63*, *Lonesome Dove*, and *Ulysses*—are listed one under the other. All of them seem meaningless other than as a way to pass the time.

Ten items left. I narrow more, penciling a star beside the generic items that seem a little ominous to me in a list made by a serial killer. It's why I hadn't bought them.

Hiking boots, rope, shovel, waterproof watch (resistant @ 300 meters), flashlight, WD-40.

Glad Press'n Seal.

I see it over a nose and a mouth.

Just three things remain:

Baby Head

Muleshoe

Mystery Lights

They are all destinations. Carl has made three X's, Austin being one of them. I spread the map across my lap.

Baby Head is a cemetery six hours southeast of Muleshoe—a few dozen forlorn graves that are a blur outside the window. Indians kidnapped a young white girl in the 1850s and stuck her head on a pike at the bottom of a mountain to warn settlers away. That's the lore.

The reason I even know Baby Head exists is because Carl took a photograph of the cemetery's historical marker with plastic baby doll heads dangling off it like cans on a honeymoon car. Not Carl's doing, I learned while researching. He was merely documenting a local tradition.

There is no X near Baby Head.

But there are X's close to the other two.

Muleshoe is the West Texas town near where Carl's grandfather ran his farm.

Marfa is the town closest to the desert phenomenon of the Mystery Lights.

Carl had shot a photograph of the strange lights in the sky and lived to tell. He made it the opening picture in his *Time Travel* book.

He also tucked a picture of a girl on parched desert land in his suitcase. He wears her necklace with a key around his neck. The desert girl means something to Carl, too.

I shift the truck in gear. I'm heading to the Mystery Lights. I can spend the night in Marfa. If he isn't there, I'll drive to his grandfather's farm.

Carl has no idea how far I am willing to go. No one but me does.

TITLE: *MYSTERY LIGHTS*

From *Time Travel: The Photographs of Carl Louis Feldman*
Marfa (off Highway 90), 2000
Hasselblad 50mm, tripod

Photographer's note—I've always been a skeptic about the ghost lights, the Mystery Lights, the Chinati lights, the Marfa lights—whatever the natives want to call them. On my West Texas jaunts, I'd occasionally see them jitterbug in the sky like aliens as I looked across Mitchell Flat toward the Chinati Mountains. Until this night, I'd left documenting them to the tourists who draw up here right after sunset. Scientists debunk them as high-energy particles or electromagnetic currents, or even bouncing headlights. Believers will remind you that Indians talked about these "ghosts" long before cars existed. On this night when I pointed my camera at the stars, six round orbs appeared, floating in a straight line across the flat. They collided into a bright balloon that began to speed toward me. I ran. My camera was on a timer or this shot wouldn't exist.

49

I'm only an hour out of Austin when Carl crawls into my brain.

If he were sitting in the seat beside me, he'd have his head out the window, snapping his real or imaginary camera at the puffy *Toy Story* clouds, begging me to stop for peach stands or roadkill, insisting he pan for gold every time we cross the meandering Pedernales.

He'd be sneering as we pass a town called Hye and a winery named Fat Ass.

I don't miss him. It would just be nice if he were keeping me awake.

It will take about seven hours driving straight through to the Mystery Lights. That's going to be my first stop. The "official" viewing area used to be pretty much just a turnout on a desert road until a rich Texas ranch family helped legitimize the phenomenon with a small parking lot and bathroom.

I'm limiting myself to three pit stops to pee and water Barfly and to comply with my gas-tank-never-less-than-half-full rule. My company on the drive is eighty percent pickup trucks, at least half of them white. I try to keep an eye out for Carl, but I'm not the only Texan hiding behind tinted windows and sunglasses.

I'm feeling more vulnerable and insignificant as the bowl of Texas sky expands and I shrink. Somebody once described this piece of earth as The Big Empty, and nothing was ever so aptly named.

The rolling green Hill Country has transformed sharply in the last half-hour to scrubby brown desolation and cacti with stiff arms.

The irritant keeping me alert at the moment is an old blue VW Bug driven by a woman with stringy blond hair that hangs out of a red baseball cap. Her car windows are wide open, which in a Texas July means she's as poor as the dirt flying in.

There's either an animal or a furry blanket on her lap. She weaves and dawdles outside the lines. She passes me. I pass her. We do this dance four times before I decide *enough*. The gas stations are getting sparser every mile, the trucks fewer.

The blue VW charges past me as I pull off at a run-down gas station sporting a pole with a Texas flag big enough to wrap the whole place like a present. The sign planted in the pale dust outside: *Don't Die a Virgin: Terrorists Are Up There Waiting for You.*

No other vehicles. Bars on the windows.

I decide something cold to drink is worth venturing inside. As soon as I push open the door, I'm hit with a chilly blast of window air-conditioning, the smell of tamales, and the jangle of Tejano music.

I say, "Dr Pepper," and the teenage boy in the Houston Astros cap behind the counter points to a tub of beer. He looks too young to be selling alcohol but I'm guessing his customers aren't complaining. The Dr Pepper bottle caps are deeply embedded in ice with a selection of Corona and Ozarka water.

Only three drink choices in the whole store because the owner knows his audience. I grab two glass bottles of Dr Pepper, Carl's high-end, pure-sugar kind from over the border. I pick up a string of beef jerky and the last five tampons in an open box that are being sold as singles for $2 apiece. The owner knows his desperate market, too.

While I'm paying the kid, including for the high-dollar gas I'm about to pump, I notice through the dirty fog on the door that the blue Volkswagen is pulling in. The boy hands me my change, barely glancing at me. Good, because I made no effort at disguise or makeup today.

When I push open the door, the blue Beetle is nowhere in sight. I suck down the Dr Pepper and toss the bottle and the receipt into an old plastic bin marked Recycling. It feels liberating not to subtract this spree from my budget. Since Carl took off, I'm not counting. Not money, not steps.

I yank on the pickup door.

The woman from the Volkswagen is sitting in the truck's passenger seat, facing forward, as still as a crash test dummy, like there's a gun leveled at her head on the other side. I see a slice of profile, a baseball cap, and caramel blond hair that's the matted, tangled texture of an old Barbie doll's.

Now she's turning, removing the hat and hair simultaneously.

Carl.

"Funny, huh?" He's grinning. "It's all one piece. I bought it at the Goodwill on Lamar. It's an old Six Flags Over Texas souvenir."

"Where have you been?" My voice is angry, but the relief is seeping into every pore.

"I thumbed a ride with a pair of girls going back to Austin."

"And then."

"Don't know. Think I lost a little time." He taps his forehead. "And then I got a car. I found you on Guadalupe. Thought you saw me. Anyway, I followed you to the donut place. Thought I'd wait until you looked a little less pissy."

I scan the front of the store. No blue Volkswagen. "Did you steal the car? Where is it?"

"Parked behind the store. Keys inside."

"You took off on me, Carl. We had a deal. Conditions."

"The girls were cute. A little high." He tosses the cap into the backseat. "Go ahead. Ask. I can see it on your face."

"Did you . . . hurt them?"

"I certainly did not." Emphatic. Enjoying himself. I want so badly to believe him.

I fill the tank, $50 worth, and climb back into the cab. Carl has taken my beef jerky out of the bag and is tearing his teeth into it. The extra Dr Pepper I left in the cup holder is half-gone.

I reach into the seat behind me for my backpack. I don't want Carl to see the bag of loose tampons. Instead, my hand brushes against something soft.

I know the smooth blanket feel of Barfly, and this isn't it. I flip around. The dog is stretched out in the back, unfazed, with company.

"There's a cat in here."

"Baloney. He does better than I thought he would on three legs."

Baloney. The cat pictured in the flier that was stuck under my windshield wipers. The handicapped one that hits the litter box every time.

"We don't have a litter box," I murmur.

"What did you say?"

"Carl, we can't keep the cat."

"I've heard that before." He swallows the last dreg of Dr Pepper. "Which dead girl are you on now?"

50

Carl won't confirm why he drew his second X in the middle of the desert near the Mystery Lights. He's noncommittal about the importance of driving there. I spread out the map in the cab to show him.

"Who drew all those lines?" he demands. "It's confusing. By the way, Walt's upset you didn't say hello."

I tamp down my frustration and remind myself that we are not necessarily on a journey to a grave but to that place in Carl's head where he keeps his secrets. Our trip, as much as I want it to be, might not be a physical destination.

And it isn't just about my sister—it's about all the girls. Not just Vickie and Violet and Nicole, not just the little Marys or the lady in the rain or the one in the desert, but every other murdered or lost girl whose name I ever wrote down on a list.

I know I'm teetering, that my boots are over the edge of the same pretty precipice as the desert girl in the picture and if I don't pull back soon, the canyon will slam up to meet me.

But I also know the truth. No one else but me will ever carry it this far.

Jack Kevorkian was a lunatic who assisted suicides in the back of his van before it was ever considered humane. A principal contributor to the first Oxford English Dictionary was a patient in an asylum for the criminally insane after killing a father of six. The mathematical genius Pythagoras had an aversion to beans because he thought part of the soul exited the body with every fart.

Crazy people get shit done.

There has to be a reason why Carl kept that picture of the girl in the desert with the little key around her neck. Somewhere in this vehicle, her photograph is still riding along in his suitcase. That same key is still hanging off Carl's neck, hidden under his shirt. The sun reflected off it when he bared his chest at the beach.

"First stop," I tell Carl firmly, "the Mystery Lights."

He shrugs. "You're the boss."

Carl naps most of the ride. As the sun drops and his chest rises and falls in steady rhythm beside me, I imagine how it would feel to stop the truck, pull my gun out of the console, and shoot him in the middle of the Chihuahuan Desert. I'd watch his blood land like black raindrops on the dark leather. It could be the most satisfying second of my life—the price maybe being every single second afterward.

When I wake him at our destination, it's gently. We're standing on the dark side of a road, waiting for aliens or ghosts or swamp gas or whatever it is to prick Carl's conscience.

We stare up at the giant handfuls of shiny sugar tossed into a wasteland of night, the most stars I've ever seen in my life. The desert and its shadows stretch all the way to the rippling muscles of the Chinati Mountains.

We're a little late for prime-time viewing. There's no free show tonight, no kaleidoscope of lights dancing around. There is never any guarantee the lights will materialize.

I think that tonight it is maybe more profound without them. The air is expectant. There's a deep spiritual stirring in my gut, even with Carl at my side. Maybe even more because of him.

I'm holding hands with the past—the stars above me that died light years ago, the dinosaurs and Indians who are cobwebs in the sand, the girls Carl killed.

The light tickle of laughter floats from two couples leaning against a car behind us, drinking wine.

"I saw the picture of the girl in your suitcase," I tell Carl. "Did you take that out here? It's beautiful. Why didn't you put her in your book?"

"You're a goddamn snoop. There are thousands of pictures I didn't put in my book. Dozens of girls."

"This one must mean something special."

"I don't know why you just don't straight up ask if I killed her, too."

"You marked an X here," I persist.

"I marked the X because it's one of my favorite spots. I want to be buried around here." And then he mumbles, "We're nothing but exploded matter."

Tell me something. Anything. Please. It's the first time I've pled with him, even in my head.

"The lights aren't coming tonight," Carl says curtly. "I don't feel it."

Carl heads back to the truck. One more time, I've learned nothing. I linger a little longer, waiting, wondering if Rachel is out there somewhere in the dark.

We slide onto the barren streets of Marfa, population 2,000-minus, around 9:30 P.M. No people. No other cars. Flickering streetlights.

The town is so desolate, so dusty and dreamlike, we could have time-traveled to the empty set of some zombie Western. It is like we are the last living things on earth—killer, cat, woman, dog—all crammed in the cab of this truck.

Carl is chattering away about Dostoyevsky, of all things. My brain feels like it might burst if he doesn't shut up.

My own head jibbers away, too. *Where the hell is this old hotel with the Spanish stucco that Carl's been talking about for twenty miles? How many waters are left in the cooler? How am I going to get rid of the cat?*

Is a point-blank shot to the head the most efficient way to kill a cowboy zombie?

"Marfa was a railroad hub in the 1880s. There are still conflicting stories about whether the town was named for a character in *The Brothers Karamazov* or the Jules Verne book *Michael Strogoff*," Carl is saying. "Are you listening?"

"Yes," I say, while my head pounds. "Keep going." *Keep the peace.*

"A railroad executive's wife who settled here picked the name out of a book. But no one is sure which book the lady was reading."

This, Carl can remember.

"Turn right up here," he instructs impatiently. Since I climbed back in the truck eight miles ago, Carl has been offering rambling directions to the Paisano, a historic hotel close to the town's court-house. He's insisting on staying there tonight, one of his haunts on photography pilgrimages.

Now he's pointing. Sure enough, an oasis of white lights is inter-rupting the dark. "Hotel Paisano will be my treat." Carl delivers this with a completely straight face. "And let me work at getting Barfly in the door. Trust me. You'll get a good night's sleep. You'll love Marfa in the morning."

I don't tell Carl I've already been to Marfa, little desert city of the surreal. I've read all about its artsy hipster personality in *Texas Monthly* and *The New York Times*, a paper I will likely finally find here for Carl in the morning in some shop that will offer Viva La Feminista coffee.

I know all about the minimalist art movement ignited by Donald

Judd in the 1970s when he abandoned New York and began installing his large-scale art projects in the Texas desert.

His rows and rows of aluminum boxes transform into abstract, shimmering beauty depending on which way the brutal Texas sun falls on them through the windows of an old artillery shed. They've been playing with the blinding light here for almost fifty years.

I know all about the Prada store erected in dusty nowhere, handbags and a lineup of right-footed shoes in the window, that is really not a store but a sculpture meant to degrade into the natural landscape.

It's profoundly creepy.

So is the expression on Carl's face right now. He's fiddling with his Nikon even though it's pitch black in here except for the blue glow of the dashboard.

"Please don't shoot me," I say.

The boyfriend who said I had suicidal tendencies brought me to Marfa once on the way to Big Bend National Park. He was interested in Donald Judd's titanic sculptures and hiking, but not at all in what he called *the pagan lights* or *prissy lattes*.

We stayed in a colorful, retro trailer park outside of town, where the rental campers sat like pretty pastel blocks on a dusty floor. By then, I'd already taken a few secret lessons with my trainer, and my boyfriend had noticed the new bruises.

He was on the brink of breaking up with me because I wouldn't explain. Halfway up a mountain in Big Bend, I told him a small portion of the truth, and he screamed at me that I had a death wish. It echoed. It still does.

My trainer, of course, had highly approved of a week traversing scorching sand and tricky canyons. He'd told me to lug a gallon of water a day if I wanted to survive.

That seems like centuries ago. I'm inexplicably passive as soon as I park the truck on the street looking into the courtyard of the Paisano, twinkling away. Carl maneuvers Barfly in, no problem, by laying out three hundred-dollar bills in front of an assistant manager and saying "my daughter's poor dog was shot in the ass."

There's only one room left: the Rock Hudson Suite. We are perfunctorily told that the movie star used to hang out in the hotel during the filming of *Giant* in 1956. Barfly and the cat will be allowed to sleep outside the suite on a shared second-floor patio that extends from its French doors.

The hotel manager doesn't care. It's a slow night. I'm sure that way out here, Carl and I are on the low end of weird.

The suite itself is a little dated but in a pleasantly retro way. A massive old white-bricked fireplace dominates a wall. A tinge of ash sits in the air. There's a small kitchen we won't use, two baths, and one bedroom without a lock on the door.

Before I can bring it up, Carl announces that he and Walt are camping out with the animals on the patio, in the sleeping bags.

"Lock us out, if you want," he says. "I'm sure you will."

As soon as he shuts the French door behind him, I feel desperately alone. The Chihuahuan Desert is 200,000 square miles, most of which extends south over the border. I have limits. Not many. But letting Carl's memory lead me around a desert with two handicapped animals in tow is an absurd journey I'm not going on.

Through the glass, Carl's shadow is bustling around, laying out the sleeping bags. Finally, his shadow stills in one of the patio chairs. A tiny familiar glow begins to float up and down. I don't have to ask where Carl bought more pot. He was hanging in Austin, Pot Paradise.

I wonder how much of my money he has left and how hard it will be to steal it back. I did have the sense to sneak away the extra set of keys from Carl and hide them in the wheel well.

I take a deep breath and grab some peanut butter crackers and two apples out of a bag.

I open the French doors to a serene milieu. The lights from the courtyard are shooting their warm glow upward. The cat is perched on the ledge, peering over at things only cats can see in the dark. Barfly is curled up on one of the sleeping bags.

Carl heard the creak of the knob as soon as I turned it. He has kicked out a chair beside him for me to sit, which I do without saying a word. He offers me a toke, and I offer him some crackers. I lean back and suck in.

"This weed is called White Widow," he says. "She's very nice."

I don't question why I can't stand to touch Carl's skin but I'll put his spit, his wet DNA, to my lips. Why I keep feeding and watering him like a nice plant.

Two puffs, and my head tumbles in a new orbit.

"We sometimes encounter people," Carl remarks, "even perfect strangers, who begin to interest us at first sight, somehow suddenly, all at once, before a word has been spoken."

I want him to shut up.

I close my eyes and float. I see Carl behind the trees as the lady in the rain runs by. The pretty desert girl asking for a ride. Two little girls disappearing into the forest. Nicole pushing her small son on the park swing. Vickie's blood on the walls of an abandoned Victorian house. Violet's footprints along the ocean.

My sister, straddling her bike, turning to smile. She was such a cynical sweetheart.

The toke drops from my hand to the floor. Carl bends to pick it up.

"That's Dostoyevsky," he says. "*Crime and Punishment*. Good line. Kind of my motto. It's how I choose. How I decide who is special enough to live forever. On paper, of course."

How to eat one of my mom's ghost peppers

1. Eat four Tums.

2. Suck on a lemon.

3. Hold your nose.

4. Bite.

51

Like always, Carl shuts down. After sucking the life out of his toke, Carl is not so much hazy as ravenous. Says he isn't talking anymore until I provide real food. Crackers and an apple aren't going to cut it. He insists he knows a place open after 10 P.M. in Marfa, a town that operates on its own bizarre and unpredictable sleeping schedule.

My high has already crash-landed by the time we get to Carl's "place," a picnic table under a tree at an outdoor beer garden with the name Planet Marfa.

The other seating options are inside an old bus or in an underground area covered by a lighted teepee. We order a plate of cheese nachos with a side of extra jalapeños and two Coors. Carl's treat.

Half the plate of nachos has disappeared before he notices the book I've placed in the center of the table. *His* book. Pink Post-its stick out of the specific pages I marked before we left the hotel.

He runs a finger along the duct tape and traces the title, lingering over the words *Time Travel*. "Where'd you get this?" he asks.

"Where I got the book is not important. When I was eight, I found a copy of one of your photographs hidden under the staircase in my house."

He glances up, eyes sharpening. "Well, isn't that a pip. Why didn't you mention this before? Now we're getting somewhere. Maybe you open up a little, I open up. You ever think of that? Which photograph? What house?"

"I'll get to that. It depends on how you do." I'm enjoying a bit of control. I think about pretending to ask Walt to play, too, but Carl and I seem to have a flow going.

Carl runs his finger lightly over the duct tape on the spine. "You know I'd be happy to sign my book for you if you'll agree to take better care of it."

"I've looked at it almost every night for the last six years, trying to figure you out."

"Honored."

"I'm going to show you a selection of photographs in here. You just say the first word that comes to mind."

He silently stacks seven jalapeño slices into a little silo on top of a single nacho.

"Memory is processed more clearly if there is an old emotion connected with the picture," I say formally.

At first, I had thought when I laid out real pictures of victims and their families, he just didn't remember or was lying. But maybe the problem is that he felt no emotion at all. Maybe he was just that cold. What could move him more than his life's work—photographs he captured in his mind's eye before he snapped and dodged and burned?

"Just one word?" Carl asks.

I nod.

I open the book to the picture of the lonely white cross peeking out of the weeds under the 17th Street bridge in Waco, where cops searched for Nicole Lakinski's dead body. "First word that comes to mind," I command.

"*Barfly*. I hope he's isn't howling his head off on top of the Paisano roof right now."

"Barfly is your answer?"

"Yep. It's where we found him. I love Barfly. Got lots of emotion about that. Final answer."

"Did you kill Nicole Lakinski?"

"They declared me not guilty."

I flip several pages to his portrait of the decaying Victorian house in Calvert, where Vickie Higgins was murdered, then hauled away by her killer.

"*Skeleton*," Carl says, stuffing in another nacho. "How am I doing?"

"Are you talking about Vickie Higgins's body?"

"I am not."

I flip again, to the orbs of light exploding over the desert.

Carl hesitates at this one.

"We were just there," I say impatiently. "First word."

"If I'm being honest?" Carl drawls out. "*Bullshit*. Is that one word or two?" Now he's grinning.

"Did you bury the girl in the desert out here? The one whose key you wear around your neck?" *Anyone else?*

"I did not. I didn't know you knew about the key. This game is kind of fun."

My fingers fumble for the next one. The screaming face swirling in the water off of Galveston. A hundred years after the Great Galveston Hurricane, Violet Santana came to this beach to play. She never left.

"*Sad*," Carl says. "That's my word. Hard to imagine just how sad. Tell me, what's the saddest thing that's ever happened to you?"

"Did this dress belong to a girl named Violet?" I can't resist side-stepping the rules of the game.

"How would I know? It's a found object. I made quite a few dollars off this shot. So much, I felt a little guilty. I donated most of it to the Galveston Historical Foundation for restoration. They get the royalties now."

Guilty. It's almost midnight. I leaf through a few more pages to *Lady in the Rain.*

"First word," I say.

"First."

"Yes. The first word. Just like you've been doing."

"First *is* my word. She was the first. Well, the first that I cared about. It's probably why she shows up to bug me every now and then. She's up on the patio right now, drying out, talking to Walt. One of the reasons I needed to get out of there."

Carl pushes the plate of nachos in front of me. Five are left. He reaches across and dumps a heap of fiery jalapeños on top of them.

"Now it's my turn," he announces. "I'm going to call my game Truth or Nacho. You don't answer, you eat a nacho. Use as many words to answer as you like. Are you ready?"

"I'm not done with my turn."

"Too bad. Why do you tell everyone you're my daughter?"

I shrug. "It was the best way to get you out of Mrs. T's. It's a good cover for the road."

"Truth or Nacho. How did your sister die? Was she shot? Knifed? Choked? Drowned?" He enunciates every word.

"We never found her." It comes out in a whisper. *Why am I answering?*

"That's a damn shame." He slides the book back at me. "Which photograph is the one you found in your house?"

An opening. I fumble with the pages and prop up the book on the picnic table, facing it toward him.

He's silent for a few seconds.

"The Marys," he says grimly. "Of course."

"What do you mean 'of course'?"

"Did you love your sister?" he fires at me. "Truth or Nacho: Did she ever make you mad?"

"Stop it, Carl."

254

"Truth or Nacho. *Truth or Nacho*. Did your sister ever make you mad?"

"Yes, Carl, *I loved her.* Yes, she made me mad sometimes." *Rachel liked to take everything to the edge.*

"Why?"

"Everyone thought . . . Rachel was the brave one."

"That's a pretty name, Rachel. Is that the real reason for this little road show? So you can prove yourself to *Rachel*?"

I glare at him furiously.

I pick up a nacho and let it explode in my mouth.

He slams the book shut.

52

We've exited Planet Marfa by silent mutual agreement. I'm half-way across the street to the parked truck, ten steps or so in front of Carl, when the car swerves around the corner, lights off.

Carl calls out a warning a millisecond before I figure out what is happening. I dive forward toward the curb. The car squeals by, inches from striking me.

Never fall on your dominant hand. I remember that in the flash before I hit the concrete and a bone snaps in my left arm like a piece of dry wood.

The pain, excruciating. A shapeless black shadow hovers in my vision, a familiar indicator that I'm going to faint. I turn my head and can barely make out Carl furiously waving his arms in the mid-dle of the street, mouth open wide.

Whatever he is yelling is at the top of his lungs, but I can't hear him. The contents of my purse litter the street. The book of photo-graphs is lying at my ankles, once again split in two.

The white noise in my head is deafening. I throw myself into a sitting position on the curb in case I have to defend myself. Two women are running at me from the direction of the bar; one is punching numbers into a cellphone.

As soon as they reach me, the one without the phone drops to her knees, places her hand gently on my shoulder, and speaks, pointing to both of them, mouthing something. I shake my head. I wonder if my brain has finally imploded. *So much noise.*

I watch her lips shape the same word over and over. *Nurses.* The women are nurses. *Maybe drunk ones,* I decide abstractedly, *because I can smell the tequila.* Both of them are laying me back down, arranging my limbs. Keeping my arm, bent at such an odd angle, across my body. *Still. Be still.*

By the time the ambulance arrives, my vision has restored itself. My hearing is creeping back. A terrible blaze roars in my arm. "I don't need to be on a stretcher." My voice sounds squeaky and small, like it's coming from a tiny, tiny person at my feet. "I'm fine."

"Nice to meet you, *fine,* I'm Andrew," one of the EMTs cheerfully replies. "Just relax, sweetheart. Let us do the work." I'm lifted onto the stretcher like I weigh nothing at all.

Carl is bending over me with jalapeño breath, whispering: "Who the hell did you piss off? Those two guys were *aiming* for you."

I shudder as his lips brush my ear. His hand roams purposefully under my shirt, near my waist, before he steps away to let the EMTs load me into the ambulance. They are about to take me somewhere in the desert with the siren howling and the lights flashing. This is *not* invisible.

Carl isn't climbing in the back of the ambulance with me, although I don't know why I thought he would.

He's waving cheerfully outside its doors, my purse slung over his shoulder and the pieces of the book jammed under his arm. I'm pretty sure that when he leaned over and stuck his hand under my shirt, he swiped my gun.

My purse, which I rarely carry, holds the keys to the truck and a chunk of money I'd transferred from my suitcase. The rest of the money Carl hadn't taken is concealed in the Rock Hudson Suite's master bathroom. While I hid the cash, I'd thought about secrets: mine, Carl's, and Rock Hudson's.

"Don't worry!" Carl is yelling, as the doors to the ambulance slam shut.

Somewhere turns out to be Alpine, which possesses the emergency room closest to its dreamy cousin Marfa. It's thirty miles down the road, so I'm glad I'm not having a massive stroke. Every mile to Alpine, a static-filled West Texas radio station is blasting a countdown of the best country music lyrics ever written.

If my nose was running money, I'd blow it all on you.

Andrew put a little something in my IV, so I had some trouble with the brain twister: *If the phone doesn't ring, it's me.*

I also have trouble distilling the idea of two strangers trying to kill me. Maybe twice. Could they possibly be Carl's partners? Or am I really just that bad at being invisible?

Two hours after my "accident," the young emergency room doc is scowling at an X-ray. I've sustained a complex fracture. Surgery will be required, which is way out of his league. He'll apply a splint tonight. I'll wear that until the swelling goes down and I can get in to see an orthopedist. "Three days max," he says firmly. "Don't let it go too long."

I nod my head. I've given him a fake name. Smiled when he said my face reminded him of the secretary on *Mad Men*, which he is finally watching on iTunes. Wondered with every escaping minute where the hell Carl is with the truck, my gun, my money, my research, my fake IDs, my clothes, and my hair dye, which won't be so easy to apply now with one hand.

"Are you ready?" the doctor asks. "We're about to do the splint. It's not going to be a picnic."

"My arm . . . already hurts," I say, instead of reciting my own country song lyrics. *A serial killer stole my dog and truck. Now I'm shit out of luck.*

"No worries. I'm going to get you a prescription for that," he promises.

The doctor gently wraps my arm while I grit my teeth. "Do you live around here?" Such a sweet man, trying so hard to distract me.

"No, I don't live here," I say. "I'm just on my way to visit my sister."

DAY EIGHT

How not to be afraid of shots

1. Mentally prepare.

2. Squeeze my leg muscles.

3. Have my big sister hold my hand.

4. Don't ever look at the blood.

53

I'm staring at white ceiling plaster swirled by a Van Gogh wannabe. I've lost time. I've lost Carl. Again.

My arm rests in a sling across my stomach. It aches, and so does my back from lying flat for hours on an examining table, the same table and the same room where I was treated. The lights are off, shades pulled, but I can see the glimmer of sunshine through the slats.

The nice nurse who poked my arm with a shot of woozy said I could lie here until they needed the room, which apparently never happened.

I'm trying to remember where things stand. Before I conked out, I had depleted a ream of paperwork, not one word of which was the truth. I had promised to pay later, which is possibly the truth.

I roll my body up, grimacing. I crack the door and read the clock hanging over a nurse's pod. 10:17 A.M.

I gather my only belonging at the moment, a scrap of paper. There's one person in the waiting room, a large man with arms folded across his chest, asleep and snoring. I step outside and blink in the sunlight. My arm is killing me. I'm clinging to the paper and trying to figure out what I could sell on my body to get the prescription filled.

That's when I hear a light honk. It reminds me of Barfly's single short, polite bark when he requires something.

A white truck is sitting about fifty yards from me across the parking lot. The beams flash once. Twice. I start to walk toward the truck. It starts to roll toward me.

"Did they have to grow you a new arm?" Carl asks, as soon as I open the truck door.

This must be how Patty Hearst felt, grateful to a person who stole everything from her. The first thing I'm surprised to notice after climbing in is that my gun is sitting on the console between us. My purse is on the floor at my feet.

The second is that there is no room for Barfly to lie down. He's sitting up, panting cheerfully. The backseat of the cab is loaded with our luggage, the cooler, the unrolled sleeping bags, some loose dirty clothes, an open "party-size" bag of Cheetos I don't remember. The cat is missing.

"How long have you been here?" I ask.

He shrugs.

"We aren't going back to the hotel?"

"Are you kidding? And risk meeting up with the assholes in that car again? They were aiming for you. You might have a death wish. I don't. Time to go."

"They could have followed the ambulance. They could be watching us right now."

"We'll just have to deal with that." He hands me one of the pink Post-its that were marking pages in the photography book. I stare at a series of numbers and letters written in his distinctive scrawl. I blink a couple of times. The characters are jumping around like fleas.

"You look dizzy," Carl insists. "That's the license plate of the guys who tried to run you down. Don't you have someone who can run it so we know what we're dealing with?"

"You seem certain this accident wasn't random."

"Not the way that motor gunned."

"I can't think," I say. "I need pain pills." I ransack my purse one-handed and pull out my wallet. It appears nothing is missing. I count out some bills on the dashboard. I grab the ID with the name that matches the prescription. "I'm going back inside to the hospital's pharmacy to fill this. Give me twenty minutes."

I'm halfway out of the truck when I remember.

"Did you happen to run across some money hidden in the hotel bathroom?"

"Two rolls tucked inside the extra toilet paper. They are relocated to the inside pocket of your luggage. Is that it?"

"That's it." Interesting, what Carl sees and doesn't.

I turn back again, reluctantly. I have to ask. "Where's the cat?"

"Gave a pretty little waitress at the Hotel Paisano a hundred dollars to keep him for a few days. Told her there would be another three hundred in it for her when I get back. Baloney's not the traveler Barfly is."

I can't resist asking sarcastically: "Where are you getting another three hundred dollars?"

"Where do you think?"

I'm still holding my wallet with the wad of cash. I don't know how much of my money Carl has left, but I count out three hundred-dollar bills anyway.

Carl came back for me. I can pretend he's coming back for the cat.

54

"Before you swallow those, I have some questions," Carl says grimly.

"OK." I'm tearing open the stapled pharmacy bag with my teeth. "You have sixty seconds. I don't know who those men are, if that's what you're going to ask again."

We are still sitting in the hospital parking lot, windows down, ignition off.

"You seem unconcerned," he complains.

"I'm concerned. You have thirty seconds." My hand is fumbling with the childproof lid. I see no reason to tell Carl about the men at the Black Pony and that I'm leaning toward the unfortunate probability that they are the same pair who just tried to run me down.

"If you want me to open that bottle for you," Carl says, "we need to call one of your guys."

"What guys?"

"You have connections. How else would you know all you do about me? Shit, you have my old camera in the back of the truck. I know for a fact that was in a police vault. Read off that license plate number to someone and get us some useful information."

So Carl did find George during his hunt in my truck bed. I'm picturing George, in jagged pieces on the ground. Regret curls up for that impulsive decision. I might have needed that camera to bargain with. Now I'm closer and closer to just pointing a gun at Carl's head.

"I don't particularly want . . . any of *my guys* to know where we are," I say.

"Then make the call and throw your phone out the window. You've got two more of them burner things in your backpack." Carl clearly wasn't taking a nap or counting his gold while I was at the hospital—he was snooping through my stuff.

"I want to make something clear: You and me? We aren't a team." I toss him the pill bottle.

"Make a call. I'm not opening this or starting the truck until you do. And you can't drive with a broken chicken wing." Carl reaches in his shirt pocket and hands me my phone. It was in the street the last time I saw it. When I press the button, it still works.

I lay the phone on my knee and punch out the cell number from memory, half-hoping it has been changed.

He picks up on the second ring.

"Where the hell are you? Are you alone?" Either Andy's lying, or I successfully destroyed all of his GPS trackers.

"Two men tried to run me down last night. I have a license plate. Will you run it?"

Silence.

"I told you to stop this. Why won't you?"

"Do you know who they are?" I ask.

"Just read me the damn plate number."

The numbers have settled in place on the pink paper, so I do.

"Do you want me to call you back on this number?" Andy asks.

"No, I'll call you."

"I will pick you up anywhere."

"You're very sweet to help out," I say into the phone, thrusting a thumbs-up into the air for Carl's benefit.

"Wait . . ."

I end the call, pull the battery out, and toss the phone out the window, under the bushes.

Andy knew more than he was saying. I also have to consider that he knows exactly where I am.

I pick up the Glock from the console and check the magazine. Still fully loaded.

"I've been wondering if you ever killed someone with that thing," Carl says as he backs the truck out of the parking space.

It doesn't seem to be a question, so I don't answer.

55

I'm alone, drowning in white. The walls are white, the floor is white, my dress is white. The only hit of color is the pink Post-it note in my hand. I'm stuck in a panic room, with only fifty-seven seconds left to get out. I know it's a nightmare. But I can't fight my way to consciousness.

This panic room is nothing like my trainer's—a boring middle-class living room, a stopwatch strapped to my wrist, clues to the combination lock on the door hidden God knows where. Consequences.

How can I be dreaming and remembering at the same time?

I stare at the pink Post-it. Twenty-four seconds left. Now twenty-three.

I recognize the riddle. It's the same set of letters and numbers that Carl gave me for the license plate. They're now jumping off the tiny piece of paper, climbing up the walls, tickling my arms.

Someone is calling out. Trying to shout the answer through the walls? I strain to hear. *Only four seconds left.*

I open my eyes to blinding sun.

Carl is vigorously shaking my shoulder. We're perched on the side of the road with an eighteen-wheeler rumbling past, so close it shakes the truck like airplane turbulence.

I'm groggy. Surveying the new scenery. This doesn't look like West Texas anymore.

"Where are we?" I bark. My arm and head are throbbing. "I thought you were driving us to Muleshoe. To your grandfather's farm."

"I'm taking you back to Fort Worth. You're a goddamn ticking bomb. I was looking for a pleasant little road trip and a lot of Whataburgers. Not this." He's easing back onto the highway, driving as carefully as a good father.

I'm the bomb.

"Why were you shaking me so hard?"

"I couldn't tell if you were breathing."

"What route are you taking?"

"We're on 67." Not the fastest way, but he's on track.

I hadn't meant to sleep. Just shut my eyes a little. "Can you tell if anyone is following us?"

"A black sedan. Then it disappeared. Are you high? You seem a little high."

"I'm fine. I had a . . . dream. Let's just talk. About anything. Tell me about *Invisible Girl*."

"She deserved better. Not a good subject. Brings me down."

"OK. How did you get the scar on your chest?"

"This feels like Truth or Nacho."

"How about Muleshoe?" I ask impatiently. "You know, growing up." I feel the pressing need for information, any information, about that farm. *In testimony, you said Muleshoe was a perfect beginning.*

"What do you want to know? My brother and I would get up before dawn in the summers to work twelve hours in the fields. We came back to the house every night with all that West Texas sand and dirt in our teeth, in every crevice of our skin. Whatever my grandmother cooked that night was the best food we'd ever eaten. My brother liked to set the wheat fields on fire and watch them burn." Carl glances at my face. "It was a controlled burn, to get rid of the residue after harvest."

"Oh." *Right*. The same brother who was a fireman, who watched the Armageddon blaze in Waco.

"Myself, I liked to plow up and down the fields all alone on the 4640 John Deere. My grandfather owned a thousand acres. I just stared into infinity. It was monotonous, beautiful solitude. It trained me to like my own company. It trained me to see pictures. I could watch big storms moving across the sky from way out in the distance. It was like a little movie only I could see."

I wonder if that boy ever felt like he was in an old rerun of *The Twilight Zone*. I'd felt that way as a kid sometimes, when I'd prowled a neighborhood in the dark, while everything slept.

I picture young Carl on a monster machine, nothing stretching out in all directions but land and sky. Was he ever frightened that the storm was coming for him? Was it terrifying staring into an orange inferno of burning fields?

Or was that boy already developing into a savvy killer with nothing but time and space to make his plans?

The pain in my arm is unbearable.

"Try to sleep," Carl says. "You look like shit. I got some pain pills out for you a while ago. They're right here." He taps the cup holder. "I've been thinking. I *might* be able to help you find your sister. If you're not pushy."

I toss down the pills, but there's not a chance in hell I'm going to sleep.

56

I jolt straight up in the seat, disoriented. We're slowing down on a two-lane strip of black, a wall of forest on either side. It's night, and this isn't a dream.

The moon hangs directly over the open sunroof like a half-shut eye. The sunroof was closed before, wasn't it?

How long have I been out? The air is tickling my nose, sweet and spiced. The signal on the dash is blinking, beating in time to the dull throb in my arm.

That must be what woke me up—the steady, clicking sound of the signal, like a camera that won't stop shooting. Either Carl has forgotten to turn it off or we are going left, eventually. I'm trying to process why Carl has strapped a piece of duct tape over the clock. The gas gauge is at a quarter-tank. My neck is struggling to hold up my head. I have no idea where we are or what time it is, if I've been out for three hours or ten.

"Hard to see on this road," Carl says grumpily. "Our shortcut is four-point-two miles past the *Deer Crossing* sign. Town still hasn't cleaned the graffiti off it. Some ass drew the *D* into a *B*. It's disrespectful to deer."

What sign? What town? The pine trees indicate we overshot Fort Worth and are deep into East Texas, unless I've been out longer than I think and we're in the woods of Oklahoma or Arkansas. Exhaustion and a little pain have tricked me into godforsaken nowhere. It's like I never trained.

"Where are we, Carl?"

"Changed my mind again. Decided to follow your map east."

My eyes are hypnotized by the blinking light on the dash. It takes extreme effort to pull them away. The drugs, still a woolly blanket cuddling my brain. Without warning, Carl powers down the front and back windows.

Damp, delicious air rushes in from every side, scattering my hair and every piece of paper and fast-food napkin on the dash. Half of it flutters into the night like space debris.

"This air will wake you up," Carl says. "Smell it. Nothin' like it."

He's not wrong. Just like that, my senses are flushed and alive again, cranked with oxygen that has been cleaned and filtered by the pine needles of a thousand trees. I feel a rush—hope, energy, resolution? Like something important is happening.

"Where . . . ?"

Carl suddenly cranks the wheel left. We're veering off the road, straight into the trees.

I want to scream but nothing comes out. I brace for impact. Instead, it feels like we are speeding through the rough and tattered brushes of an old car wash. Branches poke me through the open windows, sweep along the sides, feather across the top.

A road is slung inside here, hidden by undergrowth and kudzu, nature wild and abandoned to its own will. Carl was aiming for this forest opening by feel.

"That deer sign and the odometer have never failed me," he confirms. "Four-point-two miles."

He's slammed on the brakes in the middle of the road and

switched on the high beams. Thirty to forty yards ahead, the head-lights illuminate a bumpy asphalt road that drops into oblivion.

It's the kind of night and the kind of road where you have to edge forward trusting that there will be another thirty yards, and another and another. We are sitting less than a quarter-mile off the highway, yet it's like we've left earth.

The sky is no longer visible through the sunroof. Barfly's nose is at work behind me, whispering, orgasmic with hundreds of new scents. I turn and his tail whips me in the face. He's poking his neck out the back window, stretching like a hungry giraffe.

I've read about dogs that can hang their noses off a boat in the middle of a lake and signal to searchers where a corpse rests at the bottom. Dogs that can sniff out the unmarked graves of Civil War–era slaves and archaeological remains a thousand years old. The soil chemistry is changed for centuries when flesh dissolves into the earth. Dust to dust, everything composting for the new life to come, the way it is supposed to be. Some dogs can smell that old death in the soil.

Barfly's paws are suddenly braced up on the window, his body now leaning so far out into space that I am sure he is going to tumble out. "Barfly, come," I say sharply. Miraculously, he obeys. "Roll up the windows halfway," I order Carl, and he obeys, too.

Two small things, but it makes me feel like I've wrested back some control.

"Where the hell are we, Carl? Where are you taking me?"

"My darkroom." He floors the gas, and we shoot into black.

57

Carl forges the truck ahead with little regard for speed or a dark, bumpy road unfurling bit by bit.

"There's a deep ravine on your side," he mentions, squealing around a serpentine pass. "My uncle named this section James Dean Drive. About six cars a year used to go down there. It's a big junk-yard jungle now, vines and moss creeping all over everything. They lost a wrecker or two before they figured out it's too much trouble to pull anything up but the bodies. This curvy part just ahead? My uncle called it Marilyn Mon-road. Get it? Curvy? He liked his old movie stars. Of course, he's long dead now. He lived out here with my aunt for fifty years."

"Please slow down." My voice is tight. "I don't need you to be a tour guide."

"Relax," he says, "I'm a blind man who knows the way. All my senses heightened. You like maps. Well, it's mapped perfectly in here." He takes a hand off the wheel to tap his temple.

To my relief, he does ease his foot off the gas. It's not to appease me, I learn shortly, but to wheel off on a dirt road. I picture us driving around inside Carl's brain, a giant asteroid floating in space, packed with craters and holes. We can travel forever but never leave.

My head knocks back against the seat as Carl smacks into a particularly deep rut. I think about rough terrain puncturing the tires and only one spare riding in the back. Running out of water, food, and gas. Hiking or driving out of here with a broken arm and limited supplies.

All of these loom as threats just as big as Carl right now. The last time I glanced in the cooler, which was yesterday, it was a chocolate-tinged lake of water and scattered ice with one Ozarka water bottle, a Stella, and two Hershey bars.

I don't expect help. We've crossed the desert into the Pine Curtain. People out here thrive on isolation and survival. We had to carve our way in. The road is neglected. I've glimpsed the shadows of a few abandoned, sagging cabins.

I'm gripping the plastic handle above my head, the one meant to help old ladies climbing in. My fingers itch to rip off the duct tape covering the clock so I can know the time. My backpack with the extra burner phones and my laptop are on the floor behind Carl, all of them turned off.

But I've only got one working hand. I don't want to lose my grip as Carl hits every pothole in the road like he's aiming for them.

No, it definitely wouldn't be smart to piss off Carl at the moment by reaching around to get something. His driving is getting more erratic every minute. My dim hope—to fire up one of the extra burner phones and use a GPS app—is fading. There will be no cell towers able to filter through these soaring trees. No drones or satellites that are going to stretch their eyes and ears down here just for me.

Nightmarish questions pelt my brain. *Did he turn that junkyard ravine into his own private cemetery? Did he roll Rachel down its cliff, listen to her tumble through the brush to the bottom?*

Are my sister's bones lying in rust? Are Nicole and Vickie and Violet keeping her company?

"How far?" I ask, instead, friendly. As much as I want him to turn the truck around, I don't. Rachel wouldn't turn around.

I wince as Carl slides the truck a little too far to the right, the paint shrieking off the passenger door as he scrapes a couple of trees.

He seems not to care, just leans forward, peering out the windshield like he suddenly can't see as well. The road appears to be shrinking. I can see twenty feet in front of us. Ten.

"Just a couple seconds," he says, suddenly confident, eyes on the odometer. "Right *here*." He thumps jerkily on the brakes, sending Barfly yipping and scooting off the seat onto the floor.

I flip sideways to protect my broken arm from colliding with the dashboard. Carl turns off the ignition, pitching us into utter darkness. Barfly lets out one sharp protest bark.

"We're here," Carl announces.

For seconds, we sit in silence. Then I recover. "You're not driving anymore. That was it." I reach in the glove compartment for the small flashlight stowed there.

I'd accidentally, foolishly, left my Maglite in the other rental. My trainer would have given me hell for that. "Flip on the headlights so I can see where we are. Carl? Turn. On. The. Lights. And put the leash on Barfly if you're getting out. He could take off and we'd never find him."

As long as I order Carl around, as long as I'm not so nice and rapidly assign tasks with no time for him to think, things will be fine.

Carl mutters and maneuvers with Barfly, and I slide myself gingerly out of the truck. We're parked in a very small, circular clearing. Carl stopped the truck inches before slamming into a tight line of trees.

Carl said, *We're here.* I expect some sort of dwelling. Instead, the smoky beams from the truck are fighting their way into dense woods, illuminating nothing.

The road, if you can call it that, has quit. Carl is still inside the truck. I circle around, sweeping the flashlight on all sides, making sure I'm right. There is nothing but forest beyond our doily of dirt, with the single exit behind us. It's going to take some maneuvering to back out.

I hear the creak of the truck door opening on the other side and the steady stream of Barfly peeing. I hope it's Barfly. When Carl emerges, he grins at the minuscule distance between the trees and the front of the truck he almost demolished. Measures it with his hands. I'm not amused. Driving out of here without headlights would be unthinkable.

"What are you still standing there for?" Carl asks, testy. "We need to turn out the eyeballs on the truck so we can get going. We have a little bit of a walk."

He's carrying a flashlight I've never seen before, an industrial, expensive one. His list of conditions pops into my head.

Shovel. Flashlight. Rope. WD-40. Glad Press'n Seal.

He got the flashlight, what else might he have purchased on that list in our time apart?

I note that the left calf of his jeans is bulging more than the right one.

Waterproof watch (resistant @ 300 meters). Did he get one of those? Is he leading me to a lake? There is no lake in Texas as deep as a skyscraper. I've done the math—300 meters is almost 1,000 feet. The only American lakes I know that deep are north. Very, *very* north. It doesn't matter. I don't plan to join Carl in water of any depth, no matter what he says he has stored there.

"The path's right here." Carl pulls aside a branch and directs the beam forward into a narrow opening. The ground slants. Carl intends for us to climb down. It *could* be a path. It is so plush with a rough carpet of leaves and dead pine needles, there's no way to know.

"Toss me the keys so I can turn off the lights," I demand grimly.

He does. He watches with interest as I trudge over to the driver's door. He snickers a little off to his side, like he has a bet going on with Walt about whether I'm going to take off. I'm not sure Carl cares whether I do or not. I can almost hear the crunch of Walt's boots myself. *Fifty bucks or a handful of your gold says she's done with us.*

The driver's door is wide open. I step up on the running board and click off the truck lights. I rip the duct tape off the clock. 9:26. Four minutes until *Family Feud.*

I grab whatever is left of the napkins on the dash and open the door to the back of the cab. The backpack is heavier than I remember. I can always dump stuff out along the way if it weighs me down too much. Still, it takes supreme effort to sling it over my good shoulder. I never trained with anything broken, just sprained. Broken would be a little sadistic, even for my trainer.

Whoosh. Crack.

The sound, swift and merciless, has traveled from the other side of the truck, where Carl was standing. Did he fall? Is someone else here? There's no outcry from Carl. No more sound at all. I duck around the truck and beam my flashlight where I last saw Carl.

A large branch is missing, leaving a gaping hole. I see a beam of light bouncing ahead in the woods. My own light catches the shadow of Carl's lean form and a flash of metal. *Crack.* Carl is slashing through the forest using an extremely sharp object. *A small sickle? A knife?*

Something pushes against my leg. I gasp, and Barfly lets out a howl that sends another, unseen animal skittering into the woods.

"I'm so sorry, Barfly." I'd forgotten about him. I've stepped on his foot. I flash my light and hold up his paw. Looks OK. He's licking my hand.

Barfly has been sitting patiently, waiting, his leash wrapped around a giant root jutting out of the ground. Carl giving me one more chance to give up? Or Carl trying to make my hike more difficult?

He knows I can't hold on to both Barfly's leash and the flashlight. I'm already considering how well I'll be able to maneuver an obstacle course of stones and roots with a backpack and my arm in a sling.

I'm going to have to trust someone. It might as well be Barfly. I worry about his stitches, even though he seems to have forgotten they exist.

I worry more about leaving him behind. What if I leash him to a tree or lock him in the truck with a window cracked and never make it back?

"Stick with me, OK?" I whisper, as I unwrap his leash. "We can always turn around." I don't know whether I'm reassuring him or me.

"You coming?" Carl calls out.

Coming . . . coming . . . coming . . .

The echo dances off the trees, almost musical.

Did Carl ever call out Rachel's name here?

His flashlight glints like fire between the branches of the trees and then it's gone, extinguished, out of sight, descending to God knows where.

Whoosh. Crack.

Whoosh. Crack.

I step onto the path.

I trained for this.

58

I shouldn't have worried about losing Carl. First, he doesn't appear to want to lose me. He even stopped so I could catch up.

The object he's swinging at every plant in his way turns out to be a machete, the kind sported by outdoorsmen and maniacs.

I'm staying a good fifteen yards behind him, not because I think he plans to use it on me but because I want time to duck if it flies out of his hand by accident. Barfly is trotting along a few feet in front of me, similarly wary.

This does appear to be some sort of old trail. My flashlight has illuminated fading arrows painted on tree trunks—some orange, some white. For hunters? Amateur botanists? Boy Scouts? The Ku Klux Klan?

Half the time, they point different directions, sometimes even up to the sky. As far as I can determine, Carl is ignoring them, walking purposefully, still following the map in his head.

I comfort myself that dementia patients often easily remember the past and there is a good chance he knows where he's going. I wonder if Carl's darkroom is not a room with four walls but a whole damn forest.

For about half an hour, Barfly and I trudge behind Carl, while he slashes plant life and sings "The Battle Hymn of the Republic." It floats back in bits and pieces. *Mine eyes have seen the glory of the coming of the Lord.*

We splash through a shallow, rocky stream.

Glory, glory, hallelujah.

I check Barfly's wound. It's holding up fine. All along the path, I'm attaching scraps of fast food napkins to the branches as markers, little white flags for me to follow on the way out.

I'm feeling more optimistic now that we're out of the truck. I've felt more certain than this that I was going to die, and for no reason other than a trainer did exactly what I paid him to.

No more singing. Carl has halted in a clearing. Above us, there's a jagged circular patch of dark gray sky like a kid cut a hole out of construction paper to help us see better.

Directly ahead, a small house is settled among the trees.

It's dressed in worn green shingles and accessorized with black trim and shutters—an attempt at camouflage, maybe. A porch widens out, with a decrepit white swing. Two Mexican flowerpots sit in the front yard, cracked and depressed.

If this place wasn't buried in the woods and falling apart, if there weren't dead girls to consider, I'd think nice people used to live here.

The screeching of the hundreds of cicadas living in this hole on earth is so deafening I wonder if that's why Carl still isn't moving. If he's confused and the noise is crowding all thought out of his head. I'm struggling to think myself.

"Put the machete on the ground, Carl," I say loudly when I'm three feet behind him. He grips it tighter. I repeat: "Drop it, Carl."

"Don't need to drop it. I'm not going to sling it at you. Going to go sit down on the porch."

I start to argue. Then shut up. He advances toward the porch. I move in sync behind him. When he lands heavily on the swing, it groans, something near death. I expect it to crash to the ground, but it just sinks ominously with Carl's weight, then holds. He switches off his flashlight and places it and the machete on the floor beneath the swing.

He raises his hands in front of his chest, wiggles his fingers at me like sarcastic worms, then slides them behind his head, elbows out.

"Good enough for you?" he demands. "Get that light out of my eyes. These damn cicadas are louder than a rock concert. That's a fact. Loudest insects on earth. They can get over 115 decibels. Did you know that they pee out of the trees? We used to call it honey dew."

I'm beginning to wonder if Carl belongs to this house. Maybe he was standing there, assuring himself it was empty. Maybe he just needed to sit, and he found a creaky swing.

"Homer wrote about cicadas in *The Iliad*," Carl continues.

"Is this our destination or are we just resting?" I pause. "Does someone live here?"

I'm not sure he hears me. His chin has drooped against his chest. He's pale in the meager light. His eyes are little cut slits. Barfly has settled his nose across his boots, the doggie sign that all is well. I flash the beam toward the ceiling hooks. The bolts appear surprisingly secure. Carl and his machete seem fairly secured for the moment, too.

I kneel on the concrete floor, jerk the backpack off my shoulder, and dig around inside. I hold up a Neoprene water bottle and jiggle it. Half-full. I wish I'd grabbed the last bottle of water in the cooler. I was just so afraid of losing Carl in the woods. I take a long swig and consider his wilted form. I tap him on the knee. "Heads up, Carl. Have a drink."

While he's guzzling, I try to figure out where we are. Estimating the time on the truck clock plus thirty minutes for the hike, this means Carl drove for about four more hours after I fell asleep again.

My gut is, we're still in Texas, and the landscape definitely confirms the Piney Woods.

I now most emphatically know why this stretch of forest is noted for its Bigfoot sightings and historic hideouts for Civil War deserters. The bad news is that the Piney Woods overwhelms more than 20,000 square miles in Texas and I can't Google the map in Carl's head.

I rove the light over the porch. "Are we here?" I ask again. No answer. The front door is latched tight. Up close, it's newer than I expected, considering the condition of the shingles and the swing. It's outfitted with a solid lock.

The large picture frame window behind the swing is equally unyielding, double-layered with storm glass. No damage from forest critters or vandals. The inside window shade is an eyelid shut tighter than Carl's.

I know it can't be, but I feel like I've been here before.

On this porch. *In this forest.*

Two little girls in white, one a ghostly blur. *The Marys.* In the stories I made up on my closet floor, I gave them a hundred names.

Something is traveling down my neck. I slap it away. A porch spider. *The girls, playing, giggling, dancing a bird feather on my skin. Did they bring me here?*

I wonder if I'd tried hard enough to root out their fate. I'd never wanted to enter those two little girls as numbers in Carl's dead column. It was fine for me, better even, if they existed only in his picture and I controlled their lives from my closet floor. Nothing bad happened in that forest.

In Carl's heyday, one well-known New York art critic speculated that the ghostly Mary in motion was superimposed. He said Carl was copying the disturbing feeling of a famous twins photo by Diane Arbus, two seven-year-old girls she pulled aside at a Christmas party.

The father declared it the worst likeness of his daughters ever, a photo that turned out so creepy and iconic it was said to inspire Stanley Kubrick's casting of twins in *The Shining*.

The same critic similarly disparaged two other photographs in Carl's book—the Mystery Lights in Marfa and the ghostly face swirling in fabric and algae in Galveston. He dismissed Carl as an illusionist, a trickster, not a documentarian. That was before anyone called him worse.

Carl's public response to that critic? "What's everything but an illusion? Pity you—dying alone in a toilet-size New York apartment after eating bad pasta with one of your cat's hairs in it."

I try to match Carl, the wit, the artist, with the one who brought me to this purgatory between hell and moonlight. The cicadas are still trilling. I turn to face the yard, dense with firefly glitter.

When the swing moans, I jump. The moon is suddenly gone, like it has been shot out. My light clatters to the floor, a second shot, snuffed out the moment it hits. I whip around. Carl is standing in the shadows.

"Did you know fireflies synchronize their flashing?" He's extending his hand. "You're jumpy. I'm just giving you the key."

I can't make out the tiny object he is holding to confirm that. I step forward and connect my fingers with his anyway, a little bite of electricity. The piece of metal is warm and oily with his perspiration.

I had thought it might be the little key to nothing he wears around his neck, the one that belonged to the girl in the desert. It is, in fact, a perfectly ordinary door key.

It could belong to this house, to one of our old motel rooms, to the front door of Mrs. T's. He could have picked it up in a nest of gravel in a parking lot while panning for gold.

My arm is aching from inside the bone. I crave another pain pill. Or two or three.

I yearn for running water and soap for the insane itch and burn that are beginning to trickle up my arms and ankles, the work of cunning insects and thorns along the dark trail.

I want to drop backward, fall forever, and land on a place soft and endlessly deep. It is the opposite of how I thought I would feel while I stood on the precipice of answers.

"Whose house is this, Carl?"

"Mine now. Inherited from my aunt." He picks up my flashlight from the floor and gives it a shake like an experienced magician. It cooperates, lighting up the swing's splintered frame and the floor beneath. Barfly's tail twitches under the swing, lightly tapping the machete's serrated edge.

"No electricity turned on inside," Carl announces, holding out my flashlight politely. "You're going to need this."

I stick the key in my pocket to grab the flashlight. My wrecked arm is a monster obstacle to even the simplest task.

Carl is instantly, nimbly, pulling something else out of his pants. A small can. Pepper spray?

"Why the hell do you keep jumping back?" he grumbles. "For sweet Christ's sake, it's WD-40. For the lock on the door."

I can see now that he's telling the truth. He's holding a mini-can, the familiar blue and yellow. He gives me wide berth on his way to the door. The hiss of spray fills the air.

"All yours," he says sarcastically, holding the screen door open.

"You shot those little girls in these woods, right? The Marys? Their picture, I mean. You shot their *picture*." I'm babbling. "Tell me what happened to them."

"Long dead," he replies. "Go on in and see for yourself. I hope you don't think less of me."

59

The key fits, gliding easily in Carl's grease.

Until then, a good part of me didn't believe Carl knew where we were, in spite of feeling that this porch was a familiar set piece, in spite of the disturbing legend of the James Dean junkyard ravine, in spite of Carl's last wicked remark about the little girls in the photograph as if I am about to find their skeletons with white veils tied perkily to their skulls.

The girl in the desert could be in this house. The lady in the rain. Nicole. Vickie. Violet.

My sister.

"You first," I say to Carl. The words are sticky in my mouth.

"I'm not going in." Carl is holding up empty hands in surrender again. Wiggling his fingers. "I'm staying here on the porch with Barfly, where there's a breeze. I suggest you open some windows in there. Be sure to check out my aunt's sewing cabinet. It's a gem of carpentry. Nothing like it. Her father built it right to her specifications as a wedding present."

I've nudged the door open farther with my foot, about four inches, revealing a sliver of inky black. I could wait until it's light. My gut warns that every second counts. I keep the flashlight under my armpit and use my jeans to clean WD-40 off my hand, finger by finger. Carl must have unloaded the entire can.

I think of a picture of my sister that only I will ever see. It was two nights before she disappeared, a crisp brain shot I return to again and again.

She is fresh out of the shower, smiling, sitting cross-legged on her twin bed with wet, stringy dark hair that leaves damp spots on the shoulders of her yellow pajamas. Her face is scrubbed free of makeup. Her eyelashes are blond, lacy fringe.

There's a faint shadow under her green eyes that she hates and can never get rid of no matter how much sleep she gets. I think it makes her look like a fairy, delicate and ethereal. My big sister was most beautiful like this, with no artifice.

"What are you scared of?" Carl asks impatiently.

That's just it. Now that I'm at the door and he's inviting me in, I don't know.

The first thing to greet me isn't a little girl ghost. It's the vague smell of chemicals. Formaldehyde is my first thought. Darkroom fixer, the chemical bath that embalms an image forever, is the second.

In pitch black, with one working arm, I choose my flashlight over my gun. I shoot the beam across the room to make sure nothing is moving—that Carl hasn't arranged some kind of trap with those two men on my tail.

I wish I'd thought to ask Carl for his more industrial flashlight. How weird and dysfunctional is our relationship that I'm certain my sister's killer would obligingly agree to give me the better flashlight. That, minutes earlier, without a thought, I'd let him drink the last drop out of my water bottle.

The quick sweep reveals a large, open room with a living area to the left, a small kitchen to the right, and the requisite fireplace for a little house in the woods. I quietly push the door shut behind me and turn the lock. There's a dead bolt, a good one, so I throw that, too. No way do I want Carl popping up behind me. I'll take the chance that everything in here is dead.

I flip the switch on the wall twice. Nothing, as Carl promised.

The chemical smell is nauseating, a hint of cover to an unpleasant stink.

The swing on the porch has begun a high rhythmic whine that bleeds through the walls, harmonizing with the cicadas.

Control your physical arousal. If it isn't a race, don't run. I take a minute for the 4X4 exercise. I breathe in four seconds, and out four seconds. I do this exactly fifteen times. The swing still whines.

I visualize the search ahead of me. I see myself methodically investigating every room, an inch at a time. Walking out the front door into bright sunshine in about fifteen minutes without a scratch. It's absurd, this visualization, but it has worked in the past.

I'd found my trainer on the Dark Web, where his reviews, detailed and frightening, maintained a steady five-star ranking. At the end of his insane games, he placed an icy can of Coke in my hand as a reward. I think of him now as I'm squeezed by awful silence.

He once asked if I had noticed how the long pauses in the games were the worst. The waiting for what you couldn't see coming.

I had nodded obediently. I had sucked down his icy Coke and let it burn my throat, the most delicious thing I ever drank.

My mind would be the thing to kill me, he'd warned. He could train my body. But my mind? *That is where even soldiers fail.*

"You will never die on my watch," he'd insist. I never believed him. Maybe that's why he was so good at the game. Why Carl is so good. There is an established lack of trust.

I drip the light more judiciously around the room, clockwise. Blackout shades. That's why it feels like an underwater cave.

A pine-framed couch with cushions and two oversize chairs, all obviously handmade. Photography books neatly arranged in a semicircle on a large glass coffee table. Paul Strand, Keith Carter, Diane Arbus, Robert Frank. Great photographers. The best. Henri Cartier-Bresson, master of the candid, the Hemingway of them all.

There's no TV, no stereo, no shelves, no magazines with dates. There is a worn wooden floor. A thick layer of dust that sits on everything. A charred log in a filthy grate. A stunning desert landscape over the fireplace, rich in rusty color, empty of life. Carl's mark is in the right bottom corner, a tiny, black *clf.* A rare photo from Carl not in black and white.

I scan the kitchen from where I stand. Gas stove, refrigerator, microwave, dishwasher. As soon as I step into the hallway, the smell burns and catches in my throat like airborne Tabasco.

I count three doors, all firmly closed, two to the left, one to the right.

My light flashes next on the cabinet at the end of the hall—a floor-to-ceiling behemoth of pine riddled with little doors and drawers of every size. The sewing cabinet Carl was talking about, presumably.

I couldn't have missed it. It's enormous, running all the way to the ceiling. Daisies are hand-painted on the porcelain knobs.

As I get closer, I see that almost every single drawer, every single cabinet, bears a white label with a name, written in Carl's strong, artistic hand.

Elizabeth Ann. Mary Louise. Jean. Sandy. Clara. Betty. Little Boo.

Respectful, I think, *just like the Waco memorial.*

I shakily skim the light over the cabinet.

Searching for my sister's name.

Eleanor, Belle, Sophia, Poppy. Vivian. Dixie. Lulu. Sadie.

Cinderella, Big Bertha, Gertrude, Scarlett, Penelope, Fiona, Tina.

I've been saying their names out loud.

When I stop, I can't hear the porch swing anymore.

60

Rachel's name isn't here. Neither are the names of the other girls I've linked to Carl, three little red dots on the map, or any of the others who were runners-up. I don't know what this means, or if it means anything.

I've counted. Twelve drawers and ten small doors. My imagination is roaming all over the place. I can't bear to open even one of them.

I'm going to make Carl open this fucking sewing cabinet. Let him *explain* while I point a gun at his head. Make *him* touch whatever is in there.

My pain and fury are drowning out everything else—the fact that he instructed me to stop and admire *the carpentry*.

Maybe his brain only lets him see the things his aunt stored there in the past—the rainbows of fabric and thread; the pointy needles with invisible eyes; the mix of old buttons trapped like tumbled memories in old mayonnaise jars.

It doesn't matter. Some part of him knows. He didn't bring me here to knit him socks from his aunt's yarn.

I have no idea if Carl has somehow sneaked into the house. I think I'd know. I think I'd feel him. I travel swiftly back to the living room. Slide the dead bolt. Open the front door a crack, and listen.

The moon's bulb is on. As soon as I step outside, it shows me everything.

A lifeless swing.

An empty porch.

No Carl. No Barfly.

The saucer to an old clay pot lies on the ground near the rickety porch trellis, half-filled with water. Carl has turned it into a makeshift dog bowl.

On the swing, he's neatly lined up a collection of things removed from my backpack.

A result of a bizarre sense of fair play or a way to push me ever so politely into madness? Both?

I see the pain pills with the lid considerately removed. The water bottle. Three Tampax. One granola bar. A Ziploc bag stuffed with rocks and pebbles. The tiny key to nothing with the chain that hung around his neck.

The water bottle is now filled to the brim. Where did Carl find water? I screw off the lid and take a sniff. From a stream? I sweep my light into the corner where I had tucked my backpack for safekeeping when Carl's eyes were closed.

It's gone. My laptop, a travel kit of tools, a compass, the burner phones—all of it traveled into the night with Carl. He has successfully broken my other arm.

I toss two more pain pills down my throat and chase them with a sip of water. I jam the granola bar in my mouth and chew it until the dank taste goes away.

My trainer wouldn't like these moves. Drinking from a bottle filled for me by a serial killer from an unknown water source. Dulling the edges of the pulsing pain in my arm that may be the single thing keeping me alert.

I stroll to the middle of the yard and stare up at the cemetery of stars.

"Carl!" I yell his name at the top of my lungs, in every direction.

There's no echo. Here, the sound just disappears.

61

I start with the first hallway door on the left.

A small bedroom. One window. Blackout shade drawn and undisturbed, an old pine double bed with a wildly colored quilt of mismatched squares and nothing underneath but rodent droppings. A chest of empty drawers. A closet that holds six bare hangers and a man's flowered Hawaiian shirt circa I-don't-know-when.

I rip the shirt off the hanger and throw it over my shoulder. It might be useful. A door that leads into a cramped, dank bathroom indicates this is the master suite. A beveled, clouded mirror reveals a deranged girl out of focus.

I almost miss the old bookshelf by the side of the bed. Black-and-white photographs are grouped in simple frames. I shine the light on the first picture.

A middle-aged man leans on a spade in a garden. The woman standing next to him is equally somber, face cast down. Carl's aunt and uncle? There's no skill involved in the framing or lighting of these shots. I rove the light to the next photograph.

I stop breathing.

The Marys are sitting primly on a flowered couch like they are waiting for me. Maybe a year or two older than in the shot in the forest. Hands impatient in their laps, legs on the brink of escaping, faces busting with grins. Since the first time I saw them, I'd been almost certain they were twins.

In fact, they are two very separate girls. And now that they are sitting still, side by side, I can make distinctions. The more delicate nose on one, the wider eyes on the other.

Their silky hair is identically styled in short blond bobs, not straggly and free like in the forest. I lay the flashlight on the shelf so it casts a spotlight and pull the back off the frame. The glass falls out with it, drawing a trickle of blood on my thumb. I suck its metallic taste and read.

In memory of neighbor girls Mary Fortson and Mary Cheetham, age 11, Piney Woods. Last picture. Both born on same day May 5, 1935. Died Nov 6 and 7, 1946, one day apart.

It doesn't say why they died. It doesn't matter. When they died, Carl wasn't born yet.

The critic was right—Carl was an illusionist. He never took his own picture of the Marys. He must have discovered old negatives. Stole someone else's work. Created something new out of something old.

Made up the story about the girls in his book even though the real one seems more morbid and interesting.

All this proves is that Carl's a liar. A thief. I already knew that.

I don't have time to mourn my playmates. I place the Marys back in the frame, shut the door, and leave them dead. I think I always knew they were.

The sweep of the second bedroom takes no time. A blue futon sits on naked white tile. The closet is empty except for a broom. Blackout shades smother the two windows in here, too.

I'm guessing this is where Carl slept every night after his trial. I don't have the whole picture, but I'm arranging pieces of it.

I stop at the third and final door.

The smell is worst here. I can hold my breath for ten minutes underwater, five times the average person who is in good shape and relaxed in a pool.

I can hold it with my hands and feet tied, while a Texas snake of undetermined heritage circles me. I've spent three hours in a loaded garbage dumpster on a 98-degree night with a ripe dead raccoon. I am my own lonely reality show.

I turn the knob, and my flashlight beam flies in the dark. The walls and the window are painted pitch black. Linoleum sticks to my shoes. The pink porcelain sink has a terrible, peeling sunburn. A pink toilet sits in the corner, lid down. I rake my neck on a cord that runs double across the old bathroom like a clothesline.

A piece of L-shaped plywood is fitted in the corner. It holds an old enlarger, a stack of pans, a row of bottles. Fixer. Stop bath. Developer. Hypo clear. The fixer has a hole bitten out of it and the liquid has stained its way through the plywood onto the floor.

The culprit, a rat, is lying dead six inches from my foot.

In a darkroom where there should be photographs pasted to the walls and clipped to the line for drying, there are no photographs.

I flip open the lid of the toilet. Dry, but reeking of sewage.

Two things happen.

The rat on the floor lets me know he isn't dead.

My flashlight clanks into the toilet bowl and dies for good.

62

The rotting slats of the swing scrape my back.

Back, and forth. Back, and forth.

I punch the button on the flashlight in perfect timing with the push of my foot.

On, and off. On, and off.

An exercise in madness. There is no *on*. The light is stone cold.

The extra bulb and the batteries are in the backpack. Carl is probably using the backpack as a pillow right now. Maybe he dumped the contents twenty feet from me in the dark once he figured out how heavy it is. Hell, maybe *he* is twenty feet from me in the dark.

The swing is lulling me. Now that we're acquainted, I can see it is the same swing, with the same jagged teeth, as the one in Carl's book.

Back, and forth.

If I push off hard enough, I can see a slice of sky beyond the roofline. Down here, I'm just another one of the shadows gathering on the porch like there's going to be a surprise party. We had a surprise birthday party for Rachel once. For a second, I saw what her face would look like scared. Thanks to Carl, that is how I almost always picture it.

The pain pills are a warm ocean lapping at my brain, a jazz singer humming under my skin. The pangs of hunger and the throb in my arm feel like they belong to someone else. The pine trees are rushing, a thunderstorm of leaves, the kind of sound that usually makes me feel like a little girl all tucked in.

I need to make a plan for the night before I can't.

There's no way I'm finding my way back up to the truck in the dark.

Early dawn isn't that far away. Six hours. Maybe five.

It takes some effort to drag myself up from the swing. My whole body aches. The door is still open. I fumble in the kitchen for one of the straight-back chairs clustered around the small dining table. I scrape the chair noisily down the hall in the dark until it bumps into the sewing cabinet. *Can't think about that.*

I choose the room with the futon and shut the door firmly behind me. Carl's room.

Still blind, I tilt the chair under the knob, cross over to the window, and rip away the shade. It clatters down, no problem. The more noise I make now, the more control I feel. A gray balm casts itself coolly over the room, not a lot of light, but enough.

I unlatch the window, shove it up, and suck in the harsh cinnamon of pine. I wonder if its tonic smell could cure cancer. There are tiny screen holes in my prison.

I leave the window open. Let bug and man come for me, I need to breathe. From my arm sling, I carefully remove the pain pills, the bag of rocks, and the tampons.

It was both considerate and disgusting of Carl to leave the tampons. I open the Ziploc bag of rocks and place eight of them in a row on the windowsill, another eight on the tilted edge of the chair seat. I scatter the rest in front of the door. It won't be much of a warning, but it will be something.

I pull the broom out of the closet and sweep it across the futon, hoping to disturb anything nesting there. I take my gun out of the holster and place it and the broom on my good side, within easy reach.

I lay my head down on the dirty mattress and smell Carl's scent in the fabric whether it is there or not. I feel for the key now hanging around my neck instead of Carl's.

I see terrible things inside those drawers on the other side of the door.

I force my mind back to the trail and the scraps of napkins I've left waiting in the trees to guide me out.

A sudden, delicious rush floods my ears, my arms, my legs, my toes. The pills have been patient, held back by adrenaline. Not anymore.

The ocean sweeps me out and I let it.

I can see flashes. My sister's face. The Marys. Barfly's eyes.

I'm back at the napkins. They're waving at me.

I watch them transform into beautiful white butterflies beating their wings.

One by one, they fly away, taking my way out with them.

DAY NINE

How not to be taken while you sleep

1. Super-glue your bedroom window shut.

2. Keep shade up at all times so you can
   see who's coming.

3. Plant prickly roses/transplant poison
   ivy underneath window (use gloves).

4. Every night, place eight jingle bells
   in a row across windowsill.

5. Keep gun within reach.

63

When I wake, pale light gilds the pine floor and bare walls. The eight rocks sit undisturbed on the window ledge. The chair is still propped under the doorknob. The broom and my gun are companions beside me. The shade that I tore off its rod lies crumpled in the corner.

It is 6 A.M., maybe a little earlier. Guessing the time is one thing I was born to do. My trainer could rarely trick me even when he blindfolded me. When I roll off the futon and stand, it feels like a brick struck my right temple. The aching in my arm is a quiet ping in comparison.

I slide over to the window and peer out at a peach tree, its fruit rotting on the ground where it fell. A stone well with crumbling mortar stands to the west of the tree. Beyond it, I see the glint of a stream where I'm guessing Carl filled my water bottle. My eyes settle back on the well.

Waterproof watch (resistant @ 300 meters). The thought comes unbidden, and ridiculous. That well is not a thousand feet deep. Maybe ten. At most, a hundred.

I turn my attention to the rusty umbrella clothesline sticking out of the ground and a neglected patch of dirt that once grew vegetables. Not much farther, the small green oasis ends abruptly in forest. This must have been a happy little haven for an acquitted killer.

I wiggle the chair out from under the door and let the rocks clatter to the floor.

Then I listen. Nothing but the early chirping of a few cicadas trying to get the most out of a short life after hibernating for seven or thirteen or seventeen years. The cicadas share an odd love affair with sleeping and prime numbers. *I know my cicada trivia, too, Carl.*

I run through the house and rip off every single blackout shade, wondering if they ever kept a kidnapped girl from keeping track of time.

Either the noxious smell is dissipating or now I'm immune.

In five minutes, the house is suffused with fresh air and the light of sunrise. I venture outside and walk two slow circles around the house. A piece of brittle, ruined plywood covers the well with a massive rock in the center to keep it in place. Too heavy for me to lift alone. I wonder if the well was hand-dug by Carl's uncle, or by Carl himself.

The stream is tiny, full of algae, making me regret last night's sip of water. I yell Carl's name. Nothing. I'm thinking about my trainer's warning—that it is worse to be hunted in the daytime in a strange place than at night in someplace familiar.

More cicadas are chiming in, ratcheting things up.

In the kitchen, I search out a rusted butter knife, a sleeve of saltine crackers in an old tin and three orange Gatorades that expired two years ago. I cut away the bad spots on a few peaches. The breakfast feels like a feast.

Rebooted and ready to go.

So here I am in the hall again. The daisy knobs are smiling at me with their round white faces and yellow eyes.

They are saying, *Open up.*

The largest door in the cabinet is center-perfect and labeled *Big Bertha*. It makes me think of Buffalo Bill in *Silence of the Lambs* and the way he stole only fat girls and starved them so he could use their extra skin to sew his costume. Rachel was thin.

When I yank on the door and find an old Singer sewing machine tightly strung with beige thread, ready to go, I nearly throw up.

I didn't think it was possible to hate Carl more. But every second that passes in front of this hideous cabinet, breathing in its musty stench, sinks me to a deeper, darker place.

Who do I pick next? *Cinderella* because he called her that in the notes in his book? *Scarlett* because my sister and I watched *Gone With the Wind* countless times one summer, or *Poppy* because it is my mother's favorite flower?

If I've learned anything, it's that every lost girl has exactly the same value. They all deserve to go first.

The pulse points in my body are hammering away. My hand pulls at the knob for Cinderella. Then Vivian. Mary Louise. Jean. Sophia and Penelope. I tug at the drawers and cabinets in this monster until they are all gaping wide open, and I can be certain.

I'm staring at cameras.

Carl didn't just name George, his traveling camera.

He named all of his other cameras, too.

The lenses glare back at me like an assortment of empty eye sockets. I can't place my emotions. Relief that I didn't find Carl's macabre trophies? Trepidation that Carl is still in control of the game?

I grope behind the sewing machine and come up with nothing but dust. I remove Eleanor, a boxy old Kodak Duaflex, and Jean, a vintage Canon with a long accordion neck, and place them on the floor.

When I studied Carl, I also studied cameras. I could name almost anything set in front of me. I search the back of the cubbyholes that held Eleanor and Jean. They are otherwise empty, so for the moment I'm going to assume there is nothing in this cabinet but Carl's camera collection.

A large, shallow drawer that I didn't notice last night runs across the bottom of the chest. No daisy knob, just a small keyhole.

I get it, Carl. The little key to nothing goes to something.

I strip off the necklace and kneel down. I don't find out if the key fits because I don't need to use it—when I tug the drawer, it topples out, and half the contents stuffed inside slide onto the floor.

More paper ghosts.

64

Shadows and light, angles and blurs. I'm guessing Carl stored at least a hundred photographs, all 8X10, all black-and-white, in the drawer. It took four one-armed trips to carry all of the pictures to the living room couch, where I'm hastily sorting through them.

There are no closeups of the lady in the rain or the girl in the desert. No broken bodies, no bones scattered beside rusted cars at the bottom of a Piney Woods gully. No Marys. Most of the pictures I've never seen before. At least a quarter of them are portraits of dogs.

All of them are filled with the dimensions of Carl I like to deny.

My chest tightens with all that he provokes. The regret, the triumph, the longing. The idea that we miss so much waiting for what is right in front of us, that the ordinary is magical, that the exotic is in our backyard, that every animal has a soul, that there is this terrible, wonderful novel in every human being. He shoots through a dark glass. *Nothing lasts,* he's saying. Not joy, not pain.

Carl never aimed to be in the right place to preserve an iconic moment in history. Marilyn Monroe's skirt flying up, a busboy on the floor trying to comfort Robert Kennedy after he was shot. Carl shot what was right in front of him. The proud dog, the dying tree, the poor child wearing an adult's face, the rich adult wearing a child's.

I feel suddenly exposed. It's like a camera is pointed at me through every one of the windows I've so recklessly flung open. I'm fighting the urge to leave, to be done with Carl's house in the woods.

I turn to the next photograph quickly, and the next and the next and the next, hardly seeing them as they whir by. But something registers. I stop. Go back.

Wisteria is blooming in front of a simple house.

Two story, white frame, one window box, a pitched roof. A girl is balanced on top of it, wearing an old flowered sheet as a cape.

Her arms are stretched from her sides like she's already soaring. Her eyes are closed. A thin mattress from a crib is lying on the grass to catch her if for some reason her plan doesn't work.

I don't need to use my imagination to make up what happens next in this picture. I was standing just outside the frame.

My sister jumped and broke her ankle and two ribs.

It was seven years before she disappeared. I had just turned five.

If Carl took this photo, he must have been spying on us for a very long time.

I'm tugging every white scrap off the branches as I hike up, erasing my footprint.

I shove them into the sack I created out of the Hawaiian shirt, which is hauling two orange Gatorades, a large selection of Carl's photographs, the rusted butter knife, the pain pills, and the water bottle, still full, a backup. I'm less worried about consuming old Gatorade than parasites from the stream.

Wherever I remove a napkin, I leave one of Carl's rocks at the base of the tree. In the daytime, I can see that he chose them carefully—there is a little sparkle to them in the light dribbling down through the branches.

Like all trails, it's steeper on the way up. With only one working arm, my headache still pounding, it feels like Mount Everest.

I'd gotten so used to the cicadas' cacophony and the cool cover of pine trees that I am fifteen minutes in before I realize the screeching insects have abruptly shut off like they were on a switch.

A storm is coming, maybe a bad one. The last time insects gave me such an ominous signal, the wind flattened my Girl Scout tent while I cowered in it with an anxious girl like me named Lily, the one who hid food under her bed and never ate it.

Up or back down? What if Carl managed this climb, and the truck is gone? The pine needles are beginning to chatter and dance. The breeze filtering down is raising goosebumps under my shiny sweat.

The decision is simple. I won't spend another second at Carl's cabin. I plunge forward, visualizing the truck still parked in the clearing, the extra key still hidden in the wheel well, Carl at a Whataburger mirage chowing down.

The last thirty steps to the clearing feel like a mile. The truck hasn't moved. Barfly is tied to a tree, whining. Trees are going crazy. The sky is an ugly black finger painting.

As soon as Barfly sees me, he tugs at his leash and barks in frantic, staccato beats. I can't believe Carl abandoned him out here while he probably sits inside the truck, radio blaring, chatting to Walt.

I finish that thought in my head just as I reach Barfly to untie him. Something's wrong. It doesn't match with the respect I saw in those dog portraits or Carl's obstinate affection for Barfly. Carl loves dogs more than people. More likely, *instead* of people.

I whip around. Two figures are running out of the trees straight at me. Barfly is urgent and snarling. The men from the bar? Who tried to run me down? Behind them, I glimpse Carl, a gun in his hand. A .22. *What is going on?* One of the truck windows shatters. Or Carl aimed for my head and missed.

The crack of the gunshot seems to surprise the men, too. They make the mistake of turning their backs to look. I sling the full weight of my makeshift sack as hard as I can at the closest one, stunning him.

I whip the sack again. He stumbles down easily. In the daylight, I see my pursuers for what they are: thirtysomethings with memory muscle and flab, whose current exercise rigor is probably mowing the lawn.

Barfly is going nuts, straining at his leash. The guy still standing is making his move on Carl. Carl fires. The scream is a shrill, bone-shattering sound that shouldn't ever come out of a man his size. He's on the ground, clutching his leg.

Carl has already pulled out the duct tape and rope from my backpack.

There's blood in the dirt near Carl, but I can't tell where exactly it's coming from. Carl roughly tapes the man's ankles together, then tosses me the duct tape. "Wrap that one. Hands and feet."

"Hey, wait a minute . . ." My guy, groggy as he is, has started to assess his future. The threatening sky, the snarling dog, the wild-eyed old man now looping a rope a few feet away.

"No talking," Carl admonishes. "Shove him over here when you're done."

In minutes, both men are expertly coiled to a tree.

"Cartoon bandits." Carl stands back, grinning. "Nice job with the luau purse. We'll wait out the storm with Barfly in the truck. Then we'll get their story."

He grabs Barfly's leash to unwrap it and whispers something in his ear. Barfly licks his cheek.

"We are not a team," I protest dully, but the thunder drowns me out.

65

"Explain," I demand.

We're in our old positions. Barfly in the back, Carl at the wheel, me in the passenger seat. The wind and rain are slamming away, the thunder almost constant. I'm not afraid of the storm. I'm pretty sure nothing will flatten this Chevy truck.

"I took a walk," Carl says, "and look what I found when I got back."

"Explain better."

"I tied Barfly to the tree and went to take a dump in the woods. We had just woken up. I heard a car engine. These two parked about two hundred yards back and got out. Same car from the other night. I just waited while they chatted. Couldn't hear much. Fat one's named Marco. They mentioned something purple. What took you so long? Did you find the girls?"

It takes me a second to realize that by "the girls" he means "cameras." I have no idea what his purple reference means. The name Marco, though, is ringing a distant bell. "Where did you get the gun?"

"Lucky, huh? Got the gun out of the Volkswagen. Under the front seat. Those college girls are pretty damn careless now that they can conceal and carry. I almost didn't take the gun with me while I did my business in the woods, but I wasn't sure what kind of a mood you were going to be in when you got up here."

"Who are these guys?"

"How the hell do I know?"

It's sinking in. Carl stole a car *and* a gun. I'm aiding and abetting a weapons charge. I just concussed a human being. I transformed into someone I didn't recognize when I swung that sack.

It's still raining furiously. I can barely make out the two men through the wet blur of the window. I pray the tires won't be mired in mud. In twenty-four hours, Mrs. T, the police, will be looking for us. Someone will be looking for these men. I pull out the key on the chain around my neck.

"I'd like that back. The key belonged to my aunt. Did you use it on her sewing cabinet? She used to wear it all the time as a reminder of her dad. Also, so none of us cousins would get into her private stuff when we were kids." Carl chuckles. "That turned out to be a box of Fannie Mays, her honeymoon negligee, some slutty novels, and that photo of her in the desert, which my uncle took when they were dating. He was a shutterbug, too. Taught me a lot. Got several of the girls from him when he died."

"You wore the key to remember your aunt? The photograph in your suitcase—your uncle took it? You used her drawer to store your photos?"

"Now you're getting it."

"The cabin . . ."

"I inherited it when she died. You see why I was so fond of her."

"Was the whole purpose of this visit for me to find the photo of my house in that drawer? Of my sister?" *Do those cameras in any way represent your victims? Ones I don't know about?*

"As usual, you're full of questions. We need to get out of the truck. Marco is beginning to move."

It is clear that Carl is excellent at tying people up. Marco is jerking his arms and legs but not going anywhere. His friend is awake and trying more subtle moves, which aren't working, either.

I got out of the truck holding a garbage bag over my head for cover. I don't need it. The storm is slacking off, leaving oppressive humidity. The mud is thick pudding under my feet.

Carl rips the tape off Marco's mouth. He spits at Carl and misses. "I'm going to sue the shit out of you."

"I doubt that," Carl says smoothly, untaping the mouth of the other guy. Carl removes the .22 from the back of his jeans and aims it at Marco's other bright yellow Nike, the one that isn't bloody. "I want you to tell my friend why you are so pissed at her."

The other man attempts to sit up. He's soaked and clearly miserable. "Marco, I'm done here. I've got a wife and kids. You've taken it way too far."

"Shut up, Fred. Do you want your wife and kids to know what you did?"

"That was all *you*! You were almost through before I saw what you were doing to her in the water. I never touched her!"

"You're just as guilty. Texas likes to fry the people who let things happen as much as the ones who do the deed."

Fred's cheeks are turning an ugly shade of maroon. "You—"

A gunshot rips the air. It ricochets into a deep puddle in front of Marco, slinging mud into his eyes.

"Carl!" I yell.

"Those two are making my head hurt," Carl complains. That's not hyperbole. He's beginning to look confused.

I'm less confused now. Water. Marco. Fred. Purple. *Violet.*

"Carl, I've got this, OK? Don't shoot anymore. Is one of you married to Gretchen?"

Fred appears almost grateful, as if this is going to be our bond, the thing that saves him. "Yes, yes, that's me. Ten years in May. We're going to Hawaii to celebrate. Let me explain. When Marco and I got out of the water that night, I figured Violet was just lagging behind. Mad because Marco went too far. You know, worried I might try to screw her, too. She screamed once."

"You walked into the water with Violet," I say quietly. "Your friend raped her, maybe drowned her, and you just left. Now you're married to her best friend."

"Like I said, I didn't do anything back then. All I did now was tell Marco that some woman was bugging Gretchen, wanting to meet at the beach. He thought you might be a cop. You sure as fuck don't act like a cop."

"What's a girl expect if she skinny-dips?" Marco asks.

"I just got all that on tape," Carl announces.

"What?" I'm confused.

"It was a condition," Carl explains impatiently. "The girls helped me pick out an iPhone back in Austin. Paid $34.99 extra for the gold case but worth every penny. You want me to play it back? It's easy."

"Just give me that gun."

"Why?" But, to my relief, he hands it over.

I empty out the bullets. I use my sack to wipe Carl's prints off the gun. Then I throw the bullets and gun as far as I can into the woods. Not brilliant, but it will do. The rain is starting to fall harder again. It will help clean things up.

I'm getting much more efficient with one hand. I look at Marco's shoe. A lot of blood, but Carl just winged him. What a baby.

"Take their picture, Carl. Then let's go."

"You can't abandon us here in the middle of nowhere," Fred whines. "Creeks could rise. We could drown."

I check their rope. A snug, wet snake. "Don't worry. We wouldn't leave you here to die."

"That's sarcastic," Carl tells them. "She's not as nice as she looks. She's mean as a hornet."

66

"Oh, geez," Carl complains. "Now she stinks like well water."

That's all it takes to remind me that even though Carl didn't point his gun at my head or tie me to a pine tree, he's not benign.

The lady in the rain is sitting in the backseat again, apparently after mucking around in Carl's well. I don't want to think about what this means. I wonder where Walt is. Marco and Fred are yelling their heads off outside the window, struggling against the rope, as Carl turns the key in the ignition. Rain sloshes down the windshield. Barfly's whine is set to A-sharp.

I want to plug my fingers in my ears but I know that won't erase the noise. Ever since I hurled a sack at the heads of those men, I've been attempting to hold back a flood of emotions and doubts about how deep the moral scar will be when I'm done with Carl. My gut feels like it's being torn apart. My head, beating with questions.

Carl is reversing into the narrow road of pine walls where he tore a shrieking scratch across the side of the truck less than twenty-four hours ago.

"Shut the f up!" Carl is yelling at the backseat. I don't want him fighting with a ghost while he attempts this maneuver. As much as I'm itching to ask questions about her, I turn around: "Please leave Carl alone right now, OK?"

"Don't worry. She'll leave. She hates my driving." During the ten terrifying minutes it takes for Carl to back out an eighth of a mile, I wish I could slip through metal into the wind, too.

By the time he spins us onto a more decent road, my teeth are hurting from gritting them so hard. The back fender of the truck is wrecked. The good news is that I almost immediately see a cell tower peeking out of the trees up ahead, outlined against a blue-gray patch of transitioning sky. So we aren't as buried alone in here as I thought.

"Good job." I've been praising Carl every couple of minutes no matter what he bangs into. We're back on James Dean Drive, and he's navigating the loopy road at the pace of a John Deere tractor. I'm worried about when he'll jam on the gas. I try to peer over the edge of the ravine to the junkyard cemetery, but it is too overeaten with kudzu.

"Where are we going now?" Carl asks.

I think about the two men we've left back there in the mud. The pressure of my timeline. Carl is supposed to be back at Mrs. T's tomorrow by midnight. If he isn't, she will most certainly call the police. She'll lie about why he's missing but still blame me. Anything to keep the money coming.

"We can go wherever you want," I say. "Wherever Walt wants. I need to make a call, OK?" I pick up Carl's gold iPhone glittering on the console.

Carl's mouth twitches. "You aren't worried about somebody finding us through that thing?"

"I'll be fast." I'm thinking that people seem to be tailing me without a problem, no matter what I do. I had to have missed another tracker. Were Fred and Marco following me since the beach? Was Gretchen in on it? Or had her grief and guilt blinded her to a bastard who swore marriage vows while knowing he let Violet, her best friend, sink into the murky Gulf?

The phone trembles in my hand as I stab out the number.

When I hear Andy's steady voice on the other end of the line, I feel a rush of gratefulness. A warm hand on my cheek.

"Thank God," he says. "Are you OK?"

"Yes."

"Is Feldman with you?"

"Yes."

"Are my guys correct that you left a hospital with him in Alpine with a splint on your arm?"

"What guys? FBI guys? You were really following me?"

"You didn't think I was going to leave you out there on your own, did you? They caught hell for losing you. A truck jackknifed in front of them. I'm tracing this call, OK? But I'm going to keep talking. The license plate you asked me to run was a rental to a Marco Barone out of the Woodlands. His name popped up in my computer as someone who was a witness way back in a Galveston disappearance. Violet Santana. Does that name mean anything to you?"

"Yes. He and a friend of his are ready to be picked up."

Dead silence.

"OK," he says. "If you're not going to add to that right away, I will just keep talking. I'm reluctant to make you feel justified in any way whatsoever, but your poking around is giving life to the Vickie Higgins case in Calvert. The woman who gave Vickie's husband an alibi—his second wife, it turns out—walked into the police department yesterday. She admitted she lied about where he was the afternoon wife number one was killed. Apparently, a little chat with a serial killer and his nutcase daughter scared the shit out of her the other day. Now she's having nightmares about a wedding veil smothering her. I'm guessing all of this means something to you."

When I'm silent, he continues.

"So Feldman probably isn't guilty of killing either Vickie Higgins in Calvert or Violet Santana in Galveston, correct?"

"No. It seems not."

"And these are two cases you connected to Feldman, correct? Are you going to give me a clue what you know about Violet?"

Two of my three red dots on the map, eliminated. Redeemed. I'm struggling to remember how much I told Andy a year ago while I was looped up on a Lemon Drop martini and how much he has figured out on his own.

I do know when he uses the word *correct* in a question, it's not sweet talk to a former lover. I'm an interview subject. A lead. Useful. Why he hasn't stopped me. Still, I'm going to have to trust him a little.

"Do you still think Carl Feldman killed your sister?" he asks.

And there it is. The big, ugly question.

The forest is crawling by. Carl seems like he's in a daze. We are still only a couple of miles from the clearing where we left two killers.

"I have your location," Andy says.

I hang up. Then I text Carl's recording of Fred and Marco to Andy's number. I hesitate over the picture of them roped to a tree. Then I send that, too.

"What are you doing with the phone?" Carl asks suspiciously.

"I'm turning it off." And I do.

The windshield wipers are beginning to squeak. The rain, letting up. Ahead, the sky is light. Once we're on a smooth section of highway, Carl swings us over to the shoulder. I take the wheel. His eyes are glazed. I'd rather drive with one arm than worry about him falling asleep or forgetting that he's driving.

If I keep it to forty-five miles an hour with a crunched fender and friendly, blinking taillights, if I scoot over for every trucker rumbling by at eighty-five, I think things will be fine. Carl hasn't told me yet where he wants to go, so I'm just trying to keep myself on the right side of the yellow line using one hand.

I'm battling any doubts about giving up by reciting the Moscow Rules in my head, a mantra of John le Carré. My trainer used to bark them at me when I was at my lowest, a rat at his feet.

Trust your gut.

Assume nothing.

Everyone is potentially under opposition control.

Don't look back; you are never completely alone.

"Walt wants some collard greens and black-eyed peas," Carl announces.

Lull them into a sense of complacency.

"OK," I agree. "Where? I need my bearings."

"We like the Pickett House up at the next exit in Woodville. I used to go there with my aunt and uncle. Mashed potatoes, biscuits, fried chicken. Real food."

Vary your pattern and stay within your cover. Go with the flow; blend in.

I'm not sure what my cover is anymore. I'm filthy. Smelly. And I can't remember the rest of the Moscow Rules.

I begin to mentally number a new list in my head.

I stop at No. 1.

Seven years before Rachel disappeared, Carl stood in front of my house and snapped a picture of my sister on the roof. He had to see a five-year-old me through his lens, too.

67

Carl saved me.

It really is his most brilliant play yet.

It takes me all the way to the Pickett House to figure that out and to push away feeling grateful.

I slip my hand into the Hawaiian sack and bring out the old photograph of my sister balancing on our roof. I lay it on the plastic tablecloth near my amber-filled iced tea glass that reminds me of my mother's whiskey.

I slide the photo toward Carl, who is shoveling black-eyed peas into his mouth. His plate is loaded with fried chicken, gravy, greens. There's something obscene about his appetite, like he'll never get enough.

We're sitting at the end of a long picnic-style table with a grim old East Texas farmer who probably slaughters wild pigs for pleasure. Right now, he has no interest in us.

If he knew what Carl was, the information I was trying to dig out of him, I think he'd retrieve his shotgun from his pickup and take care of business for me.

"I found this in the drawer in your aunt's sewing cabinet." I keep my voice low.

"That girl's about to fly," Carl replies.

"Did you take this photograph?"

"A spontaneous classic. Almost made it into my book."

"Do you know this girl's name?"

"Have no idea."

"Right," I say sarcastically. "Her name is Rachel. She's my sister."

"Well, there's a coincidence. Is that why you think I killed her?"

"Carl, you *led* me to this picture. You *know* whose house this is."

"Sure. My cousin's."

A grim chill rolls over me. "What was your cousin's name?" I can't bear to think we're related, that Carl's blood runs in mine. In Rachel's.

He pulls over a small bowl sloppy with peach cobbler. "Edie is what we called her. She was a lot older than I was. We didn't get along."

I snap to. "You mean Edna? Edna *Zito*?" *My Edna? Nursing home Edna? The Edna who lived in the house before us?*

"Edie, Edna. We called her Ed, too, when we wanted to bug her. What difference does it make? The day I showed up, she'd already moved away. A little girl in the front yard told me that the lasagna lady didn't live there anymore. And then the kid on the roof jumped. Total chaos."

I was that little girl on the lawn. That whole afternoon is a blur— neighbors, an ambulance, my mother on the ground alternately cuddling my sister and screaming at her. Now I know that Carl was there, too.

"Is there a particular reason you were visiting your cousin Edna?" I struggle to keep my voice even.

He glares at me for a few seconds. "Oh, what the hell. In honor of your sister, I'll throw you a bone. Edie was blackmailing me. After my uncle died, I put that photo of the Marys out there as mine. It ran in an international photo magazine. Won a little prize. Edie had one of my uncle's original prints. She'd been threatening to expose me for months. People weren't as forgiving back then. There was a code. I'm not saying I don't regret it. I'm damn good on my own."

I let this sink in. Unromantic, despicable, with the ring of truth.

"You still let them print *The Marys* in your book." I don't keep the contempt out of my voice. "Your *published* book."

"That was years later. My editor insisted. Everybody loves a prize winner." He shrugs. "A small risk. I'd searched her room at the nursing center a few days after I shot this picture of Supergirl. And her house, top to bottom." He pauses. "*Your* house at the time, I suppose."

I'd dreamed of Carl's fingers roaming our drawers. Fingers that stank of darkroom fixer. Tainting my sister's things. *My* things. *Were we home? Sleeping?*

Rachel's photograph is still flat on the blue-checked tablecloth, facing Carl. He couldn't know that her Superwoman cape was made out of an old flowered sheet inherited from our grandmother. He couldn't see the clothespins clipping it to the shoulders of her T-shirt or the purple stain when she spilled grape juice in bed the year before.

"Tell me," I say coolly, tapping the picture, "is this also the day you started stalking my sister?"

Carl shoves his bowl away. "You have it all wrong," he grumbles. "Don't *push*."

A weird calm settles over me. You think I'd be boiling with frustration and rage, reaching across the table, curling my fingers around his neck. Even the farmer with his knotted arms should not be unable to pull me off of him.

Instead, I don't move. I press my hips harder into the wood bench.

It is on my lips to ask Carl: *What did you do with Rachel's body?*

But now I know he wants me to.

I know Carl has a lie all ready to go. So I don't.

Tomorrow will be different.

Tomorrow, this is going to end.

Carl is smiling at me across the table. "Did you sleep under a little bedspread with blue unicorns?"

DAY TEN

How to find your sister's killer

1. Make a plan.

2. Be willing to die.

68

It is one minute past midnight on my cheap watch.

D-Day. The day I'm supposed to return Carl to Mrs. T's or decide to kill him instead. The day I round up the final answers so I can bury my sister properly in the Weatherford cemetery where she twirled and flew and lived forever young just like Peter Pan. I've already bought her a plot that opened up twenty feet from Sophronia's under a beautiful live oak tree. I've picked out her epitaph.

The clock is ticking while Carl and I stand still. We're laid up at a tacky motel named the Ten-Star, a little outside of Fort Worth. Carl is on the other side of the adjoining door, chattering away to Walt, to Barfly, to his wet lady ghost, who knows.

He hasn't spoken to me since right after we ate. I'd refused to take him on a hike at the nearby Big Thicket preserve so he could witness the work of a rare carnivorous plant called the Texas trumpet pitcher. He seemed to have completely forgotten our surreal to and fro over fried chicken minutes earlier. He wanted to shoot the trumpet pitcher with his new iPhone.

"It's such a clever damn thing," Carl had enthused. At first, I thought he was talking about the phone.

He was referring to the killer trumpet, which lures insects down a long, tall shoot that is like a vase for its sweet nectar. The insects either drown in the water that collects at the bottom or exhaust themselves struggling to climb out the slippery sides. "Their dead bodies are liquefied by enzymes," Carl informed me. "Just wiped off the planet like they never existed."

It made me imagine the inside of his well in the Piney Woods, a basin of green soup with walls cloaked in slime, impossible to scramble up. It reminded me that serial killers have been part of evolution for millions of years.

"It's a condition," he had demanded angrily when I said no.

"Your conditions are closed," I replied firmly, "until I know what happened to my sister."

In return for my threats, I get silence. I had turned the truck toward Fort Worth, not knowing what I'd do when we got there. In the end, I'd stopped short at this motel dump on the side of the road.

I walk over and lock the adjoining door. There's no chain. The Door Jammer is in the truck bed. I'm not sure I could shove it in place with one hand anyway.

I tuck the Glock under my pillow.

Carl is looming over my bed. Everything's dark except for a spooky blue light dancing on his face.

"Walt thinks he knows where your sister is. He wrote down the address for you."

I sit up and switch on the bedside lamp. The faint hee-haws of *Family Feud* are floating through the adjoining door, which is wide open.

"Didn't you hear me? Walt has an address for your sister. I thought you'd be more excited."

Carl is holding two things: his iPhone, which is what made him glow in the dark, and a piece of paper ripped from the motel pad. A row of red, white, and blue stars is stamped across the top of the pad. Below that, some scratchy handwriting that doesn't look like Carl's.

I wonder how long Carl has been playing with his phone. How many minutes before Andy or his "guys" track us to this room.

I reach for the paper Carl's holding. I can tell by the way he grips it just a little longer than he needs to that he's still furious with me.

He wasn't lying, though. The scribble is an address on a farm-to-market road near Burleson. Not that far out of Fort Worth. Maybe ten miles from the house where Rachel slept beside me, where I last saw her face.

"Sure, let's go," I say casually, as if it's no big deal. As if we're heading to the movies or to see a carnivorous plant. "Hand me your phone and I can map it."

"Check out of this crap place first," Carl insists. "We're not coming back."

The sky is light with wispy white cloud cover. *Mood lighting,* my dad used to call it when he got up early to go hunting. The kind of cool light that makes it easier to see where you're going and harder to put a hole in a pretty animal without any guilt.

Carl is navigating from the passenger seat, highly entertained by the friendly GPS arrow pointing the way to a red dot.

The country road is just as lonely as I imagined it would be. Endless, biting barbed wire. Neat round blocks of baled hay on flat land. A chilling, hot quiet, like everything is dead and the earth is done.

"Go right at this next road," Carl instructs. "It's that ranch house up there on the hill."

As the truck steadily climbs the dirt drive, I'm not looking at the house. I'm focused on the red barn that sits beside it.

I was numb when we left the motel. Now I'm afraid.

"There's a light in the window," Carl observes, "but I did call ahead. If this road trip is about you being as brave as your sister, now would be a good time to prove it."

69

I don't want to beg Carl for answers anymore. I shut off the headlights as we crawl up the drive.

The ranch house is ordinary, white brick, hugged close to the
ground. The weathered red barn is the kind my sister leaned against
for her senior portrait. It seems surreal to rap politely after we climb
the porch steps, but that's what I do.

A sixtyish woman, dressed in a man's faded T-shirt, Wranglers,
and pale lavender Dearfoams slippers, opens the door. She's clearly
not surprised to see either of us. She reminds me of my mother—not
so much her features or the Dearfoams as the weariness she wears
like extra skin.

"I'm Mrs. William Sherman," she says. I don't respond, or take her
outstretched hand. Carl pumps it cheerfully and introduces himself.

She ushers us into her living room—vacuum tracks on the brown
carpet, couch patterned in colorful autumn leaves, a pair of recliners
facing the TV. A pitcher of iced tea and three glasses sit on the glass
coffee table beside a small plate of Lorna Doones.

She gestures for us to sit on the swath of autumn leaves. I shake my head. Carl sits.

That's when I notice. Carl is clutching the photograph of my sister and the red barn—the one he snatched out of the hotel in Houston. When he reached around to the backseat a few miles ago, I thought he was settling Barfly; instead, he was retrieving this picture.

Carl snatches a Lorna Doone off the platter and places my sister on the coffee table, facedown. I open my mouth but nothing comes out when I read the red rubber stamp on the back.

A-Plus Portrait Photography.

I hadn't thought about this stamp for a very long time. Rachel had disappeared more than a year after this portrait was taken. A woman at church had recommended the photographer to my mother. Seven of Rachel's friends had used him for graduation pictures, too. None of them disappeared.

I had dialed the phone number on the back anyway. Three or four times, I got an answering machine with a woman's sweet drawl. I was thirteen.

I left messages that were never returned.

Now the hairs on the back of my neck are standing. Because the stamp also includes an address. *This* address.

"Somebody needs to tell me what's going on." My voice sounds calm. But the thirteen-year-old girl inside me is screaming. Carl has started to hum.

He turns one of the picture frames on the coffee table toward me so I can see.

The delicate face smiling out of the silver frame looks a lot like my sister. But I've never seen this girl before.

"Don't touch that," Mrs. Sherman repositions the photograph exactly the way it was, facing the TV like the recliners, a happy little family.

"We should just go on out to the barn," she says.

The barn is cavernous, almost empty. A raked dirt floor. A fluorescent light, buzzing. There's the faint smell of dung. A rope dangles from a rafter in the far corner.

"That's where my husband hung himself after he killed your sister."

Mrs. Sherman points to the rope like a docent in a museum. "When he took your sister's portraits, he couldn't believe how much she looked like our Audrey."

My head is exploding with Carl's humming, Steve Harvey guffawing, cicadas screeching. *I need to pay attention to Carl. Are they in this together?* He's on the move, over at the rope now. Tugging, testing it out.

The woman isn't paying attention to anything but her story. "Our daughter had died a few years before that. He thought your sister was sent, you know. Asked her to visit us just once a week as a sweet reminder. She came a few months—out of pity probably—and then she wrote us a real nice letter that she couldn't show up anymore. I thought my husband gave up. But turns out, he'd been following Rachel here and there when she was home from college. Told me later he'd just wanted to talk. When they showed up, she was in the back of the truck, already dead. Just a very, very little bit of blood. William said it was an accident."

The woman is now curling her arm around my shoulder. Carl is still messing with the rope. I shove her off.

In my head, new pictures are flashing. So many, many pictures.

"Mr. Feldman told me on the phone that you're her sister," she says brightly. "Rachel sure loved you. Talked about you every time she was here. Would you like to see her grave?"

70

Carl has been tossing the rope back and forth like a pendulum. Outside, the wail of a siren is traveling down the lonely country road.

"Lying is a delightful thing, for it leads to truth. That's Dostoyevsky. Lots of shit happens in a barn. That's pure Carl Feldman."

Carl is gripping my elbow, edging me away from Mrs. William Sherman, who still proudly carries the name of my sister's killer. "She's not going anywhere with you," he tells her. "You're a pure-grade lunatic. Get the fuck back to your house before I do something about it."

Carl releases my arm. I can't help it—I bend over, hands on my knees, stare into the dirt, try to quiet the pounding in my head, my chest. *Breathe.* I hear the barn door click shut.

When I pull myself back up, Mrs. Sherman is no longer there and Carl is chuckling. "I thought you'd believe it more from her. She was ready to spill. Still remembers that you left voicemails when you were a kid. Thought you'd figured it all out. Still expected you to show up any day. Look, get ahold of yourself. I'm sure you've got your gun. Those sirens sound like somebody's coming. And I'm not going back to Mrs. T's. I took the rest of your money stash. Didn't you leave the keys in the truck?"

He doesn't wait for an answer.

"For the most part, I've had a very nice time, whatever-your-name-is. If I *had* a daughter, I wouldn't mind you. And if it makes you feel any better, I'm not innocent of everything, you just didn't pick the *right* things."

He's standing in the barn doorway, bathed in morning light, the kind photographers crave and farmers barely notice. "I thought it was one of your little games at first. In that hotel room, showing me the picture of your sister. That you thought *I* shot it. Then I realized. You had no clue." He places his hand on my chin and tilts it up, like he is posing me. "It was your sister's face in that photograph that made me think. Her body language. She was looking at someone she didn't like. Someone who made her squirm. Most people see whatever they want in a picture. But a photographer *knows*."

He pulls his invisible camera up to his face. Snaps off a shot. Grins.

Carl, this man I'd hunted, *hated*, didn't kill my sister. Instead, I'd handed him a photo and he took a lucky guess. He would say, an educated one.

"My real name is Grace," I say, but he is already gone.

71

I can't see anything in that picture of my sister now except the fear in her face. I can't glimpse red barns without thinking of swinging ropes, or live oak trees without remembering the one Rachel was buried under in the backyard of that ranch house on the hill.

There was just a simple wooden cross under that live oak, painted white. It was a more respectful burial for Rachel than I'd ever imagined—except for the fact that Mrs. Sherman placed her in the ground two feet from her killer.

Andy and his crew burst through the front door of the ranch house to find me sitting in one of Mrs. Sherman's recliners, the Glock in my lap. Mrs. Sherman sat in the other chair, cradling the picture of her daughter. Barfly was lying between us. I have no memory of what I was thinking or planning to do next.

Every second since—in public, to the cops, to the lawyers—Andy has made me as invisible as possible. He has erased my sins.

I'm the shadowy little sister in the stories about Mrs. William Sherman's upcoming trial. Obstruction of justice, withholding evi-

334

dence, concealing my sister's body—I've stopped keeping track of what she's charged with.

I've been quietly subpoenaed in the grand jury trial of Marco and Fred, although Carl's tape says it all. A headline in the *Houston Chronicle* read, *Sweet Violet's Redemption*.

In Calvert, Vickie Higgins's husband is now the prime suspect in her death. His stick figure wife has left with the kids. Every scrap of evidence is being retested for his DNA.

I've cleaned up my debts from the road—paying off the fake credit cards and closing out the accounts, fixing the damage to the rental truck, mailing an anonymous package of money to the Alpine emergency room.

Telling my mother that she'd introduced her daughter to her murderer was one of the hardest things I ever did. I didn't look at the glass of liquid amber she clutched. It was the first time I was glad she was holding one.

Andy, my mother, my lawyer—they think I went to extraordinary lengths to get the truth. They only know the smallest bits of the story.

Three days after he'd driven off in the truck, Carl tipped most of my money to an autistic woman cleaning tables at a Whataburger and the rest to the taxi driver who brought him back to Mrs. T's at his request.

"The world's gone nuts," he'd told me emphatically. "I'm hanging here for a while." That was ten visits ago, and he still hasn't said a word about leaving a place he swore he'd never return to.

Now I'm back on Mrs. T's porch steps, still trying to pull broken glass out of Carl's mind, one splinter at a time.

I hold one of the broken halves of the *Time Travel* book. The Marys are as lovely, as haunting as ever. I worry someday I will pick up this book and they will be erased, the forest cold and empty. Snatched out of the air, like Rachel. I imagine silly things like that even though I found Mary Fortson and Mary Cheetham in a 1946 registry of flu deaths.

Carl is munching on the contents of a sack of Dairy Queen grease I brought, an old condition, and petting Baloney, a new condition. Mrs. T and Carl struck some kind of deal that involved him not telling lurid Discovery Channel stories to the woman with the wedding veil.

I hold up the photo of the lady in the rain. I believe in my gut that Carl killed her.

"I told you," Carl snaps, "I don't want to look at that damn picture again. I see her plenty. She's sleeping with me this week. She's so wet, Mrs. T thinks I'm peeing the bed."

"Let's play your game," I persist. "Truth or Nacho."

He shrugs, mouth full. His arm vibrates as he lifts a French fry to his lips. Mrs. T tells me the tremors are getting worse.

"Do you know her name?"

"You didn't say Truth or Nacho."

"Truth or Nacho, *do you know her name?*"

"Nope. Ask me something else. Ask me if I killed that girl in Waco."

"Did you kill Nicole Lakinski?"

"Acquitted. Sorry. Double jeopardy."

Some days I think I'm just messing with an eccentric and mortally sick old man. Some days, I think he is messing with me. Mrs. T has shared the imaging from Houston. His brain is being eaten away. I don't care. If there is the slightest chance to get any answers for Nicole's young son, to find her body or anyone else's, I have to try.

Some days, I just let him drift. He'll talk about the stories behind his favorite photographs. Giggle about how much Baloney likes baloney or quote Walt (or Dostoyevsky—usually hard to tell which). This is the way I found out that he stole the negatives for *The Marys* the day of his uncle's funeral. He swears it was the only time. The other photos, he insists, are his.

A year ago, I had attended a workshop on how to build a trusting relationship with a dementia patient. One man stood up to talk earnestly about his mother, who was brutal and demeaning to him as a child. *What is the point of still being full of anger? My mother doesn't exist anymore. How can I hate this sweet old lady who now loves me unconditionally?*

I don't waver on an answer for that for a second. Even if Carl's no longer a killer, there is still a witness buried inside him. Even if he can't remember, he can't be redeemed.

There are just way, way too many coincidences with Carl. So I pick up a photograph. I keep up the game.

"Truth or Nacho," I say. "What was your pillow talk last night with the lady in the rain?"

"Stupid, stupid, stupid," he mutters restlessly. "Let's play chess. You don't understand the concept of Truth or Nacho anymore. You don't even have any damn nachos today."

A tremor got Carl. He fell in the shower and hit his head. All of us were camped at his bedside the day he died: Walt, the lady in the rain, Mrs. T, me. In his last moments, he insisted the lady in the rain had tried to help him get up.

It was a simple graveside service. Mrs. T and her priest were the only other people who attended.

I felt torn about speaking, about eulogizing Carl. But it felt . . . necessary. I rambled a little about how a great photographer records both the seen and the unseen, the fragility of life and inevitability of death. Carl would have asked why I was putting him to sleep when he was already dead.

I hesitated about which Dostoyevsky quote to use to finish the eulogy and almost chose one Carl loved about not depriving animals of their happiness. But I caught myself. I kept replaying that moment in the barn, when Carl said I just didn't pick the *right* things he was guilty of.

I see the violent scar drizzled down his chest. I hear the whip of his machete in the woods. I remember the expert way he roped two men to a tree and callously shot one of them. I summon up the terror I felt when he played with me in the dark using a simple motel door chain or placed two fingers on my throat to probe my heartbeat. I think about missing women, grief that hangs like smoke.

So I ended with a compromise—a line from Dostoyevsky's *The House of the Dead*.

Bad people are to be found everywhere, but even among the worst there may be something good.

Right after the service, I searched Carl's room. He had duct-taped his five-line will, witnessed by Mrs. T, to the back of his headboard. There were two things stapled to the piece of notebook paper. A Ziploc bag that held Nicole Lakinski's silver owl pinky ring.

And a deed still in his aunt's name.

He left that dark, wild piece of woods to me.

Epilogue

"My name is Grace. I was twelve when my big sister disappeared. No one touched her unmade bed for ten days until I started curling up in it. I wouldn't let them wash the sheets. This wasn't supposed to happen to us. One month passed. One year. One less place set at the Thanksgiving table. One less toothbrush in the holder. One less birthday to celebrate. One less, one less, *one less*.

"Two years passed. Five. Reminders of Rachel, every minute of the day. The Minnie Mouse juice glass she'd drunk out of since age three untouched in the kitchen cabinet. Any hint of musky shampoo. The chatter of *Friends,* Green Day crooning, fireworks, Shakespeare, the Christmas ornament with her first-grade picture, the smell of spearmint dental floss, wind chimes, the color blue. Clouds.

"The stupid hope for years every time the phone rang. The ache when it turned out to be a telemarketer, or a cop preparing my parents because they'd found unidentified female remains in Mississippi or Oklahoma or Houston. *Did you forget to tell us she had a mole on her back? A touch of scoliosis?* We'd turn to each other: *Did she have a mole we didn't know about? Was her spine a little crooked?* It was never Rachel.

"I was a child obsessed. Then an obsessed adult. Six years passed. Ten. Rachel would have been thirty-one years old the day I buried her where she belongs. I don't feel peace. But I think she does."

I sit down. Four women and one man are crowded into this tight circle. No one has touched the coffeepot. There are no cellphones, no chatter, no one but us in this anonymous room. They are assessing me. Each other. They know it is their turn to say as much as they want or as little, to use only first names.

The youngest says she is twenty-one, which is the bare-bottom age requirement for the group. I'm guessing she's eighteen. I like her. She's exceptionally mature—a dreamer, a wannabe actress, a musical theater major at a community college, a mother to three of her younger siblings while her mother works nights. Despite her youth, I think it's OK if she stays; I think the others will, too.

Her father disappeared in Mexico a year ago without a trace, his car abandoned in the desert after visiting her grandmother in Juarez. She says way too many people vanish in Mexico for the government to bother with anything but the barest of paperwork. She bites her nails. I'm going to help her stop.

The oldest claims to be forty-five. I'm guessing closer to fifty. Twenty-six years ago, her husband was shot to death in front of her on their San Francisco honeymoon. The cold case is listed in the files as a robbery-homicide. She doesn't believe that. He was an ambitious assistant district attorney snuffed out by a single shot to the back of the head.

The young man directly across from me piques my interest the most. He says he's twenty-five. I believe that's the truth. He says little else. His body is already lean and toned. A tattoo of a woman's name snakes across the upper part of his right arm. He chooses not to explain it. Later, I will tell him why the tattoo is a mistake.

I won't ever tell these people certain, personal things—that I'm married to an FBI agent, that by day I'm a popular second-grade teacher, that mothers enthuse about my detailed classroom lists and skill at counseling the shyest children to stand up to playground bullies. My little students love that I own a dog named Barfly and a three-legged cat named Baloney. They wait eagerly for Monday to find out which photograph I will tape to the chalkboard so we can together imagine its story.

I officially changed my last name, so no one gets to decide who I am anymore before I tell them. I love Andy so deeply that sometimes it wakes up the pain for my sister.

Andy is busy. Works weekends. I want to tell him everything, but I don't.

He knows I lead a support group for people who grieve for family members who died violently.

He doesn't know exactly how it operates. He doesn't know how people find me. He doesn't know about the equipment stored in the large lockbox in my truck bed.

Andy knows I run a scholarship fund for the children of murder victims.

He doesn't ask where I got the money.

Four years ago, right before the police finally invaded Carl's woods, I hired two East Texas boys. They scoured Carl's property with their hunting dogs. I trust hunting dogs to sniff things out and East Texas boys to keep their mouths shut. They didn't find Nicole or anyone else. Neither did the police. Carl couldn't make the game that easy. So I play on, without him.

The only interesting thing the boys discovered was hauled up from Carl's well. It took both of them to drag the heavy, muddy bag to the cabin porch. I didn't cut it open until they left. I had to laugh. It was stuffed with gold bars.

I still return to those woods.
I almost always have company.
Two little girl ghosts.
And strangers who seek me out.
I survey the room one last time.
I ask: "Are you ready to train?"

"Never say goodbye because goodbye means going away and going away means forgetting."

—J. M. BARRIE, PETER PAN
Epitaph on the grave of Rachel Lynne Barrett,
Greenwood Cemetery, Weatherford, Texas

Acknowledgments

First, there are spoilers in here. If you haven't read this book yet, stop at this period.

One of the killers roaming *Paper Ghosts* confounds me more than any I've written about. It steals someone for no reason. It taunts us with bits and pieces of the person we love like a kidnapper holding up a phone so we can briefly hear the voice. Dementia is like any other serial killer—except there's no way to fight back. Not yet.

In these pages, I let dementia play out like the dark comedy it can be. Laughing is sometimes a necessary part of the upside-down, imaginary world that both patient and caretaker live in. I thank everyone who has shared stories of beloved parents with me, particularly my friends Kirstin Herrera and Tommie McLeod and my editor, Kate Miciak.

The "ghosts" in this book jumped to life with the help of *Hallucinations,* by the late neurologist Oliver Sacks. He shares the torrid history of hallucinations and points out that many of us will experience one at some point. He lets us know there should be no shame in that; it's a common part of the human experience. The anecdote about Grace seeing the ghost of her sister at the stove is adapted from my own mother's history. Shortly after my grandfather died, she saw him stirring his trademark chili in her kitchen. He grinned and said, "Fooled ya, didn't I?" and disappeared just like the goofball he was.

That same grandfather, who shot crime scene photographs and coal mines, inspired the deep love of photography that runs through these pages. Jill Johnson, one of my favorite photographers and journalists on earth, was the muse for the artistic side of Carl. I cannot thank her enough for her expertise and generosity. She shared stacks of well-thumbed photography books from her coffee table and talked passionately over bottles of wine. She created the otherworldly shots of the twins that appear on the cover and inside this book. She spent her summers just like Carl did, waking up at dawn on her grandfather's West Texas farm. She turned me on to photographer Keith Carter's beautiful, eerie eye (*Holding Venus, The Blue Man, Mojo, Bones*). His work inspired me more than I can say. Carter mostly lives and shoots in East Texas, proving his philosophy that you don't need to travel much past your backyard to tell life's great truths. If you haven't seen his photographs, please do.

One of the murders in this book sadly happened in real life. Haruka Weiser, a beautiful University of Texas dance and theater major, never made it back to her dorm on a spring night in 2016. A homeless teen was charged with her murder in the days after she was found near a creek on campus. Her death felt personal to me. My own son was a UT student who had walked the same path many times. Grief and prayers for her infused my writing at that time. I included Haruka in this book to honor her life and also her family, who set the tone for love in the aftermath. Their public statement after the suspect was caught is presented word for word in this book. It is remarkable in its quest for peace and understanding. The Haruka Weiser Memorial Fund is now set up at the University of Texas.

All of my thrillers are an ode to Texas. In *Paper Ghosts,* two mysterious people drive from the gray beaches of Galveston to the existential desert town of Marfa and then back across the state to disappear into the Pine Curtain. A huge Texas map has been plastered to my kitchen wall for more than a year as I plotted. (Repair guys gave me very funny looks when I told them the crooked line I'd drawn was the path of a possible serial killer.) Texas travel writer June Naylor Harris was kind enough to double-check my facts and mileage. If there are any mistakes about real places, they are mine. I took only a little bit of license in this book. Hotel ZaZa, I love and recommend you; I imagine you *do* have a bridal suite of mirrors like that. Also, the Black Pony bar was inspired by Austin's White Horse, but only the good parts.

Alyson Ward, a lovely, funny writer and my dear friend, helped this book along by introducing me to the haunting places of Waco, Texas. We stood under the 17th Street bridge by a mysterious cross with no name; wandered through the beautiful, sprawling Oakwood Cemetery; marked the approximate spot of one of history's most terrible lynchings; stared out at the lonely ruins of the Branch Davidian complex, where eighty-six people died when hell exploded on earth in 1993. Because of Alyson, I will forever remember the children and the sad poetry of their names engraved on brick and stone in a barren field.

Many, many more thanks to:

—Kate Miciak, my editor at Ballantine, for her magic pen and all she continues to teach me; Kara Welsh for believing in *Ghosts*; Jennifer Hershey and Gina Centrello.

—Maxine Hitchcock, my fairy godmother across the ocean at Michael Joseph/Penguin Random UK, who waved her wand over me long before we met in person. I'm grateful for all of your efforts on my behalf, and that of Louise Moore, Lee Motley, and the rest of the team.

—Kimberly Witherspoon, my agent, for her fire, humor, creative advice, and for caring so much about everything.

—My husband, Steve Kaskovich, who does endless, loving things to make my books happen, and for my son, Sam, who inspired me with his passion for *The Brothers Karamazov*.

—My parents, Chuck and Sue Heaberlin, on the other side of eighty-five—still begging for the first loose-page copy of my manuscript and still volunteering at the library. Dad, thanks for dreaming up titles in your sleep.

—My brother, Doug Heaberlin, for coming up with Barfly's name, which makes me happy every time I write it.

—Amy Rork, my social media guru, for adding joy and Instagram to my life. I love you as much as I love London.

—Timothy Bullard, who shot an inspirational and iconic image of a mysterious lady running in the rain for the *Houston Chronicle* in 1993. Google it.

—Michael Hall, for the *Texas Monthly* article "The Truth Is Out There," a terrific, timeless piece on the mythic lights of Marfa.

—Alex Coumbis, my enthusiastic Ballantine publicist, and Gaby Young, her first-class UK counterpart, who inspired the first line of this book, and always wears the best skirts.

—All of the people behind the scenes who worked so hard to catch my mistakes and package this book so beautifully: Loren Noveck, production editor; Pam Feinstein, copy editor; Dana Leigh Blanchette, interior designer; Angela McNally, production manager; Caroline Johnson, jacket designer; and Paolo Pepe, cover art director.

—Allie Honeck, for advice on Grace's quick-changes and for the phrase "*Toy Story* clouds." Good luck on your own writing adventure.

—J. R. Labbe, for her diligent efforts to teach me about guns. Anyone who knows J.R. knows that any mistakes in this book on that topic are my own.

—My extended complicated family and friends *again* for their rousing support—with special citations to Jennifer, Emme, Morgan, and Isaac Bennett, and Cara Clark, for their artful photography and promotion; Stephanie Heppenstall, Rhonda Roby, and Laura Di-

Caro; Rob, Paul, Val, and Chelsea Kaskovich and Pablo Croissier; Seth and Sean Stapf; Mike and Mikie Haney; and Kate, Michele, and Laura Heaberlin. You can find Laura at the Flying Pig bookstore in Burlington, Vermont, where she will hand-sell you my book. You can listen to her fantastic indie folk music (which Grace and I love!) at www.cricketbluemusic.com. You can blame Kate and Michele for introducing me to *Family Feud*.

—Miguel Suarez, for spouting funny country music lyrics, and his wife, Judy, for always buying my books.

—Pam Ahearn, always, for both our continuing professional and personal relationship, and for seeing something in my writing from the very beginning.

—The readers, book clubs, booksellers, tweeters, Instagrammers, Facebookers, neighbors, friends, and librarians who have embraced my books here, in the UK, and elsewhere abroad: You bring the sun.

—And finally, Sarah Grace and Elizabeth Marie Claire, the lively, incandescent Texas twins who modeled for this book's eerie photos in the Fort Worth Botanic Gardens, and to their parents, David and Tanya Claire, who shared their daughters' spirits. Someday, I hope to meet the ghost that makes that cold spot in your house.

By Julia Heaberlin